Ascension

The Veil of Shadows

A
Novel

Daniel Wheeler

First Edition

ISBN 13: 978-0-9853284-4-3

Front Cover Artwork: © photobank.kiev.ua Fotolia.com
Back Cover Design: © Lulu Templates. Lulu.com
Photo and Graphics: © Daniel Wheeler
Author: Daniel Wheeler
Self-Publisher: © Daniel Wheeler
Published in the United States of America

First Printing: Lulu.com
Print is the last number listed:
10 9 8 7 6 5 4 3 2 1

Disclaimer: This book is a work of fiction. Names, characters, places, and incidents either are the product of the author's imagination or are used fictitiously. While this novel may draw inspiration from historical events, places, or concepts, certain details have been altered for dramatic effect. The author makes no claims to the authenticity or accuracy of any such similarities or material used, and any resemblance to real events, persons, places, or creatures, living or dead, is entirely fictional and coincidental.

"For He shall give his angels charge over thee, to keep thee
in all thy ways." "They shall bear thee up in their hands,
lest thou dash thy foot against a stone."
~ Psalms 91: 11, 12.

❧ CHAPTER ONE ❧

My name is Sarah Hope, bestowed upon me by the ascended ones to provide me with an identity during my temporary sojourn in the human realm. As a Light Being, some may recognize me as a Guardian Angel, or a Divine Messenger tasked with guiding and protecting souls on their earthly journey. The decision to assume human form for a limited duration is a rarity among angels, requiring extensive preparation and adjustment to the constraints of physical existence. Despite prevailing misconceptions, this transformation is not taken lightly, and the challenges of adapting to the intricacies of mortal life are ever-present.

In this physical incarnation, I navigate the complexities of human experiences with a sense of purpose and duty, knowing that my time here is brief. While my celestial nature remains unchanged, the limitations of the physical realm necessitate a different approach to my divine responsibilities. As I strive to fulfill my mission, I am mindful of the delicate balance between the seen and unseen worlds, seeking to bridge the gap between human understanding and spiritual truth. Though my presence may be fleeting, the impact of my guidance and assistance resonates far beyond the confines of mortal time, echoing throughout eternity. I grapple with the notion of time running out, which feels alien to me in my celestial understanding. The guardians have imparted upon me the knowledge that time holds significance solely within the confines of my physical form, a realization that proves challenging to assimilate. Aware of the brevity of my earthly tenure, I am compelled to redouble my efforts to fulfill the purpose for which I was sent. The impending return to the angelic realm looms ever closer, driving me to maximize every moment in service of my divine mission.

With the awareness that my time here is finite, I am driven by a sense of urgency to complete my tasks. The weight of responsibility presses upon me as I strive to leave a meaningful impact before my departure. Despite the overwhelming workload that lies ahead, I am resolved to meet each challenge head-on, fueled by the knowledge that my actions carry profound significance in the cosmic tapestry. As the countdown to my ascension accelerates, I am spurred onwards by the unwavering determination to fulfill my sacred duty and leave behind a legacy of light and guidance.

As an angelic being, I am intimately familiar with how we make our presence known to humanity. Whether appearing in dreams, manifesting as ethereal visions adorned in silk and linens, or softly whispering guidance into receptive ears, our interactions with mortals are nuanced and diverse. Contrary to common belief, we do not materialize in physical form only to vanish into the ether; instead, our manifestations are filtered through the lens of human perception, tailored to align with individual understanding and belief systems. Through this symbiotic exchange of energy and interpretation, our ethereal essence permeates the human experience, offering solace, guidance, and enlightenment to those in need.

Yet, the delicate balance between reality and imagination remains fundamental to human consciousness. The mind, equipped with its intricate sensory apparatus, processes stimuli and constructs interpretations that align with personal understanding and cognitive frameworks. While this hidden censor mechanism safeguards against overwhelming exposure to realms beyond conventional perception, exceptions to this rule abound, allowing for fleeting glimpses into the ineffable mysteries of the divine. As angels, we navigate this interplay between perception and reality with grace and subtlety, ever mindful of the profound impact our interventions may have on the human psyche.

As a celestial being assigned specific tasks by the guardians, I understand the necessity of embodying a physical form akin to that of humans. Without this vessel, I would be utterly powerless to connect with and guide individuals within their physical realm. Through this tangible manifestation, I can bridge the gap between the ethereal and material worlds, facilitating communication and interaction with those I am tasked to assist. While most of my work primarily entails engagement with beings of the physical plane, there are exceptions to this rule, particularly within the animal kingdom. Animals possess a heightened extrasensory perception that often surpasses that of humans, enabling them to communicate through non-physical means such as telepathy and clairvoyance. However, even among humans, there exist individuals who transcend the earthly confines of conventional perception, demonstrating an openness to the unseen world that defies the materialistic worldview perpetuated by mainstream society.

Despite the skepticism perpetuated by human science and the prevailing materialistic worldview, I have come to recognize the existence of exceptions—those who embrace the belief in the unseen and acknowledge the profound influence of spiritual forces in shaping their reality. Before delving further into my narrative, it is essential to elucidate the intricate hierarchy and dynamics of the angelic realm from which I descend, shedding light on the origins and significance of my celestial existence.

Within the celestial realm, an expansive multitude of angels stand ready to intervene in the affairs of humanity. Guided by the archangels, these ethereal beings serve as messengers and ministering agents, offering comfort, guidance, protection, and provision to those bound to the earthly plane. At the behest of higher powers or guardians, angels swiftly respond to the needs of mortals, transcending the boundaries between the natural and supernatural realms with seamless grace and efficacy.

As intermediaries between two worlds, angels possess the unique ability to navigate the intricate tapestry of existence. While invisible to human eyes within the confines of the physical realm, they maintain a keen awareness of both supernatural beings and earthly creatures in the unseen world. This dual capacity allows them to fulfill their divine mandates with precision and insight, orchestrating subtle interventions that shape the course of human destinies in ways both seen and unseen.

The angelic hierarchy, composed of nine distinct orders, is a celestial ranking system in various religious texts and theological doctrines. Divided into three spheres, it categorizes angels based on their proximity to the divine and their roles within the celestial hierarchy. The highest sphere comprises Seraphim, Cherubim, and Thrones, beings closest to the divine presence primarily engaged in worship and contemplation. In the middle sphere, Dominions, Virtues, and Powers govern and oversee the cosmic order, ensuring harmony and balance in the universe. The lowest sphere encompasses Principalities, Archangels, and Angels, tasked with roles related to human affairs, protection, guidance, and divine messages. Each order within the angelic hierarchy possesses specific characteristics, duties, and levels of closeness to the divine source.

Guardian angels, regarded as spiritual beings assigned to individuals, provide protection, guidance, and support throughout their lives. Acting as messengers from the divine realm, they deeply understand individual circumstances, nudging individuals toward paths that align with their spiritual growth. As an intermediary between the spiritual and material realms, my role is to uphold cosmic balance and serve as a bridge between the divine realm and the material world, with my purpose and tasks gradually unfolding as my journey progresses.

Soaring through the celestial expanse, my wings ablaze with the brilliance of a thousand stars, I carry the unwavering resolve of a guardian angel. Christopher Daniels, my cherished charge, occupies my thoughts with purpose as I descend from the heavens. With each graceful descent, the heavens part to make way for my celestial presence, my luminous form casting a radiant glow upon the earthly realm below. Descending and alighting upon the threshold of Christopher's residents, the air shimmers with anticipation, the very fabric of reality bending to accommodate my divine presence. With a gentle touch, I impart a sense of peace and serenity upon the surroundings, a prelude to the encounter that awaits. Stepping across the threshold, I enter his abode, my ethereal aura suffusing the space with sacred tranquility. With Christopher's well-being foremost in my mind, I stand ready to offer guidance and protection, a beacon of light in the darkness of mortal existence.

As I hover unseen in Christopher Daniels' study, I am a silent observer, my presence veiled from mortal eyes. Though my form remains invisible, I feel an intimate connection with Christopher, a bond woven through the threads of fate that bind our souls together. As he delves into the depths of his research, I linger in the shadows, my essence permeating the air around him with a whisper of celestial energy. With a gentle touch of my ethereal hand, I reach out to Christopher, imparting my thoughts and feelings into his consciousness. Though he may not see me, he senses my presence like a soft breeze brushing against his skin, a subtle shift in the atmosphere that stirs his soul. In the quiet solitude of his study, I become his silent confidante, a guiding spirit offering solace and inspiration in moments of uncertainty.

As Christopher ponders the mysteries of the universe, I envelop him in a cloak of divine guidance, illuminating his path with the light of celestial wisdom. Though our connection transcends the bounds of mortal understanding, he feels the warmth of my presence deep within his heart, a comforting reminder that he is never truly alone. And as the stars twinkle in the night sky outside his window, I remain by his side, a silent guardian watching over him with unwavering devotion and boundless love. Leaving Christopher's study, I ascend from his earthly sanctuary; the echoes of his thoughts and aspirations linger in the air, a testament to our bond. With each ethereal step, I feel the pull of the celestial realm growing stronger, beckoning me back to my divine origins. Yet, as I prepare to transform into human form, a sense of excitement courses through my celestial being. With a serene resolve, I unfurl my majestic wings one last time, their radiant feathers shimmering with heavenly light. Preparing to embrace the uncertainty of what lies ahead, I am eager to immerse myself in the intricate tapestry of human existence.

As I descend from the celestial realm, my luminescent wings gently fold behind me, shedding their radiant glow to reveal the soft contours of my mortal frame. With each graceful movement, strands of ethereal light intertwine with my golden locks, transforming them into a cascade of sunlight that frames my face. The celestial essence that once emanated from my being now melds seamlessly with the earthly realm, infusing my porcelain skin with a radiant glow that mirrors the brilliance of the heavens. Stepping onto the mortal plane, the fabric of reality shifts around me, weaving together threads of divine energy to fashion a garment befitting my newfound form. Soft fabrics materialize around my figure, caressing my skin with their silken touch as they fashion themselves into an ensemble of ethereal elegance. A gown of iridescent hues envelops me, its shimmering fabric reflecting the colors of the cosmos as if woven from stardust itself. Embroidered patterns of celestial motifs adorn the garment, hinting at the celestial heritage that lay veiled beneath my mortal guise.

With each delicate movement, the fabric swirled around me, accentuating the grace of my celestial descent. A gentle breeze carried the scent of wildflowers and the promise of new beginnings as I embraced the sensations of mortal existence with wonder and delight. My blue eyes, once mirrors of the infinite depths of the cosmos, now sparkle with the curiosity and innocence of a mortal soul, reflecting the beauty of the world unfolding before me. As I ventured into the realms of humanity, I carried with me the essence of the divine, a beacon of light and hope in a world filled with darkness and uncertainty.

As I emerge into the mortal realm, the sensation of inhabiting a human body is exhilarating and disorienting. Every movement is a discovery, every touch a revelation. The weight of gravity pulls at me, grounding me in this earthly existence, yet I yearn for celestial flight's weightlessness. With each step, I learn to navigate the nuances of balance and coordination, stumbling at first but gradually finding my stride as I adapt to the limitations of this mortal form. The sensations that course through my human body are a symphony of new experiences. The cool caress of a gentle breeze sends shivers down my spine, while the warmth of sunlight against my skin ignites a newfound appreciation for the senses. I marvel at the intricacies of touch, the way my fingertips can trace the texture of rough stone or the softness of velvet, each sensation a testament to the richness of mortal existence. As I learn to wield this body with increasing proficiency, I discover the power of human expression and the subtle nuances of facial expressions and gestures that convey myriads of emotions. However, the most profound transformation occurs within my voice. At first, the sounds that emanate from my lips are foreign and stilted, lacking the ethereal resonance of celestial speech. But with each passing moment, I refine the cadence and timbre of my voice, shaping it to convey the depth of human emotion. I experiment with the nuances of tone and inflection, discovering the power of words to evoke laughter, tears, and everything in between. As I speak, the resonance of my words reverberates through my human vessel, a reminder of the profound connection between voice and soul in the tapestry of mortal existence. With anticipation and nervous excitement, I prepare to take my first steps into Christopher's world as a human.

Accommodation was made for me before my descent. I have been granted a room within walking distance of the Silver Ridge Institute and Christopher's Silver Ridge, Oregon, residence. Silver Ridge is nestled in the heart of the Oregon wilderness, surrounded by ancient forests and mist-shrouded mountains. It is located within the Mount Hood Corridor off U.S. Route 26. It is one of the communities that surround Mount Hood. Upon my arrival at my new abode, I find a portfolio; the contents are proper identification cards, dated birth records, a resume, bank account information, and cash in the form of American paper currency. In addition, there is a wardrobe of proper female attire and accessories—everything I would need to assimilate into society. I find solace in the familiarity of my surroundings, even as I navigate the intricacies of mortal life. Tomorrow marks the beginning of a new chapter in my journey as I prepare to meet Christopher face-to-face for the first time in my human guise. As I settle into my accommodations, the weight of anticipation hangs heavy in the air. I envision our meeting rehearsing the words I will speak and the gestures I will make in my mind's eye. Though I have been among mortals in my celestial form, this encounter feels different, imbued with a sense of significance that transcends the bounds of ordinary human interaction. With each passing moment, my excitement grows, mingling with a trace of apprehension as I prepare to unveil my new identity to Christopher.

Tonight, I will sleep, and tomorrow, as the sun rises over the horizon, I will venture forth to meet Christopher in his office at the institute, my heart aflutter with anticipation. Armed with the knowledge and experiences of both the celestial and mortal realms, I stand ready to embark on this new adventure, eager to forge a deeper connection with the man whose life I have watched over. As I step out into the world, I carry with me the hope of a newfound understanding and the promise of a bond that transcends the boundaries of time and space.

———

Christopher Daniels sat at his desk in his study, surrounded by the weight of his thoughts and the anticipation of something significant about to unfold. The room, usually a sanctuary for his research and contemplation, now seemed charged with an inexplicable energy. He could not shake the feeling of being watched and accompanied by a presence beyond his understanding. During his musings, memories of his childhood flooded back; memories tinted with the innocence of youth and the gradual awakening to the world's complexities. Christopher had always felt out of place, as if he were meant for something beyond the ordinary course of life.

"My name is Christopher Daniels," he whispered, reaffirming his identity in the face of the unknown. His parents, now gone from this world, had bestowed upon him a name that resonated with a sense of purpose yet to be fully realized. From an early age, Christopher had sensed a difference within himself, a subtle but undeniable feeling that he was meant for a destiny more than just the average. While others pursued conventional paths, he found himself drawn to mysteries and hidden truths, searching for meaning in the vast tapestry of existence. As he delved

9

deeper into his studies, gathering testimonials and research papers from the enigmatic Silver Ridge Institute, Christopher felt the puzzle pieces slowly coming together. There was a convergence of forces, a gathering storm on the horizon, and he was poised at the center of it all, a beacon amidst the encroaching darkness. With each passing moment, the sensation of being accompanied by an unseen presence grew stronger, enveloping him in a shroud of uncertainty tinged with anticipation. Amidst the uncertainty, there was a flicker of recognition and familiarity, a sense that he was not alone in his quest for understanding. As he gazed out of the half-open window, the gentle breeze whispering through the room, Christopher felt a stirring deep within his soul. This was no ordinary moment, no mere coincidence of fate. It was the beginning of a journey into the heart of mystery and revelation, where the lines between reality and imagination blurred, and the true nature of existence awaited its unveiling.

As a philosophy professor deeply entrenched in exploring life's profound inquiries, I find myself drawn to the realms of metaphysics, morality, and the perennial questions that have echoed through the ages. By teaching students about the writings of both modern and historical philosophers, I aim to ignite their curiosity and guide them through the intricate tapestry of philosophical thought. Whether pondering the existence of a higher power or grappling with the complexities of mortality, I encourage my students to delve into the depths of philosophical inquiry with an open mind and critical eye. Over the years, my philosophical journey has led me to contemplate the existence of a censor mechanism within the human psyche. This hypothetical entity, residing somewhere between the conscious and unconscious mind, is a barrier that prevents us from accessing specific memories and perceiving the unseen spiritual realm. While not a well-established scientific concept, the notion of a metaphysical censor raises intriguing questions about the nature of consciousness and reality. Could it be that our perception of the world is filtered through this censor, shielding us from experiences that might challenge our understanding of existence?

In exploring the boundaries of human consciousness, I am reminded of the inherent limitations of our physical form. While we may inhabit a three-dimensional plane of existence, our thoughts and dreams transcend these spatial confines, existing within the realm of the mind and spirit. Although the concept of a 'metaphysical censor" may remain speculative, the ongoing discourse between science and spirituality offers tantalizing insights into the intricate workings of the human brain. As we continue to unravel the mysteries of consciousness, we are confronted with the awe-inspiring complexity of our existence, prompting us to ponder the profound questions at the heart of philosophy.

If I had to describe myself, I'd say I'm a Caucasian man in my mid-forties with brown hair starting to show subtle signs of gray, hinting at the passage of time and the wisdom that comes with it. My brown eyes hold a depth of experience, reflecting the journey I have traveled and the knowledge I've gained along the way. Standing six feet tall, I maintain a medium build, a testament to a balanced lifestyle that includes work and leisure. I'm not saying that I always maintain a perfect balance. Certainly not so much lately. However, I've always felt comfortable in my own skin, whether lecturing at the institute or diving into research projects. Regarding fashion, I prefer to keep things laid-back and casual, regardless of whether I'm teaching at the institute or lost in the depths of research. Comfort is key for me, so you'll often find me in relaxed attire that allows me to move freely and focus on the task at hand. As for my hair, let us say I tend to let it go untamed, especially when the intricacies of exploration and discovery consume my mind. It is not uncommon to see a few stray strands framing my face, a reflection of the unbridled curiosity that drives me forward in my pursuit of knowledge.

As an existentialist, I grapple incessantly with the existential crisis punctuating modernity's landscape. At times, I find myself enveloped in a disquieting disillusionment, haunted by the weight of existential questions that linger ominously, like shadows cast by the glaring light of existence. The specter of evil looms large, its presence a stark reminder of the complexities and ambiguities inherent in human nature and society. I believe in the existence of evil, which is not solely confined to human actions but extends to the presence of otherworldly beings such as specters, demons, or entities beyond our comprehension. This conviction stems not from blind faith but from a deep-seated intuition nurtured by a lifetime of grappling with the inexplicable and the unknown. Within me, there is a profound acknowledgment that the universe is far vaster and more mysterious than our limited human perceptions can grasp, and within its depths lie forces, both benevolent and malevolent, that shape the fabric of reality in ways beyond our understanding.

That is why I am immensely grateful for the opportunity to serve as a faculty member at the Silver Ridge Institute, where I am granted access to a wealth of historical and philosophical works. Amidst the hallowed halls of academia, I find refuge in the timeless wisdom of the ages, delving into texts that offer insights into the complexities of human nature, the enigma of existence, and the eternal struggle between light and darkness. Pursuing hidden knowledge and understanding, I seek to illuminate the shadows, discern the patterns that underlie the chaos, and confront the manifestations of evil with courage and conviction.

❧ CHAPTER TWO ❧

The Silver Ridge Institute of Existential Studies is not just a place of learning; it's a sanctuary for seekers of truth amidst the chaos of existence. As a professor there, Christopher is immersed in profound discussions about the nature of being and the essence of existence. The classrooms resonate with the echoes of philosophical debates, where students eagerly engage in questioning the very fabric of reality. Existentialism is not just a subject to be studied; it's a way of life—a relentless quest for understanding in the face of uncertainty. Stepping into the institute feels like entering a realm where time slows down, and the weight of existential dilemmas hangs heavy in the air. The smell of brewed coffee drifts through the hallways, fueling the intellectual fervor that permeates every corner. Amidst the book-lined shelves and cozy reading nooks, existentialists from all walks of life converge, seeking solace in shared contemplation. It's a place where the complexities of existence are embraced rather than avoided and where the search for meaning is as vital as the air we breathe. At the Institute, self-discovery unfolds with each passing moment amidst the hushed conversations and the clinking of coffee cups.

As a believer in the divine and benevolent beings associated with kindness and goodwill, Christopher finds solace in the notion that entities are actively dedicated to promoting positivity and goodness in the world. These beings, whether angels, deities, or spirits, embody virtues such as compassion, empathy, and a sincere commitment to uplifting others. It is comforting to think that amidst life's challenges, there are forces at play that genuinely care about the well-being of humanity and strive to inspire acts of kindness and generosity. Across many cultures and belief systems, the idea of these benevolent beings manifests in various forms, each carrying its own symbolism and significance. Whether they're guardian angels watching over us, benevolent gods guiding our paths, or spirits of nature nurturing our souls, the essence remains the same: a beacon of light in times of darkness, a source of hope in moments of despair, and a reminder that love and goodness prevail. Embracing this belief instills a sense of gratitude and humility and encourages him to embody these virtues in his interactions and actions.

As a child, Christopher was always aware of a comforting presence surrounding him, a sense of warmth and protection that seemed to wrap around him like a gentle embrace. He could not quite put his finger on it, but it felt like a benevolent being was watching over him, guiding him through life's uncertainties. It was as if he had his very own guardian angel, a celestial being assigned to safeguard his journey through the world. Christopher thought: what struck me most about this presence was its unmistakable femininity. Though I could not see her with my physical eyes, I caught glimpses of her form in the depths of my imagination and perhaps in fleeting moments of clarity. She exuded a sense of serenity and grace, her ethereal presence offering solace during moments of fear or doubt. Whether in the quiet of the night or the hustle of the day, I felt her gentle guidance, nudging me towards paths of kindness and understanding. Her silent presence became a source of comfort and reassurance, a beacon of light in the darkness of uncertainty.

Even as an adult, I continued to feel the reassuring presence of this benevolent being that had been with me since childhood. Though life had taken me on many twists and turns, there was a constant sense of guidance and protection that never wavered. It was as if my guardian angel had remained steadfast by my side, navigating me through the complexities of adulthood with unwavering support. In moments of challenge or despair, I would often close my eyes and sense her ethereal presence enveloping me, offering peace and clarity amidst the chaos. I cannot help but wonder if the presence I felt earlier could have been her, here to guide, join, or protect me as I wrestle with the complexities of my existence and the foreboding feelings of uneasiness invading my mind lately. In moments of uncertainty, her ethereal presence offers a sense of reassurance, reminding me that I am never truly alone in my struggles. Whether she is here to offer guidance, companionship, or protection, I find comfort in knowing she is by my side, ready to lend her celestial support.

As the evening's hues dim and the night unfurls its deep cloak across the sky, Christopher moves through the dimming ambiance of his home's study, gently extinguishing the glow of lamps and fixtures. The soft click of switches echoes in the quiet space as he bids farewell to the day's activities. Papers neatly stacked, books resting on shelves, his sanctuary awaits tomorrow's endeavors. With a final glance around the room, Christopher leaves, pulling the door shut behind him, leaving only the faint scent of aged parchment and the lingering warmth of a day's contemplatives. In the solace of his bedroom, Christopher finds respite from the world's clamor. The tranquility wraps around him like a familiar embrace as he sinks into the softness of his bed. With a quiet sigh, he allows himself to succumb to the gentle pull of sleep, surrendering to the dreams that dance at the edges of consciousness. The night whispers its secrets outside his window, the only sound punctuating the stillness of the hour. Within the cocoon of darkness, Christopher finds solace, ready to embrace the mysteries that await in the realm of dreams.

In the depths of Christopher's slumber, his mind ventures into the surreal realm, where the boundaries between reality and imagination blur. Amidst the celestial expanse, a cosmic battle unfolds as forces of good and evil clash in a spectacle that defies mortal comprehension.

Swirling vortexes of light and shadow dance across the heavens, casting ethereal hues upon the celestial canvas. Drawn into this otherworldly conflict, Christopher finds himself standing amidst the fray, his heart pulsating with fear and determination. As the forces of darkness loom menacingly on the horizon, a figure emerges from the luminous glow of the heavens. She is a vision of divine grace, an angelic being adorned in flowing silk robes as white as the purest snow. Her golden locks cascade like molten sunshine, framing a visage of unparalleled beauty, while her eyes, a mesmerizing shade of radiant blue, shine with an inner light that pierces through the darkness.

With a gentle touch, the angel beckons Christopher to her side, her presence imbued with an aura of serenity and strength. Together, they stand as beacons of hope amidst the encroaching shadows, their spirits intertwining in a symphony of valor and righteousness. As the battle rages on, they fight side by side, their movements synchronized in a harmonious ballet of grace and power. Against the backdrop of the celestial battleground, Christopher and his angelic companion wage a valiant struggle, their resolve unyielding in the face of adversity as they strive to tip the scales in favor of light and goodness.

As the first tendrils of dawn gently infiltrate the darkness of Christopher's room, he stirs from the depths of sleep, his mind reluctantly emerging from the realm of dreams. With a faint sense of disorientation, he blinks away the remnants of slumber, the vivid images of the celestial battle still lingering in the recesses of his consciousness. As he slowly rises from his bed, the memory of the ethereal encounter with the angel and the cosmic conflict floods back to him, leaving him momentarily breathless. Sitting on the edge of his bed, Christopher contemplates the nature of his dream, its intensity and clarity defying the usual haziness of nocturnal visions. Could it be, he wonders, merely a product of his subconscious mind, a manifestation of his thoughts and emotions seeking expression in the silent theater of sleep? Or a tantalizing possibility whispers in the recesses of his mind: could it be a glimpse into something more profound, a window into a dimension beyond the confines of ordinary perception?

As he ponders the enigma of his dream, Christopher can't shake the feeling of awe and wonder that still lingers within him. Could it be that the censor mechanism of his brain had momentarily faltered, granting him access to a realm beyond the grasp of mortal understanding? The thought tantalizes him, stirring a sense of curiosity and intrigue that lingers long after the last traces of sleep have dissipated. With a sense of anticipation tinged with uncertainty, Christopher embarks upon the new day, carrying the echoes of the celestial encounter that had unfolded in his subconscious mind. Savoring the simplicity of his morning ritual, Christopher indulges in a light breakfast of warm toast and a cup of freshly brewed coffee. With contentment lingering on his palate, he gathers his belongings. He sets out for the Silver Ridge Institute, within walking distance of his residence, a familiar path illuminated by the sun's golden rays. The sound of birds chirping fills the air, harmonizing with the gentle breeze that caresses his skin, infusing the morning with a tranquil energy. Embarking on his journey, Christopher feels a sense of anticipation, eager to embrace the day's opportunities for growth and discovery awaiting him at the Institute.

As Sarah Hope gradually awakens, her senses tingle with newfound sensations, the tangible weight of humanity settling upon her. As her eyelids flutter open, she is greeted by the soft, filtered light seeping through the curtains of her small studio-style room. The sensation of cotton sheets against her skin feels novel, almost foreign after centuries of ethereal existence. Her breath catches in her throat as she reflexively touches her face, marveling at the warmth and

17

solidity beneath her fingertips. The transition from celestial being to mortal flesh is a surreal experience, one she's both intrigued and apprehensive about.

As she sits up in bed, a rush of emotions floods her soul. A profound sense of vulnerability mingles with a burgeoning curiosity about human experience. Her heart beats with a rhythm she's never felt before, a steady reminder of her newfound mortality. Glancing around the compact space, Sarah takes in the modest furnishings of her studio-style room—the minimalist decor, the cozy kitchenette tucked into one corner, and the compact bathroom nearby. Despite its simplicity, the room feels comforting, grounding her amidst the whirlwind of emotions. She cannot help but marvel at the mundane beauty of it all, each detail a testament to the vibrant tapestry of human life she's now a part of. With a deep breath, Sarah braces herself for the day ahead, uncertain yet hopeful of the adventures that await her in this newfound existence.

Stepping into the shower, the warm cascade of water envelops me, sending shivers down my spine. Each droplet feels like a revelation, a reminder of the physicality I have chosen to embrace. I close my eyes, allowing the sensation to wash over me, feeling the water cleanse away the remnants of my angelic essence. I savor an intimate experience with a newfound appreciation for the corporeal world. As I lather soap onto my skin, I revel in the tactile sensation, relishing the simple joy of feeling clean and refreshed. With each passing moment, my celestial existence washed away, replaced by the raw, visceral experience of being human. Emerging from the shower, I wrap myself in a plush towel, marveling at the sight that greets me in the mirror. The reflection staring back at me is undeniably human—my human form is a marvel of flesh and bone, a vessel for experiences yet to come. I trace the contours of my face, marveling at the softness of my skin, the curve of my lips, and the depth of my eyes. It is a sight that fills me with wonder and humility, a reminder of the beauty and fragility inherent in mortality.

With a sense of purpose, I dress myself, choosing clothes that reflect my newfound identity. I carefully selected a semi-casual outfit that exudes professionalism with a touch of feminine charm. I opted for a pastel-colored knee-length dress in a soft shade of lavender, its gentle hue lending an air of sophistication. The dress boasts a tailored silhouette, accentuating my figure without being overly revealing, while the modest neckline and cap sleeves add a refined elegance. Paired with burgundy tassel penny loafers, the ensemble exudes practicality, confidence, and poise, striking the perfect balance between professionalism and approachability. However, beneath my morning's excitement and discovery lies a gnawing hunger, a sensation I've never felt before. It reminds me of the earthly needs that now define me, propelling me towards the kitchenette in search of sustenance to fuel my body and soul.

Rummaging through the sparse contents of the kitchen, a slight pang of disappointment washes over me as I find it devoid of any food. However, my spirits lift slightly as I uncover the modest array of kitchenware provided by the manager—a small range, a handful of dishes, glasses, cups, and a tea kettle. My gaze falls upon a metal tin nestled among the other items, its contents a welcomed surprise. Inside, an assortment of flavorful tea bags awaits, a comforting sight amidst the barrenness of the cupboards. With gratitude, I prepared a cup of tea, a humble offering to quell the persistent hunger gnawing at my insides. As I take my first sip, the warmth of the tea floods my senses, enveloping me in a comforting embrace. The delicate blend of flavors dances across my palate, each sip a symphony of sensations—earthy notes of chamomile mingling with the subtle sweetness of honey, a hint of citrus teasing my taste buds. With each swallow, I feel a sense of physical and spiritual nourishment, as if each drop of tea carries a fragment of humanity's collective wisdom and experience. As I sit cradling the cup in my hands, I realize that this simple act of nourishment is just another step on my journey into the intricate tapestry of human existence.

Stepping out of my residence, I'm greeted by the crisp morning air, a gentle breeze carrying the scent of dew-kissed grass and blooming flowers. The streets are alive with the vibrant energy of the early hours as pedestrians bustle by on their way to work, and the soft chirping of birds provides a melodic soundtrack to the bustling townscape. Walking towards the Institute, I pass by quaint parks with charming gardens, their colorful blooms nodding in the breeze. The grassy areas along the sidewalk are dotted with dewdrops, glistening like miniature diamonds in the early morning light, while the soft rustle of leaves overhead adds to the tranquil ambiance.

Along the way, I pass by small shops and boutiques, their storefronts adorned with cheerful merchandise displays. The smell of coffee from a nearby cafe mingles with the sweet scent of pastries from a bakery down the street. I pause to admire the intricate window displays of a boutique; the mannequins dressed in the latest fashion trends beckoning passersby with their effortless elegance. The streets are alive with the hum of activity, a symphony of sights, sounds, and smells that invigorate my senses and fill me with anticipation for the day ahead. I have passed this route in my celestial form, and now I am experiencing it in human form by taking in all the sensations.

Christopher Daniels has arrived at the Silver Ridge Institute. He walks up the front steps and reaches the entranceway adorned with Greek-style columns. The entranceway consists of two large, ornate modern doors. As soon as he enters, he is greeted by a receptionist sitting at a desk in the lobby. Christopher greets her with a smile and says, "Good Morning, Julie." She responds, "Good Morning, Professor Daniels." Christopher asked if there were any applicants for the open research assistant position. Julie informs him that one applicant is referred to them by an agency. Christopher thanked Julie and proceeded down the hallway to his office.

Christopher's office at the Institute is a sanctuary of scholarly solitude, adorned with shelves laden with philosophical tomes and journals that speak to his intellectual pursuits. Behind his mahogany desk, he sits amidst a clutter of papers and research notes, the faint scent of old parchment mingling with the aroma of freshly brewed coffee. Behind his desk, shelves brim with eclectic artifacts, ranging from ancient relics to modern art pieces. As he gazes out the window, his mind drifts back to the dream that had haunted his sleep the night before, pondering its cryptic symbolism and the existential questions it raises about his journey and purpose in life. With a furrowed brow, he delves into the recesses of his mind, seeking to decipher the enigmatic symbols that may hold the key to unraveling the mysteries of existence itself.

Sarah arrives at the institute, which she recognizes as an ivy-covered building overlooking the town square from her previous visits in celestial form. She must climb the stairs to the entrance this time, but she does so gracefully. As she enters the building, she approaches the reception desk and greets the young woman behind it. Using her human voice, she introduces herself as Sarah Hope and explains that Elysium Staffing Services has sent her for the Research Assistant position. The receptionist, Julie, confirmed they were expecting her, and that the agency had emailed her information. Julie then informs Sarah that she will be working as an assistant to Professor Daniels.

Sarah's heart fluttered with anticipation as she listened to Julie's words. She had long awaited this opportunity to delve into the realm of earthly research, a realm she had

21

only observed from the celestial plane until now. With a polite nod, Sarah thanked Julie and followed her directions down the corridor toward Professor Daniels' office. Each step she took resonated with a newfound sense of purpose, her celestial grace seamlessly translating into earthly poise.

Upon reaching Professor Daniel's door, Sarah took a moment to collect herself before gently knocking. The door opened into a warmly lit office adorned with shelves of books, papers, and philosophical, esoteric, and scientific items. Christopher, whom Sarah recognized, greeted her; his warm eyes and gentle handshake welcomed Sarah inside. As she met Christopher's gaze, she couldn't help but feel a surge of familiarity wash over her. It was as if their souls recognized each other despite inhabiting different planes of existence. Sensing the mixture of awe and admiration in Christopher's demeanor, Sarah smiled gently, her heart fluttering with warmth and comfort. Sensing his heart racing and his mind whirring with thoughts, Sarah extended a warm smile, seeking to ease any apprehension he might be feeling. With a gentle voice that mirrored the soft caress of a summer breeze, she greeted him, her words carrying a sense of familiarity that echoed their celestial encounters. As they began discussing the intricacies of the research assistant position, Sarah felt a surge of excitement coursing through her veins, eager to embark on this new chapter of her existence as Sarah Hope, human research assistant to her earthbound charge, Christoper Daniels.

When he heard a gentle knock on his office door, Christopher was engrossed in his work, lost in a sea of papers and calculations. Curious, he set aside his pen and approached the door, opening it to reveal a sight that momentarily took his breath away. Standing before him was a woman of breathtaking beauty, her presence emitting an ethereal glow that bathed the room in warmth. Her fair skin seemed to shimmer in the soft light, complemented by cascading light blond hair reminiscent of the sun reflecting on newly fallen snow. But her blue radiant eyes captured Christopher's attention the most. Deep pools of blue, clear as the sky on a crisp morning, seemed to hold secrets untold and mysteries waiting to be unraveled. As their gazes met, Christopher felt an inexplicable pull, as if drawn into a world beyond his comprehension. He could not help but stand mesmerized by the vision before him, captivated by her beauty and the enigmatic aura surrounding her. He felt a sense of familiarity towards her and could not shake the feeling that he had seen her somewhere before. However, he was unable to make the connection now. Despite this, he felt an immediate connection as if his soul recognized her, even though his mind could not recall.

Sarah introduces herself to Professor Daniels, saying, "Good morning, Professor. I am Sarah Hope, and I am here for the research assistant position. Elysium Staffing Services referred me to the institute." Christopher greets her and says, "Welcome, Ms. Hope. It's a pleasure to meet you." Sarah thanked him and said, "Please call me Sarah." Professor Daniels then asks her to call him Christopher. "Of course, Christopher," Sarah smiles, appreciating the informal gesture. She sits across from him, feeling a sense of ease in his welcoming demeanor. As they converse, Sarah is not only enthralled by human conversation but also drawn to Christopher's passion for research and teaching, which she has already witnessed when gazing at him from her celestial form, but also because it mirrors her aspirations. Their exchange flows smoothly, transitioning from discussing her background and qualifications to the details of the research projects they will be involved in.

Christopher, too, feels a sense of promise after meeting Sarah. Her enthusiasm and qualifications align well with what the institute seeks in a research assistant. He appreciates her professionalism yet is pleased by her willingness to engage more personally. Christopher envisions a fruitful collaboration where he and Sarah can learn and grow together. As they settle into the conversation, Christopher gestures towards a nearby table strewn with research materials, inviting Sarah to join him. "Let's delve into the specifics of the position and how your skills align with my project objectives," he suggests. Sarah nods eagerly, ready to display her passion and expertise in the field. The atmosphere in the room becomes charged with intellectual curiosity, setting the tone for a fruitful collaboration between the two. Sarah and Christopher embark on a journey of discovery fueled by their collective enthusiasm.

Sarah thought as she sat across from Professor Daniels; my celestial and human aspects understand why I am here and the tasks that await. While I present myself as Sarah Hope, a potential research assistant referred by Elysium Staffing Services, I know there is a deeper purpose guiding me. With time, I will gradually reveal my true self to Christopher, unveiling the nature of my mission and the celestial realm I hail from. Despite the guise of a mere mortal, I harbor an innate sense of duty, eager to intertwine my celestial wisdom with Christopher's pursuits, forging a mutual path toward enlightenment and understanding.

CHAPTER THREE

Christopher and Sarah sat amidst a sea of papers and manuscripts, their task daunting yet exciting. They meticulously sorted through the wealth of the material Christopher had amassed from various sources. The room buzzed with the rustle of paper as they delved deeper into the intricacies of their research. As the clock ticked towards noon, Christopher glanced up from his work and turned to Sarah, a hint of hunger in his voice. "What would you like to eat for lunch?" he asked, a note of consideration in his tone. Her focus was still on the document before her; Sarah replied without missing a beat, "Something vegetarian. I refrain from eating meat and prefer vegetarian foods." Taking note of Sarah's dietary preferences, Christopher reached for the phone on his desk, dialing Julie's extension at the reception desk. With a courteous tone, he requested her assistance in placing an order for lunch. "Could you please arrange for a garden salad for Sarah," he instructed, "and I would like a club sandwich for myself?" Julie acknowledged his request with a friendly affirmation, and Christopher returned his attention to the papers spread out before him, grateful for the brief respite that lunchtime would bring.

Julie knocked on Professor Daniel's office door, and upon receiving a welcoming gesture, she entered with a tray holding their lunch order. Christopher expressed his gratitude as she placed the food on the desk, and with a polite smile, Julie then left the room, closed the door behind her, and returned to the reception desk. Julie Clark, a slender blond-haired woman with hazel eyes, possesses soft, pretty features that complement her pleasant demeanor. Always ready to lend a hand, Julie Clark exudes warmth and kindness in her interactions. As the Institute receptionist, she greets visitors with a welcoming smile, and her willingness to assist is evident in every gesture.

Single and residing close to the Institute, she shares her home with an adorable cat, her constant companion. Having been a resident of Silver Ridge for three years, Julie's tenure at the Institute spans the same duration, her dedication to her role unwavering as she navigates her daily tasks gracefully and efficiently.

Taking a lunch break, sitting across from Christopher, Sarah thinks to herself, I can't help but feel relieved as the hunger pangs that had nagged me earlier have finally subsided. My taste buds dance with delight as I delve into the garden salad, relishing the fresh vegetables' crispness, the croutons' satisfying crunch, and the subtle tang of the light vinaigrette dressing. With each bite, I feel a sense of rejuvenation, nourishing my newfound body and celestial soul. The accompanying crackers and sourdough bread add a delightful contrast of textures, completing the meal with a comforting touch. As I enjoy this simple yet satisfying dish, I feel grateful for the opportunity to nourish my body amidst the flurry of our research activities.

As Christoper savors his club sandwich, his gaze instinctively drifts toward Sarah, and he observes her quietly as she enjoys her salad. He tries not to be too obvious, stealing fleeting glances whenever possible. He thinks there's a certain innocence about her demeanor as she eats, a captivating quality that draws my attention. It's as if she's discovering the flavors and textures of her meal for the very first time, her genuine curiosity shining through with each bite. At that moment, he admires her simplicity and authenticity as he silently appreciates the subtle beauty in her every movement. After lunch and as they continue working through the afternoon, Christopher and Sarah immerse themselves further into their research, delving into records, news clippings, testimonials, and maps for forgotten accounts that detail the areas surrounding Silver Ridge. Their fingers trace the delicate pages of weathered books and articles, uncovering descriptions of the misty mountains and dense forests that have long captured the imagination of residents, adventurers, and scholars alike. Detailed accounts paint vivid pictures of towering peaks lost in perpetual fog and lush greenery teeming with wildlife, offering glimpses into the untamed beauty of the region.

Among the various articles and testimonies, intriguing references to legends and folklore speak of an ominous presence lurking within the shadows of the land. Whispers of an evil force, ancient and unfathomable, permeate the pages, weaving tales of dark entities that are said to haunt the misty mountains and dense forests. Stories passed down through generations warn of spectral figures and eerie phenomena, hinting at a dormant sinister power waiting to trap those who dare to venture too far into the unknown. Intrigued by these accounts, Christopher and Sarah find themselves drawn deeper into the mysteries of Silver Ridge, their quest for knowledge intertwining with the allure of uncovering the truth behind the enigmatic legends that shroud the landscape.

Christopher says, "I have heard stories about the area and rumors of peculiar goings-on within the institute's walls and about strange disappearances on the Silver Ridge Institute's campus and surrounding grounds. Students are not showing up for lectures or classes and are not being heard from again." He continues, "Local law enforcement has investigated these rumors, and missing person reports but has not shared them openly with the community. Perhaps they have no leads or are keeping things quiet."

Sarah nods in silent acknowledgment, her mind racing with the weight of the secrets she carries. She understands the gravity of the disappearances haunting Silver Ridge and the delicate balance required to navigate the murky waters of truth and danger. With a calm exterior masking her inner turmoil, she replies, "Yes, we must look further into these rumors and stories. As your assistant, I will assist you in every step until we find the underlying cause of all this. There is much more here than meets the eye."

Christopher's facial expression softens with gratitude as he acknowledges Sarah's dedication. "Thank you, Sarah. I could not ask for a better assistant and research partner. Your insights and commitment will be invaluable as we delve into this investigation's intricacies and twisting turns. The day is getting late, so we should start fresh tomorrow morning; you can help me decipher some of the strange writings and symbols on some of the parchments, maps, books, and scrolls I have gathered in my studies." He concludes. Sarah thanked Christopher, and with a gentle handshake, she left his office, nodding a friendly goodbye to Julie at the reception desk.

Christopher sat back in his chair and folded his hands behind his head. He couldn't help but think about how enchanting Sarah was and how well-informed and intuitive she seemed. Lately, he had been feeling a sense of dread and confusion, sensing that something terrible was on the horizon, but he could not quite grasp what it might be. He felt things weren't right at the institute where he works and teaches. Perhaps Sarah could help him uncover the truth. With those thoughts lingering in his mind, Christopher leaned forward and stacked the articles and research papers in front of him. He then placed the books and scrolls back on the shelf behind his desk and put notes and an artifact of a gold cross with a ruby gem embedded in its center into his briefcase to take home with him. He had discovered the artifact within a peculiar wooden box with Sumerian symbols inscribed on its lid and sides in his office left by the previous occupant. Finally, he turned off the light and left his office. Christopher bids Julie a good night in the lobby as he passes the reception desk and leaves the building.

Sarah steps out into the mid-afternoon sun, feeling its warmth embracing her as she departs the institute. A gentle breeze dances through the air, carrying the scent of blooming flowers and distant whispers of life in the bustling town square. She takes a moment to pause and admire the quaint charm of the surroundings, her gaze lingering on the historic buildings and colorful storefronts that line the streets. She is pleased that the first day went so well and happy about the ground she and Christopher covered today. They accomplished a lot in such a brief time, and she also feels pleased with herself for acclimating so well to her physical body and surroundings. In this tranquil moment, Sarah finds solace in the simple beauty of the town square, a serene oasis amid what is to come.

Silver Ridge is nestled in the heart of the High Cascades on the western edge of Mount Hood National Forest, northeast of the Willamette Valley, and the coastal Old Cascades, surrounded by lush forests, mountain peaks, and east of the majestic Misty Falls State Park, home to the famous Kaskali Falls. This 150-foot waterfall cascades into a moss-covered basin. Locals believe the falls hold ancient secrets and serve as a gateway to other realms. The town of Silver Ridge is located within the Mount Hood Corridor, off U.S. Route 26. Silver Ridge is a hidden gem, accessible via winding mountain roads that lead to its picturesque center. With just 9,500 residents, Silver Ridge is an example of small-town life in the Pacific Northwest. Its streets include historic buildings, cozy cafes, and vibrant murals that tell the town's story.

The town's intellectual heart began with the Silver Ridge Institute of Existential Studies. Founded by the enigmatic philosopher Professor Elias Hawthorne, the institute attracts thinkers, poets, and seekers from afar. Its courses delve into questions of existence, free will, and the human condition. Hawthorne believed that true wisdom could only be attained through deep contemplation and rigorous study. The Silver Ridge Institute of Existential Studies overlooks the town square, hosting lectures, seminars, and late-night discussions. Students gather to ponder life's mysteries.

Silver Ridge fosters a keen sense of community. Residents gather for the weekly farmer's markets, where fresh produce, artisan crafts, and lively conversations abound. The community takes pride in its public art scene. Around 30 brightly colored murals adorn the town's walls, depicting scenes from local history, folklore, and everyday life. Visitors can embark on a mural tour and art walk, discovering hidden gems around every corner. Every year, during the Silver Ridge Symposium, scholars, poets, and seekers gather to engage in Socratic dialogues and ponder the meaning of it all. The town's origins trace back to early settlers who sought refuge in the Cascades. They named the town Silver Ridge after the shimmering streams that flowed through the hills. Legend has it that a silver-haired woman, believed to be a guardian spirit, guided them to this fertile land. Locals claim that the town's mist-kissed air carries whispers of ancient philosophers, and the nearby Silver Ridge Springs—where the water flows from a hidden source—holds the key to unlocking the universe's secrets.

Leaving town, you cross a bridge that spans one of the many creeks fed from wellsprings beneath the forest floor. The bridge's wrought-iron rails are adorned with silver bells. Legend claims that when the bridge tolls at midnight, it opens a path to forgotten memories and lost dreams. Those who cross it may find themselves reliving moments from their past or glimpsing their future. Beyond the town lies the Mistwood Forest. There, ancient oaks guard hidden glades. The mist here is thicker, and the trees seem to whisper forgotten names. Whether strolling along the cobblestone streets, sipping coffee at Hawthorne's Cafe, or hiking the area's many forest trails, Silver Ridge invites you to contemplate life's mysteries and find solace in its natural beauty and rich history. Silver Ridge, where contemplation meets community, awaits those who seek more than what meets the eye.

Walking along the main street sidewalk, as late afternoon approaches, the quaint charm of the small town envelops Sarah with every step. Sun rays glow warmly over the colorful storefronts, as a gentle breeze carries the scent of freshly baked goods from nearby bakeries. As she approaches the end of the main street, Sarah's eyes light up at the sight of the farmer's market. Tents adorned with vibrant banners line the marketplace, offering locally grown produce, artisan crafts, and homemade delicacies. The chatter of vendors mingles with the laughter of shoppers, creating a lively ambiance that beckons Sarah closer. Entering the market, Sarah is greeted by a feast for the senses. Tables overflow with plump tomatoes, crisp lettuce, and juicy berries, showcasing the season's bounty. Nearby, artisans display handcrafted wares, from intricately woven baskets to delicate pottery.

Sarah's eyes twinkle with delight as she spots a charming woven basket nestled among the array of artisan crafts at the farmers market in Silver Ridge. Its sturdy yet elegant design speaks to her, promising to be the perfect companion for her future market visits. With anticipation, she approaches the stall and runs her fingers over the smooth wicker weave, admiring the craftsmanship that went into its creation. With a decisive nod, Sarah chooses it, exchanging a few words with the artisan before completing her purchase. The basket is now cradled in her arms, and she feels a sense of connection to the community, knowing that her support extends to the local farmers and the skilled craftspeople who call Silver Ridge home. With a grateful smile, she thanks the vendor and tucks the basket securely under her arm, eager to return to the market and fill it with the treasures of each visit.

Sarah's journey through the small town's farmers' market is as much about connecting with the community as it is about shopping for essentials. With her woven basket swinging lightly from her arm, she navigates the bustling aisles, her steps guided by the vibrant displays of locally sourced produce. A loaf of artisan bread catches her eye, its crusty exterior promising a perfect accompaniment to her meals. Nearby, she selects an assortment of crisp vegetables, their earthy aromas mingling with the scent of freshly baked goods. From plump tomatoes to leafy greens, each selection is a testament to the dedication of the farmers who nurture the land.

But Sarah's shopping excursion does not end with just vegetables. The lure of ripe fruits beckons her to another stall, where she carefully selects a medley of juicy berries and fragrant citrus. With each purchase, she feels a deeper connection to the rhythms of the seasons and the demanding work of the local growers. As she makes her way through the market, her basket brimming with wholesome goodness, Sarah cannot help but marvel at the vibrant tapestry of flavors and colors that define Silver Ridge's agricultural heritage. As she bids farewell to the vendors and heads home to her human dwelling, she carries with her provisions for the week ahead and a sense of gratitude for the bounty of nature and the warmth of the community surrounding her.

Christopher walked the short distance to his residence, which is located on Cascadia Maple Drive. Christopher's residence, situated at the terminus of Main Street on Cascadia Maple Drive, is a serene retreat enveloped by the tranquility of nature. The two-story home is gracefully set amidst a lush landscape of maple and pine trees, imparting a sense of seclusion and harmony with the surrounding forest. From its vantage point, the residence offers a picturesque view of the majestic Cascades, their peaks towering in the distance, creating a breathtaking backdrop against the canvas of the sky. Walking up the pathway to Christopher's house, a two-car garage is to the left, with a newer model Sports Utility Vehicle parked in its driveway. To the right is a front yard grassy area, neatly maintained and inviting. A front porch awaits at the top of the walkway, leading to the house's main entrance. Crossing the threshold, the ground floor exudes an inviting ambiance characterized by a spacious living area bathed in natural light filtering through the verdant foliage outside. A cozy study tucked away in a corner boasts rich mahogany bookcases lining the walls, laden with literary treasures spanning various genres and eras. Intriguing curio cabinets display an eclectic assortment of statues and artifacts, each with its own tale to tell, adding a touch of intrigue to the space. A spacious kitchen and dining area are set off to one side, perfect for gatherings and meals. Adjacent to these spaces is a cozy guestroom, offering a comfortable stay for visitors. To the rear of the house, a deck extends outward, providing serene views of the surrounding wooded areas.

Climbing the stairs, the second floor reveals a realm of comfort and repose. The bedrooms, adorned with simple furnishings and soft hues, offer an oasis of serenity for rest and rejuvenation. A masterful study awaits in one corner, furnished with oak bookcases, a writing table, an oak desk, and a console adorned with antique maps and globes, beckoning contemplation and scholarly pursuits. Among the sounds of rustling leaves and the gentle whisper of the wind, Christopher's residence embodies a harmonious fusion of refined living and the untamed beauty of nature.

Christopher entered his residence with a sense of weary determination, the heavy weight of the day's responsibilities evident in the furrow of his brow. Stepping through the doorway, the familiar home scent enveloped him, offering a momentary respite from the outside world. He went upstairs to his study, where the lamp's soft glow welcomed him warmly. Setting down his briefcase with a sigh of relief, Christopher carefully placed an ancient artifact on his desk. A ruby-colored gem embedded into its

33

cross-shaped front surface, its intricate carvings, and weathered surface, a testament to its storied past. With a brief glance, he silently acknowledged its significance before returning to the downstairs living space. Sinking into the plush fabric of his recliner chair, he let out a contented sigh, grateful for the tranquility of his sanctuary.

As Christopher succumbed to the heavy drowsiness enveloping him, he drifted into a restless slumber in his cozy recliner. The flickering light from a nearby lamp cast eerie shadows across the dimly lit room. A chill crept up his spine as his eyelids grew heavier, sending shivers down his weary frame. Suddenly, a sense of dread washed over him as if an unseen presence had materialized in the room. With a jolt, Christopher snapped awake, his heart pounding. In the hazy twilight between wakefulness and sleep, Christopher's surroundings seemed distorted, twisted into grotesque shapes. A sinister figure emerged from the shadows, its malevolent presence palpable in the air. Its eyes gleamed with malice as it reached out towards him. It whispered in a language he could not understand, but its meaning was clear: malevolence and despair. Its voice became more profound and clearer, urging him to abandon his research about the mysteries at the institute and the malevolence lurking within its hallowed halls. The figure stood in front of him, its form indistinct yet horrifyingly real, with eyes like burning coals and a smile that seemed to stretch beyond the limits of its face.

Christopher felt a cold grip tightening around his soul, pulling him into the abyss of fear and uncertainty. Christopher could feel its hatred seeping into the walls, a palpable presence that made his skin crawl. He knew, deep in his bones, that this was no mere ghost or figment of his imagination—it was a demon intent on breaking his spirit and claiming his soul. Desperate to resist the entity's dark influence, he clung to his resolve, determined to uncover the truth behind the malevolent forces at play in and around the town of Silver Ridge, the forest, the springs, and within the institute itself, even in the face of such overwhelming evil. As the entity's whispers grew louder, Christopher's resolve strengthened, and with a jolt, he sat straight up, the echoes of the entity's presence fading into the recesses of his mind.

Christopher's heart was pounding with a newfound sense of dread. The tendrils of the entity's influence lingered in his mind like a dark fog, intertwining with the uneasy feelings that had plagued him for days. He could not shake the conviction that something significant loomed on the horizon, something vast, something ominous that threatened to engulf him whole. The encounter with the entity confirmed his deepest fears, solidifying his belief that the institute and the evil lurking within its walls were not mere figments of his imagination. It was a chilling validation of the whispers that had echoed through his subconscious, warning him of the impending danger ahead. With a steely resolve born of fear and determination, Christopher vowed to delve deeper into his research. He was determined to uncover the truth behind the malevolent forces that sought to trap him and the darkness that threatened to consume everything he held dear.

Christopher went to the kitchen and prepared a small meal. After enjoying a simple meal of meat and potatoes, Christopher retired upstairs to his study, the artifact he had brought home from his recent expedition beckoning to him from its place on his desk. With a mixture of curiosity and apprehension, he picked up the ancient relic, turning it over in his hands as he studied its intricate carvings and weathered surface. The ruby-colored gem embedded in the surface of a cross, a talisman of sorts, held the key to its origin. Each detail whispered secrets of ages past, hinting at the mysteries buried within its ancient origins. As he pondered the artifact's significance and the chilling encounter with the malevolent entity, Christopher resolved to share his experience with Sarah the following day. Despite the uncertainty of her reaction, he knew she deserved to be informed of the looming threat encroaching upon their lives. Though she might initially doubt the veracity of his account, he understood the importance of her being aware of the dangers that lurked in the shadows. With a heavy sigh, he put the artifact back in his briefcase, knowing that the truth he carried within him was a burden they would face together, united in their determination to confront the darkness that threatened to engulf them.

As Christopher gazed out of his study's second-floor window, he could not help but be captivated by the serene stillness that enveloped the landscape. The tall pines and majestic maples stood steadfast, their branches reaching toward the darkening sky like silent guardians. Not a rustle disturbed the tranquility of the night as it descended upon the town of Silver Ridge and its surrounding landscape and forests, casting a veil of peacefulness over the world outside. With a calm finally settling over him, Christopher turned away from the window and went to his bedroom, the allure of sleep beckoning him after a long day's work and the evening's troubling encounter. As he slipped beneath the covers, the embrace of slumber enveloped him like a comforting blanket, pulling him into its gentle embrace. In the soft cocoon of his bed, surrounded by the hushed whispers of the night, Christopher surrendered to the embrace of sleep, allowing its soothing tendrils to carry him away to the realm of dreams.

❧ CHAPTER FOUR ❧

Sarah arrived home from the bustling farmers market, her woven basket laden with fresh produce, bread, and fragrant herbs. A sense of tranquility enveloped her. She carefully unpacked her treasures, arranging them with care in the cozy confines of her kitchen. The vibrant hues of the vegetables and the earthy aroma of the herbs filled the air, wrapping her in a comforting embrace. With each item placed in its designated spot, Sarah felt a wave of satisfaction, knowing that she would soon transform them into nourishing meals that would replenish both body and soul. With the kitchen infused with the comforting aroma of simmering herbs, Sarah brewed a pot of soothing herbal tea, selecting a blend carefully crafted to ease the day's tensions. As she poured the steaming liquid into her cup, warmth seeped into her bones, soothing and comforting her. Settling into a cozy armchair by the window, Sarah cradled the cup in her hands, savoring each sip as it caressed her senses. With each tranquil moment that passed, her mind gradually relaxed, finding solace in the gentle embrace of the fragrant brew, allowing her thoughts to drift into a state of peaceful restfulness.

As Sarah sat in the quiet solitude of her studio apartment, she felt a gentle presence permeating the air around her. It was as though the very essence of tranquility had taken form, enveloping her in its comforting embrace. Soon, Sarah realized she was not alone, for before her stood Guardian Angel Ambriel, the embodiment of learning and intellectual capacity. His presence brought a sense of clarity that washed over her like a soothing balm, untangling the knots of confusion that clouded her thoughts. Ambriel is a vision of ethereal beauty, with features sculpted by celestial hands to perfection, radiating a timeless allure. His golden locks cascade in soft waves, framing a face adorned with serene, angelic features that captivate all who behold him. Every movement is imbued with a graceful elegance as if he were a living embodiment of celestial harmony and splendor.

Ambriel clears away confusion, disbelief, fear, and doubt. And he removes the mental fog that does not let you see a situation clearly. Ambriel is an excellent ally in making the best decision. He shows you the next step when you are in doubt. This beautiful angel also clears your path towards the truth. He fills you with curiosity and a desire to discern. Sarah sat in awe of Guardian Angel Ambriel's presence as he spoke with a clarity that left no room for doubt. With a solemn yet resolute tone, Ambriel revealed the location of the Veil of Shadows—an enigmatic manuscript that held the keys to unlocking profound truths—within a hidden chamber nestled deep within the institute's walls. His voice, imbued with purpose and clarity, echoed through the recesses of Sarah's mind as he unveiled this long-guarded secret. With unwavering certainty, he guided Sarah in her mind toward the heart of the institute, where the whispers of ancient knowledge lay dormant, waiting to be unearthed. The significance of this mysterious manuscript, concealed within the institute's walls, became palpable as Ambriel illuminated its importance.

In that trans-formative moment, Sarah realized that this visitation transcended mere chance—a divine intervention orchestrated by Guardian Angel Ambriel himself. His guidance was not merely a fleeting encounter but a beacon of light leading her toward a higher understanding. As she absorbed his teachings, a sense of purpose and clarity washed over her, dispelling the shadows of doubt that once clouded her path. As Guardian Angel Ambriel concluded his revelation, a powerful surge of warm energy enveloped the room, signaling his imminent departure. With a sense of gratitude and awe, Sarah watched as his celestial form ascended gracefully, disappearing into the boundless expanse of the celestial realm. Yet, in his wake, he left a lingering essence—a delicate fragrance of lilacs and lavender that filled the air with tranquility and peace. As she basked in the residual warmth of his presence, she could not help but feel a profound gratitude for the guidance and wisdom he had bestowed upon her. The memory of his visit lingered like a gentle caress upon her senses, a reminder of the divine connection that transcended the boundaries of mortal existence.

Sarah thought: with the scent of lilacs and lavender lingering around me and becoming part of my very being, I feel a renewed sense of purpose and determination coursing through my veins. Though Guardian Angel Ambriel had ascended to the celestial realm, his presence continues to resonate within me, a beacon of light illuminating my path forward. And as I embrace the lingering fragrance of his departure, I know that I carry with me the blessings of his guidance, guiding me towards a critical mystery that I will reveal to Christopher in the morning when we reconvene at the institute. Tomorrow, Christopher and I will embark on a crucial journey within the depths of the institute's archives. Our mission is clear: to decipher the cryptic scrolls and ancient manuscripts that hold the key to unraveling the enigmatic mysteries shrouding Silver Ridge. As we delve into the intricate texts, our minds will be focused on unlocking the long-guarded secrets that have eluded comprehension for centuries. With each carefully transcribed word and meticulously analyzed symbol, Christopher and I will inch closer to understanding the malevolence that lurks within the institute's walls.

With determination and scholarly zeal, Christopher and I will be resolute in our purpose. For beyond the confines of the institute lies a threat of unfathomable proportions, a malevolence that seeks to spread its tendrils and engulf the entire world in its sinister grasp. Yet, we will stand undaunted, ready to confront this looming peril head-on.

With every revelation gleaned from the scrolls, we will edge nearer to the daunting task: to confront and dispatch the darkness that threatens to eclipse all light from our earthly and celestial worlds. Tomorrow marks the beginning of our arduous journey, but it also heralds the dawn of hope as we strive to safeguard not just Silver Ridge but the very fate of humanity itself.

As the night unfurled its velvety cloak over the town of Silver Ridge, the moon's gentle glow cast a serene ambiance, illuminating the landscape with its silver beams. Wisps of soft mist hung low to the ground, lending an ethereal quality to the scene, veiling the streets and buildings in a mysterious haze. The faint rustle of leaves and the distant hoot of an owl were the only sounds to disturb the tranquility that enveloped the town. It was a moment frozen in time, a tableau of quiet beauty as nature reclaimed its dominion under the moon's watchful gaze. In the stillness of the night, Sarah made her way to her bed, feeling the weight of the day's exertions settling upon her shoulders. With a sense of relief, she allowed herself to sink into the welcoming embrace of her mattress, surrendering to the call to sleep. As she closed her eyes, she could feel the ebb and flow of her breath, the rhythm of life pulsating through her veins. In this moment of solitude, she embraced the opportunity to replenish her energy and rejuvenate her weary body and mind. And as the night deepened, enveloping the world in its comforting embrace, Sarah drifted into a peaceful slumber, carried away on dreams woven from the threads of the night.

On the outskirts of town, nestled amidst a whispering grove, stand a group of ancient stones, weathered yet imbued with a mystical vigor that defies time. These small standing stones pulse with an enigmatic energy that seems to resonate through the earth upon which they stand. It is whispered among the locals that these stones are not mere relics of a forgotten era but serve as a conduit between the tangible world and realms unseen. Some believe they delineate the boundary between our reality and the ethereal planes beyond, where shadows dance and spirits roam.

During the Silver Ridge Harvest Moon Celebration, townspeople gather at the group of standing stones clad in cloaks and masks. They dance and sing, invoking blessings for the coming year. This town-sponsored event is a joyous occasion. During the day, children leave offerings of wildflowers and shiny pebbles, hoping to glimpse the elusive forest spirits. Picnic tables and food are brought out, the townsfolk play games, and lanterns are lit as the sun sets and evening arrives, as the day's events end. The residents of Silver Ridge return to their homes after a day of enjoyment and comradeship. But tonight is not the season for the Harvest Moon Celebration. Under the cloak of darkness and the moon's glow through the mist, the standing stones become a stage for a clandestine gathering shrouded in secrecy and mystery. Figures draped in dark cloaks converge upon the sacred site, their presence both eerie and mesmerizing. Around the central fire pyre, they weave intricate patterns with their movements, their voices rising in harmonious chants that echo through the stillness of the night. Incantations uttered in ancient tongues invoke blessings and beckon forth unseen forces as wisps of ethereal entities swirl and dance around the stones, bridging the gap between worlds.

Unbeknownst to the sleeping townsfolk, the rituals at the standing stones persist into the depths of the night, hidden from prying eyes and rational minds. As the veil between realities thins, a sense of otherworldly power permeates the air, casting a spell of wonder and apprehension upon those who dare to glimpse the mysteries that unfold beneath the starlit sky. In the heart of darkness, the stones bear witness to a timeless dance between the known and the unknown, where the boundaries of perception blur and the secrets of the universe are whispered among the shadows.

At the Silver Ridge Institute of Existential Studies, the upper-floor windows exude an unsettling aura, emitting otherworldly, foreboding hues of orange and red that pierce through the darkness, illuminating the desolate town square below. These ominous colors cast eerie shadows that stretch balefully up and down the main street, imbuing the atmosphere with a sense of impending dread. Movement catches the eye in one corner of the upper floor, obscured by the haunting glow. A silhouette of a male figure stands ominously, his form barely discernible against the backdrop of the dancing colors. He peers out from behind the window, his presence shrouded in mystery and intrigue. The figure's silhouette remains still, almost statuesque, as if he is silently observing the world below with an intensity that sends shivers down the spines of anyone who happens to catch sight of him. His mere presence adds to the sense of unease that permeates the air around the institute, leaving an impression of lurking danger and enigmatic purpose.

While a spectral glow flickers and dances around him, the figure seems to merge with the shadows, becoming one with the eerie ambiance of the Silver Ridge Institute of Existential Studies. His enigmatic presence serves as a chilling reminder of the profound and unsettling mysteries within the institute's confines, leaving those who dare to venture near with a sense of trepidation and apprehension. As night surrenders to the approaching dawn in the town of Silver Ridge, the stars gradually fade into the twilight, yielding to the soft glow of the awakening morning sky. With the first hints of daylight, the sleepy town stirs from its nocturnal slumber, and the silhouettes of the majestic cascades come into view against the gradually brightening horizon.

As morning arrives, Christopher steps out of his residence and sets off towards the Institute, his footsteps echoing lightly on the quiet morning streets. Along the way, he makes his customary stop at Baker's Dozen Bakery and Cafe, a quaint little establishment always bustling with freshly baked delights' aroma. Lena, the proprietor, greets him with a warm smile as he enters, her eyes twinkling with the promise of another delightful day ahead. Christopher bids her a cheerful good morning, anticipating the day's adventures. Lena, a woman of graceful demeanor and warmth, stands behind the counter, effortlessly commanding the bustling bakery with an air of quiet authority. Her apron is adorned with flecks of flour, a testament to her dedication to her craft. As Christopher approaches, Lena's eyes light up with recognition, a familiar sight for the regular patrons who frequent her establishment. She prepares Christopher's usual order with practiced ease—a delectable cinnamon roll and a steaming cup of freshly brewed coffee.

The air in the bakery is alive with the smell of freshly baked bread and pastries, a symphony of flavors that dance harmoniously around the cozy space. Lena's creations are renowned for their exquisite taste and the whispered tales of luck they bring to those who indulge in them. As Christopher settles into his usual spot, he cannot help but smile at the thought of the day ahead, fueled by Lena's culinary delights and the promise of good fortune that seems to linger in the air. At the same time, the aroma of freshly baked bread wafts through the morning air, and Sarah finds herself drawn to the irresistible allure of the Baker's Dozen Bakery and Cafe. As she steps inside, Sarah's gaze meets Christopher's, who, seated at his usual spot, warmly gestures for Sarah to join him. With a smile, Sarah eagerly walks over, her footsteps carrying her toward Christopher's table. As Sarah settles into the seat opposite Christopher, she cannot help but feel a sense of comfort in the air. Knowing that Sarah would delight in tasting one of her cinnamon rolls, Lena brings over two cinnamon rolls and two cups of coffee, one each for each of them.

As Sarah takes her first bite of the warm, gooey cinnamon roll, a symphony of flavors dances across her taste buds, sending a wave of delight through her senses. The pastry is perfectly balanced, with just the right sweetness and a hint of cinnamon that lingers on her palate. She savors each mouthful, relishing the buttery richness of the dough and the comforting warmth that fills her with a sense of contentment. Paired with a sip of the freshly brewed coffee, its bold aroma mingling with the sweet pastry notes, Sarah feels a sense of bliss wash over her as she partakes in this earthly delight. At this moment, as she indulges in the simple pleasure of tasty food and good company, all thoughts of the task waiting ahead melt away, leaving only the sheer joy of the present moment.

Christopher observes Sarah's enjoyment of the cinnamon roll and coffee, and a flicker of recollection dances in his mind, recalling how she had reacted during their lunch together the day before. It was as if she had never tasted such flavors before; an innocence and wonderment struck him as endearing yet puzzling. Despite his confusion, Christopher is drawn to her, captivated by her genuine delight in life's simplest pleasures. There is a warmth in her demeanor, a purity of spirit that resonates with him on a deeper level, tugging at the strings of his heart. At that moment, as he watches her savor every bite and sip with such unadulterated joy, Christopher realizes that it's not just Sarah's innocence that attracts him—it's her ability to find beauty and happiness in the mundane, a quality he finds himself inexplicably drawn to.

As Christopher and Sarah bid farewell to Lena and step out of Baker's Dozen Bakery and Cafe, they embark on the short journey to the Institute together, their footsteps falling into a comfortable rhythm along the familiar path. The morning air is alive with the cheerful melodies of birds singing in the nearby trees, their harmonious tunes intertwining with the gentle rustle of leaves in the breeze. Above them, the sun casts its golden rays across the sleepy town, infusing the streets with a warm, inviting glow that envelops everything in a comforting embrace. As they walk, the bustling sounds of Main Street gradually come to life around them, the rhythmic clinking of shopkeepers unlocking their doors and setting up for the day's business, serving as a backdrop to their leisurely stroll.

Occasionally, their shoulders brush against each other, a subtle yet palpable connection that sends a tingle of awareness coursing through Christopher and Sarah. As they navigate the uneven pavement, their shared journey to the Institute takes on a new significance, each step bringing them physically and emotionally closer together. Amidst the symphony of morning sounds and the gentle warmth of the sun, Christopher and Sarah are immersed in a moment of quiet intimacy, their hearts beating in tandem with the rhythm of the awakening town around them. As Sarah walks alongside Christopher, she finds herself engulfed in a strange sensation that she struggles to comprehend. It is a feeling she's never experienced, an unfamiliarity that seems to echo in the depths of her being. Despite her outward appearance of normalcy, Sarah is keenly aware of the foreignness of her physical form, each movement, and sensation a reminder of the unfamiliar vessel she inhabits. And yet, there's something else stirring within her—a stirring of emotions she can't quite grasp, their intensity causing strange vibrations to ripple through her consciousness.

Unaware of how her emotions might manifest in her newfound physical body, Sarah grapples with unease, unsure how to navigate this uncharted territory. The closeness she shares with Christopher, the subtle touches, and shared moments awakens a flurry of emotions within her, their potency leaving her feeling simultaneously exhilarated and apprehensive. As they continue their journey to the Institute, Sarah's mind races with questions, her heart yearning for understanding amidst the swirling tide of feelings that threaten to engulf her. For now, she tells herself, I must focus on the tasks I must accomplish today.

As Christopher and Sarah arrive at the Institute, they go directly to his office, their footsteps echoing softly in the hushed corridors. The lobby is eerily quiet in the early morning hours, devoid of the usual hustle and bustle of students and faculty. Even Julie, the ever-vigilant receptionist, is nowhere to be seen, her desk sitting empty amidst the stillness. The silence hangs heavy in the air, sending a shiver down Christopher's spine as he recalls the unsettling visitation he received the night before. With each step, the weight of unease settles upon Christopher's shoulders, a gnawing sense of foreboding constantly gnawing at the edges of his consciousness. The absence of familiar faces only serves to amplify his apprehension, casting a shadow of doubt over the tranquility of the Institute's halls. As they reach his office door, Christopher's pulse quickens, a sense of urgency driving him to unlock the door and step inside, eager to confront whatever mysteries lie in wait within the confines of his sanctuary. And yet, as the door swings open to reveal the familiar surroundings of his workspace, Christopher can't shake the feeling that they are not alone—that something ominous lurks within the halls of the institute, waiting to reveal itself.

Christopher removes the gold cross with a ruby gem embedded in its center artifact from his briefcase and places it back in the peculiar Sumerian wooden box. As Sarah and Christopher settle into their usual positions across from each other at the research table, the morning sunlight filters through the windows, casting a soft glow upon their faces. There's a sense of familiarity in their shared space, a comfort that belies the underlying tension that lingers in the air. As they prepare to discuss the day's research plans, Christopher's expression is grave, his gaze fixed intently on Sarah as he prepares to reveal the unsettling events of the previous night. With a heavy sigh, Christopher begins to recount the visitation from the malevolent entity, his voice tinged with a mixture of apprehension and determination. He describes the chilling encounter in vivid detail, recounting the warning to cease his inquiries into the happenings at the Institute. As he speaks, Sarah listens intently, her eyes widening in disbelief at the gravity of Christopher's words. The weight of the revelation hangs heavy between them, casting a pall over their discussion as they grapple with the implications of what they have learned. Despite the ominous warning, Christopher's resolve remains steadfast, his determination to uncover the truth unwavering in the face of adversity. Together, they plan their approach for the day's research, their minds buzzing with the possibilities and dangers that lie ahead. As they delve deeper into their plans, a sense of camaraderie builds between them, a shared determination to confront whatever challenges may arise in their pursuit of knowledge. And yet, lingering in the back of their minds is the remaining shadow of the entity's warning, a reminder of the dangers that await them in the darkness.

As Christopher finishes recounting the unsettling events of the previous night, Sarah's expression softens with understanding. She reaches out, placing a reassuring hand on his arm, a silent gesture of solidarity in the face of uncertainty. With a gentle nod, she assures him that she believes his account wholeheartedly, her voice filled with unwavering support. Sarah understands the gravity of the situation and the risks involved in their pursuit of truth. Yet, her belief in Christopher's judgment, integrity, and powers strengthens her resolve to stand by his side no matter what happens. Together, they share a moment of quiet determination, united in their commitment to uncovering the mysteries that lie hidden within the Institute's walls.

With a solemn gaze, Sarah reveals to Christopher that her awareness extends beyond the malevolent forces lurking within the institute's walls. She confides in him, sharing insights hinting at a much broader and deeply rooted conspiracy that transcends the confines of their immediate surroundings. As Christopher listens intently, his curiosity piqued, Sarah elucidates on the intricate web of connections that stretch far beyond what they initially perceived. It becomes apparent that what they have shared is merely the tip of the iceberg, and darker forces are at play, manipulating events with nefarious intent. Together, they realize that they must tread carefully, for the truth they seek could shatter the very foundations of their reality.

Christopher's brows furrow in confusion at Sarah's remarks about her broader awareness, but a profound sense of relief lies beneath the uncertainty. Grateful for her openness and honesty, he finds solace in sharing such weighty matters without fear of judgment. As he gazes at Sarah, a newfound admiration for her intellect and intuition blossoms within him. There is an undeniable sense that she possesses a depth of understanding far beyond the ordinary, and Christopher can't help but feel drawn to her enigmatic presence. Despite the mysteries shrouding Sarah, he knows one thing for sure—there is something undeniably different about her, and he's eager to uncover the truth behind her remarkable insight.

✎ CHAPTER FIVE ✎

As Sarah and Christopher delved into the ancient texts scattered throughout his office, they slowly unraveled the mysteries surrounding the malevolent force lurking within the institute's halls. Cryptic symbols and enigmatic passages hinted at something dark and sinister, threatening to disrupt the peace Christopher once thought prevailed. Recognizing the gravity of the situation, they shared a determined glance. The sense of urgency grew with each clue they unearthed, propelling them deeper into a labyrinth of secrets and deceit. As Sarah and Christopher sift through the books and ancient texts lining the shelves of Christopher's office, their fingers brush against a weathered journal tucked away amidst the volumes. They carefully open its pages with anticipation, revealing the name "Dr. Isabella Grey" scrawled across the top in elegant script. Their curiosity piqued, they delve into the personal notes within, uncovering a wealth of insights and revelations. Dr. Grey's words vividly depict her experiences within the institute, hinting at clandestine experiments and hidden agendas lurking in the shadows. The mystery deepens with each passage they read, and Sarah and Christopher find themselves drawn further into the enigma surrounding Dr. Grey's legacy. It becomes clear that her journal holds the key to unlocking the truth behind the institute's dark secrets, propelling them into a thrilling quest for answers.

Before Christopher came to the institute, Dr. Isabella Grey occupied his current office. After he moved in, he discovered many books, artifacts, and scrolls left behind by Dr. Grey. Although he had not gone through them, he was curious about their contents. According to what he was told, Dr. Grey was the assistant to the institute's current director, Professor Edmund Thorne, about five years ago. Dr. Grey left abruptly before Christopher's arrival. He was intrigued when he heard about Dr. Isabella Grey, a young and fiercely intelligent researcher known for her relentless pursuit of truth in her work. Despite her youth, Dr. Grey had already made significant contributions to her field, earning the respect and admiration of her peers with her innovative approaches and insightful analyses. He regrets not having the opportunity to meet her.

Professor Edmund Thorne is a man of both brilliance and eccentricity. His goatee beard and perpetually furrowed brow are the hallmarks of a mind ceaselessly churning with ideas. His office, nestled in a dimly lit corner down the hall from the Institute's antiquated library on the second floor, is a testament to his scholarly pursuits. Overflowing with dusty tomes, cryptic symbols, and half-empty coffee cups, the cluttered space reflects his intellect's chaotic yet fertile landscape. Within the labyrinthine depths of Thorne's office, the air is thick with the scent of old parchment and the faint aroma of brewing coffee. Piles of books teeter precariously atop one another, their spines worn and frayed from years of exploration and inquiry. Cryptic symbols adorn the walls, etched into faded scrolls and weathered manuscripts, each one a clue to the mysteries that Thorne tirelessly seeks to unravel. His reputation precedes him—an enigma who has deciphered forgotten languages and dabbled in forbidden knowledge. Professor Thorne keeps to himself these days and rarely appears in the lecture rooms or classes when they are in session. Instead, he spends most of his time in his office on the second floor.

Christopher has spoken to him several times, briefing him on research projects or existential lecture material. He also occasionally attends the Silver Ridge yearly Symposium, where Professor Thorne briefly addresses the attendees. Besides those times, Christopher interacts mainly with the Professor's young assistant, Dr. Isadora Vale. Dr. Isadora Vale, a striking figure in academia, possesses an allure that transcends mere intellect. With her dark, almost black hair cascading in waves around her shoulders and vibrant green eyes that sparkle with intelligence, she commands attention wherever she goes. Her presence is magnetic, drawing others in with an effortless charm and an air of grace and poise that speaks volumes of her confidence and self-assurance. Despite her youthful appearance, Dr. Vale carries herself with a maturity and sophistication that belies her age.

As Christopher and Sarah delved into Dr. Isabella Grey's journal entries just before Christopher joined the Institute faculty, a creeping sense of unease settled over them. With each page turned, their suspicions about the true nature of the Institute began to solidify, the revelations contained within the journal painting a chilling portrait of deceit and manipulation. Shock and disbelief washed over them as they realized the extent to which the Institute had been corrupted by power and ambition. However, the additional references to Professor Thorne sent cold shivers down Christopher's spine. A knot tightened in his stomach as he read Dr. Grey's descriptions of Thorne's involvement in the Institute's more nefarious research. The realization that someone he had once admired could be delving into such malevolent practices filled him with profound dread. The old leather-bound journal lay open on the table. Its yellowed pages held secrets: Dr. Isabella Grey's written words etched in ink. Christopher picked up the journal, turned to the last several pages, and read it aloud to Sarah. "Listen to this," he said, his eyes wide. Isabella wrote:

"January 20th: I have always felt that the institute was steeped in mystery since the day I was hired as a research assistant to the institute's director, Professor Thorne. Its halls harbored secrets, and the air had an electric charge that made the hairs on my arms stand on end. But lately, something has changed. Darkness has crept through the stone walls, seeping into the very marrow of the place. I admire Professor Thorne's intellect, but lately, I sense in him an underlying darkness."

"January 25th: "For several weeks, Professor Thorne and I have been poring over ancient texts and deciphering cryptic passages that speak of forbidden knowledge. We have traced ley lines, drew protective sigils, and invoked long-lost rituals. I've noticed how the professor's eyes have gleamed with a mix of excitement and trepidation. However, I sense a malevolence lurking. I am worried about our safety. I fear that I am losing my grip on reality as we continue to pursue our research, deciphering forgotten languages and dabbling in forbidden knowledge in a quest to unravel the truth."

"February 5th: Last night, I had an awful dream of shadowy figures whispering in forgotten tongues, their eyes devoid of humanity. They surrounded my bed and warned me to stop my research before it was too late. As I lay in my bed, paralyzed by fear, the shadowy figures closed in around me, their gaze piercing through the darkness with an otherworldly intensity. The dream left me shaken, the echoes of the shadowy figures' warnings still ringing in my ears."

"February 7th: Today, we deciphered the texts of an ancient book. We discovered the legends preserved within the manuscript and cracked the cryptic codes, revealing the book's title: "The Veil of Shadows." "Within the manuscript, the Veil of Shadows possesses the power to open or close the portal between dimensions, depending on whose hand wields its formidable might. In the hands of the righteous, it is a beacon of hope, a tool to safeguard the realms from the encroachment of darkness. However, in the grasp of evil, it becomes a weapon of unparalleled destruction, capable of unleashing chaos and devastation upon all that stand in its path. Its significance in the cosmic struggle between good and evil cannot be overstated, for the fate of worlds hangs precariously in the balance, swayed by the intentions of those who seek to control its power."

Christopher set the journal down on the table and stepped back. Fear engulfed his whole being. His hands trembled, and his heart raced. He could hardly utter a word. Could this be the knowledge he was seeking through his research? He wondered why Professor Thorne did not share this discovery with him. He asked where this all was leading to. A myriad of thoughts raced through his head as he tried to comprehend the significance of this finding and the power the ancient manuscript held within its pages. Sarah picked up the journal and continued reading Isabella's entries aloud.

"February 10th: The professor's obsession with the Veil of Shadows has consumed him," she wrote. The ancient texts spoke about unveiling the secrets of existence. Its pages whispered of forbidden realms, malevolent entities, and the boundary between reality and insanity. Professor Thorne's demeanor has shifted. I hear his laughter echoing through the empty corridors on the second floor, and his eyes hold a feverish glow. I fear he's becoming a vessel for the malevolence we sought to understand."

"February 15th: Last night, rain drummed against the stained-glass windows on the second-floor library, and the sky was moonless. Professor Thorne beckoned me into his cluttered office. The Veil lay open on his desk, its ink shimmering like spilled blood. His eyes gleamed with fervor as he traced the strange markings on the book, muttering incantations that resonated deep within the stone walls. "Isabella," he said to me, his voice a gravelly whisper, "what if evil isn't an abstract concept? What if it is a conscious force, dormant yet awakening within our institution?" I shivered as I glanced at the shadows that clung to the corners. "You mean?"—I said as the professor interrupted me, "Yes," he said, "An entity that feeds on our doubts, our fears. It thrives on the fractured souls of those who seek forbidden knowledge. The Institute, once a beacon of enlightenment, now harbors a malevolence."

Isabella continued, "My mind raced. I can now recall the inexplicable accidents—the shattered vials, the flickering lights at the Institute, and the nightmares that plagued my sleep. Was it mere coincidence, or had something darker taken root? "I asked Professor Thorne, "But why?" "Why would such an entity choose this place?" I recall Thorne's eyes bore into mine, and he replied, "Because we are seekers. We unravel mysteries, and in doing so, we invite chaos. The Veil—it is a conduit. It whispers secrets but also madness." he added, "We must tread carefully." When he said this, I thought, "I fear that we have gone too far, and I shall lose my mind at the very least."

February 24th: "It stormed again last night. Professor Thorne summoned me to the upper floor library, revealing a hidden chamber behind one of the massive bookshelves that lined the walls. I was shocked to find out this chamber existed, and fear came over me as we entered and stood in the heart of the institute's hidden chamber. The air crackled with energy, and the walls seemed to pulse—the professor's trembling hands held an ancient cross-shaped talisman—a conduit to the otherworldly. "Isabella," he said as his voice quivered, "we are on the precipice of discovery. But beware. The veil between realms is thin here. We tread where others dare not."

Isabella's journal entries continued, "The Veil of Shadows manuscript sat on a pedestal in the middle of the chamber as we stood before it, its symbols writhing like serpents. The professor's hands shook as he recited an incantation. The room quaked, and the air thickened with dread. Shadows merged, forming a shape—a faceless specter that hungered for release. I trembled and hesitated to ask, "Professor, what if we are wrong? What if this presence—" Professor Thorne's gaze was hollow as he said, "It's too late. Isabella, we have pierced the Veil. Now we must confront our creation."

Isabella's entry continues, "The Institute shuddered as the malevolence spilled forth, seeping into the cracks of reality. I wondered if we were saviors or unwitting architects of doom. As the specter whispered secrets and nightmares, I clung to the fading light, torn between my loyalty to Professor Thorne and the desperate need to banish our awakened darkness. Horror and fear filled my mind and body, and I ran from the chamber and the institute, fleeing into the night."

Sarah paused, allowing Christopher to gather his composure and his thoughts. She knew that these revelations unfolding within Dr. Isabella's journal would have a lasting impact on him and his position at the Institute. In the heart of the Institute, where knowledge and madness intertwined, Sarah vowed to Christopher that they would unravel the truth behind the entries. Sarah handed Christopher the worn journal, and he read Isabella's final entry aloud.

"March 1st: Today, I have returned to the Institute. It is Sunday, and the lobby is empty; the students and faculty are away for the weekend, save for a handful of researchers and existentialists studying within the small cubicles and offices lining the first-floor hallways. I've decided to leave the Institute and the assistant position to Professor Thorne. I am leaving this final journal entry, and this journal, inconspicuously among the books and periodicals that occupy the wall bookshelf behind my desk. I hope the next person who occupies this office will find and read it. I desire that the right person of sound mind and understanding will find it and take heed of the happenings at the institute and perhaps find a way to put a stop to the evil forces that Professor Thorne has unleashed."

Isabella continues," I fear that if I don't leave now, something terrible will happen to me, or I shall lose my mind completely. I fear for my life. Earlier today, I cautiously entered Professor Thorne's office while he was away and removed the ancient cross-shaped talisman from his desk drawer. I have placed it within a wooden box with ancient Sumerian symbols on the outside, hopefully cloaking its true origins from prying eyes. I have also placed this relic among the other ancient artifacts and relics in this office."

Isabella's final entry states, "I dared not enter the hidden chamber in the upstairs library to retrieve the Veil of Shadows out of fear that I would be confronted by whatever evil lurks within and lose my soul to the other malevolent forces. I fear that we have opened a portal between realms. My final warning is to be careful not to sacrifice your sanity and soul or seal your fate alongside the malevolence we have set free."

Christopher closed the journal and set it on the table before him. He realized that the artifact he had in his possession, which he had studied for clues to its purpose, was the same one Isabella referenced in her journal. The ruby-colored gem and gold cross were indeed the same talisman that Professor Thorne used along with the incantations to open a portal. He thought, could the portal still be open? Did Professor Thorne close it before Isabella hid the talisman? As Christopher contemplated the situation, a sense of urgency gripped him. If the portal were indeed still open, it could threaten the safety of everyone in the institute. The possibility of an evil force lurking within its halls only heightened his concern. He knew he had to act quickly, but first, he needed more information. Christopher decided to search for any clues left behind by Professor Thorne or Isabella from that fateful night five years ago that might shed light on the portal's status. Turning to Sarah, he asked, "How do you feel about what we just read? What are your thoughts on what we have discovered?" Sarah knew she was much more aware of the Veil of Shadows than what she had shared with him until this point; however, she thought the "Devil is in the details," no pun intended. She replied, "I have something significant to share with you." Christopher, puzzled by her response but eager to hear her account, listened intently.

Sarah began, "Last night, the Angel Ambriel visited me. He is the embodiment of learning and intellectual capacity. Ambriel revealed the location of the Veil of Shadows to me. He guided me in my mind toward the heart of the institute, where, just as Isabella described in her journal, the Veil of Shadows is hidden in a chamber behind the walls of the upstairs library. This visitation transcended mere chance—a divine intervention orchestrated by Guardian Angel Ambriel himself." Sarah added, "Angels are real, Christopher. Just as real as you and I."

Christopher listened intently to Sarah's words, his mind racing with the implications of what she was saying. The notion of divine intervention and the existence of angels shook the foundations of his understanding of the world. Yet, he has contemplated their very existence and believes he has felt an angelic presence around him on many occasions. "Angels... real?" he echoed, the words feeling both foreign and yet strangely comforting on his tongue. Sarah's conviction in her belief was obvious. Christopher found himself drawn to the idea that there were forces beyond the tangible world, guiding and protecting them in ways he couldn't comprehend. His voice trembling with wonder and uncertainty, he began, "If what you say is true, then perhaps this visitation is more than just a coincidence. It's a sign, a guiding light in the darkness we find ourselves in." He opened the Sumerian wooden box, glancing again at the ruby-colored gem and gold cross, now imbued with a sense of sacred significance in his eyes. With newfound resolve, Christopher realized he was not alone in his quest to close the portal. Whether through the workings of fate or the intervention of angels, he was determined to see it through to the end.

"Thank you, Sarah," he said, his voice steady with determination. I may not fully understand this, but I am willing to believe it. Let's close this portal and put an end to whatever darkness threatens our world." Sarah decided to hold off revealing her true nature to Christopher for now because she felt it would be too much for him to absorb, along with all the other truths they had uncovered that morning. He would find out her true nature soon enough, she thought. "Let's get out of here for a while and clear our minds," Sarah suggested. With Sarah's suggestion to take a break, Christopher felt a wave of relief wash over him. He nodded in agreement, grateful for the chance to clear his mind and rejuvenate his spirit. The morning's intense session had left him mentally drained, and he welcomed the opportunity to step away from the institute for a while. Christopher removed the ruby-colored gem and cross talisman from the wooden box with the carved Sumerian symbols and placed it in his jacket pocket to safeguard it from being discovered at the institute. He closed his office door behind them as they departed.

Christopher and Sarah greeted Julie at the reception desk as they passed her on their way to the front entrance exit doors. Students milled about in the lobby, preparing for the day's afternoon lectures, unaware of the mystery and intrigue that hovered over the institute. As Sarah and Christopher exited the building, Christopher could not help but reflect on his newfound appreciation for Sarah's assistance and companionship. Her strength and leadership today are a guiding light amid uncertainty, and he felt fortunate to have her by his side. Together, they wandered down the shop-lined main street and the tranquil grounds of Silver Ridge Community Park and Gardens, taking in the beauty of nature and allowing the fresh air to invigorate their senses. With each step, Christopher felt the weight of the morning's events gradually lifting from his shoulders, replaced by a sense of peace and clarity. As they walked through the serene surroundings, Christopher shared intimate details of his past with Sarah, a vulnerability he had not previously dared to expose to anyone. He recounted memories of his childhood, describing the sense of a benevolent presence always watching over him, comforting him in times of need. With each word, Christopher's voice carried a mixture of nostalgia and reverence as he delved into this mysterious guardian's profound impact on his life.

Walking side by side, Christopher thought about the discussion earlier in the day and said to Sarah, "I've always wondered that there's more to this world than what we can see," he began, his voice steady. "Angels, demons, spirits—they're all part of it. I think they're not just figments of our imagination or ancient myths. I've wondered if they are real, existing in dimensions or realms beyond our sight and influencing our lives. Is it them when you feel that inexplicable comfort in a moment of despair or an overwhelming dread in the dead of night? We might not see them, but their presence is undeniable." Sarah nodded, her eyes filled with a quiet belief as she shared his sense of the unseen and the felt. As their conversation unfolded, Christopher couldn't shake the realization that this unseen presence he had felt all his life, this guiding force, bore striking similarities to the concept of angels that Sarah had spoken of earlier. He hesitated initially but eventually confessed to Sarah, "I guess I do believe in angels." To his relief, Sarah responded with a gentle smile and a nod, her eyes filled with understanding and acceptance. At that moment, Christopher felt a sense of liberation, as if a weight had been lifted from his soul, and he knew that he had found a kindred spirit in Sarah, someone who shared his belief in the divine and the miraculous.

Christopher suggests they visit Hawthorne's cafe for a meal and spend the afternoon pondering the existence of angels. This suggestion resonated with Sarah. She welcomed the opportunity to delve into such profound topics in a relaxed setting, recognizing the importance of reflecting on life's mysteries. "That's a great idea," Sarah affirmed, her eyes alight with anticipation. "And tomorrow, we will delve deeper into what we've discovered this morning. But for now, let's nourish our bodies and souls with good food and recreation." With a contented smile, she added, "It will be a welcome respite from the challenges we've faced and a chance to replenish our spirits for the journey ahead." Christopher nodded in agreement, grateful for Sarah's companionship and the chance to explore the universe's wonders together in the comforting ambiance of Hawthorne's cafe.

As Sarah and Christopher strolled through the town, they passed by a street artist who was hard at work. Christopher recognized him as Henry, the reclusive artist known for his vibrant murals depicting the mist-shrouded forest trees, riverbanks, and local scenery. Each brushstroke seemed to capture glimpses of other realms, adding an ethereal quality to the scenes. Sarah marveled at the detail and vividness of the colorful murals, her eyes tracing the intricate patterns and dimensions that brought the town's landscapes to life as she discovered scenes from local history, folklore, and everyday life. One mural that caught Sarah's attention depicted a thick forest with towering pines and cedars. At the mural's center, a secluded wellspring of water cascaded down rocky cliffs, shrouded by a veil of mist. In the center of a meadow, a large circle of ancient stones, overgrown with moss, could be seen through the mist, bathed in ethereal light. As she gazed at the scene, Sarah sensed that Henry had been to this place. She couldn't shake the feeling that there was more to the picture than met the eye.

✤ CHAPTER SIX ✤

Hawthorne's Cafe sits nestled amidst the quaint shops and produce stores, a cozy haven in the heart of Silver Ridge. With its weathered wooden exterior and welcoming glow from within, the cafe is a testament to the town's history and enduring spirit. Initially established in the late 19th century by the Hawthorne family, the cafe has been a focal point of Silver Ridge for generations. It began humbly as a small general store, catering to the needs of loggers, miners, and settlers carving out a life in the rugged wilderness. Over time, it evolved into a gathering place where locals would convene to share stories, swap news, and seek respite from the rigors of frontier life.

Through the decades, Hawthorne's Cafe witnessed the ebb and flow of Silver Ridge's fortunes. It stood steadfast through boom times and busts, serving as a beacon of stability and community amidst the ever-changing landscape. Tales of romance, hardship, and triumph echo within its walls, woven into the fabric of its rich history. As Silver Ridge grew and modernized, Hawthorne's Cafe adapted, embracing current trends while preserving its timeless charm. It retains much of its original character today, with worn hardwood floors, exposed beams, and antique furnishings lending a nostalgic ambiance. The aroma of coffee mingles with the scent of homemade pastries, and the smell of down home-cooked culinary delights draws patrons in from near and far.

The cafe's patrons are as diverse as the town, ranging from old-timers who remember its early days to newcomers seeking a taste of small-town life. Local artists display their work on the walls, adding splashes of color to the rustic surroundings. Musicians gather on weekends to play folk tunes and ballads, filling the air with melody and mirth. However, the true heart of Hawthorne's Cafe lies in its staff, who carry on the legacy of hospitality and warmth established by the Hawthorne family generations ago. They greet each customer with a smile and a kind word, making everyone feel like part of the family. In an age of constant change, Hawthorne's Cafe remains a comforting constant, where time seems to stand still amid the timeless beauty of Silver Ridge and the majestic cascades.

Christopher and Sarah entered Hawthorne's Cafe and found a table in a quiet corner where they could converse and still take in the ambiance and activities of the cafe. Perusing the menu, they selected their choices. Suzy, the server, approached the table and spoke. "Welcome, Professor Daniels. What are we having today?" Then she looked at Sarah and, with a smile, nodded her head in a welcoming gesture. Christopher responded, "Thank you, Suzy; meet my assistant, Sarah." Suzy greeted Sarah and asked, "What can I get for you, my dear?" "I'll take the cobb salad and iced sweet tea," Sarah replied. "And you, Professor, what will it be?" Christopher replied, "I'll have the meatloaf special, and bring me an iced sweet tea." Excellent," Suzy replied as she bustled off to place their order; Christopher and Sarah settled into their seats, enjoying the comforting atmosphere of Hawthorne's Cafe. Soft patron conversations and light café music provided a soothing backdrop as they waited for their meals.

Christopher leaned in across the table, his eyes alight with enthusiasm. "So, Sarah, what can you tell me about angels? Sarah smiled, taking in the quaint charm of their surroundings. "I can tell you many things about angels, and I would be pleased to share what I know about them with you." She replied. Sarah's smile widened at Christopher's question, her eyes reflecting a deep knowledge and passion for the topic. "Angels are fascinating beings, Christopher. They are prominent in various religious and spiritual traditions, often depicted as celestial messengers or guardians. Across cultures, people believed angels possess divine qualities, providing a link between humans and the celestial realm." She paused, collecting her thoughts before continuing. "In Christian beliefs, angels are mentioned in the Bible, appearing to deliver messages, offer protection, or carry out divine tasks. They're often depicted with wings, symbolizing their ability to transcend earthly limitations and move between heaven and earth."

Sarah's gaze grew thoughtful as she delved deeper into the topic. "But angels aren't confined to Christian theology. Many other religions and belief systems also acknowledge the existence of celestial beings with similar roles. In Islam, for example, angels are considered servants of Allah, carrying out his commands and recording the deeds of humanity. In Judaism, angels play various roles, from messengers to warriors." She leaned in closer, her voice taking on a respectful tone. "But beyond their religious significance, angels hold a profound symbolism in the human psyche. They represent purity, guidance, and protection, offering comfort and reassurance in times of need. Whether one believes in their literal existence or sees them as metaphorical symbols of divine presence, the concept of angels resonates deeply with many people. I truly believe in angels because I have first-hand experience with them."

Sarah's words hung in the air, imbued with a sense of wonder and reverence for these celestial beings. At that moment, surrounded by the rustic charm of Hawthorne's Cafe, Christopher felt a new appreciation for the mysteries of the universe and the timeless wisdom embodied by angels. Christopher nodded in agreement. "Absolutely," he added, "I wish I could see them and reach out and touch one." Sarah smiled and replied, "Perhaps you will, Christopher, perhaps you will!" Their conversation ebbed and flowed as they waited for their meals to arrive, swapping stories and observations about their work and the world around them. Before long, Suzy returned with their plates, setting them down with a flourish.

"Here you go, Professor Daniels, one meatloaf and iced sweet tea," Suzy said with a smile, placing Christopher's meal in front of him. "And for you, Sarah, our famous cob salad and a glass of iced sweet tea. Enjoy!" "Thank you, Suzy," Christopher said, lifting his fork eagerly. "Everything looks delicious." Sarah echoed his gratitude, admiring the colorful array of fresh vegetables before digging in. As they savored their meal, the gentle hum of conversation continued around them, wrapping them in a warm embrace of community and camaraderie. In that quiet corner of Hawthorne's Cafe, surrounded by Silver Ridge's rich history and friendships, Christopher and Sarah felt at home in each other's company.

As the afternoon sun descended, casting a warm golden glow over Main Street, Sarah and Christopher emerged from Hawthorne's Cafe, their hearts light and spirits uplifted after a delightful meal and stimulating conversation. The quaint charm of Silver Ridge enveloped them as they stepped onto the cobblestone sidewalk, the late afternoon light painting everything in a soft, ethereal hue. Christopher's parting words to Suzy, the server, were filled with gratitude as he left a generous tip and settled the bill. Suzy smiled warmly, exchanging pleasantries with the pair before returning her attention to her other customers, her apron fluttering in the gentle breeze.

As Sarah and Christopher made their way down Main Street, the air was alive with the sound of birdsong, the melodious chirping of robins and sparrows signaling the approaching twilight. The storefronts lining the street exuded a cozy warmth, their windows adorned with twinkling lights and colorful displays. Town residents bustled about, completing their last-minute errands before the day ended. Some stopped to exchange greetings with Sarah and Christopher, their faces reflecting the tight-knit sense of community that permeated Silver Ridge.

The fading light bathed everything in a soft, golden glow, casting long shadows across the cobblestone streets. As they walked, Sarah and Christopher took in the sights and sounds of the town, savoring the simple joys of small-town life and the beauty of the natural world surrounding them. As they reached the end of Main Street, Sarah glanced back at Hawthorne's Cafe, its weathered exterior glowing in the waning sunlight. With a contented sigh, she turned to Christopher. "Thank you for the meal this afternoon and for our talks today, Christopher," she said, her voice soft with gratitude. "It's been a truly wonderful afternoon, and one we both needed after this morning's unsettling discoveries." Christopher returned her smile, his eyes twinkling with warmth. "The pleasure was all mine, Sarah," he replied. "Here's to you and I and the days ahead; we will triumph together." With that, they continued their way, the golden light of the late afternoon guiding their path as they journeyed home. Christopher walked Sarah to her residence, and they exchanged a gentle embrace. Sarah gave Christopher a soft kiss on his cheek, bidding him goodnight. Christopher continued his way home, his heart full of memories of the afternoon talks and the meal they shared, his spirits buoyed by the magic Sarah had brought into his life when he so desperately needed it.

As Sarah settled into her studio apartment, the familiar surroundings embraced her warmly, providing solace and sanctuary after the day's adventures. She sank into the soft, inviting chair by the window, the gentle evening breeze whispering through the curtains as she closed her eyes and allowed herself to drift into a state of meditation. With each breath, she felt a sense of calm wash over her, easing away the cares and worries of the day. During her meditations, Sarah reflected on the moments she had shared with Christopher at Hawthorne's Cafe, his presence lingering in her mind like a sweet melody. When she kissed him, the memory of his cheek against her lips filled her with warmth and longing, igniting a newfound sensation within her. She could not help but savor the memory of this gentle touch between them, the feel of his skin against hers, and the soft scent of his cologne that lingered in the air. It was a sensation she had not experienced before but found strangely comforting and rewarding, nurturing both for him and fulfilling for her. She prayed for the days to come, seeking guidance and blessings for the journey ahead.

As Sarah sat in her chair, lost in her thoughts and prayers, the room suddenly seemed to pulse with warm, radiant energy, illuminating the space with an otherworldly glow. A figure materialized before her with a soft rustle of feathers, bathed in a shimmering aura of light. It was Guardian Angel Muriel, the divine angel of emotions, her presence filling the room with a sense of peace and serenity. Muriel's ethereal form radiated grace and compassion, her wings unfurled in a protective embrace as she gazed upon Sarah with eyes filled with infinite wisdom and understanding. Muriel offered Sarah comfort and guidance. "Sarah," Muriel's voice echoed like music in the air, imbued with a celestial warmth that soothed the very depths of Sarah's being. "Fear not, for I am here to watch over you and guide you through the journey of your heart. Your prayers have been heard, and you are never alone."

Tears of gratitude welled in Sarah's eyes as she beheld the divine presence before her, feeling a sense of awe and wonder at the realization that she was in the presence of the angel Muriel. With a humble heart, she bowed her head in reverence, ready to receive the wisdom and blessings that Guardian Angel Muriel had come to impart. In that sacred moment, surrounded by the divine light of her celestial guardian, Sarah felt a profound sense of peace and comfort wash over her, knowing that she was eternally cherished and protected by the loving embrace of the angels. Angel Muriel is the patron of animals and plants. She is also the angel of emotional harmony and peace. Muriel constantly

66

reminds us that every good deed will be rewarded. Muriel also brings unconditional love. Just like Archangels Chamuel and Zaphkiel, Muriel fills our hearts with kindness and compassion for every living thing and inspires us to help others. Achieving happiness is by helping others in need. She inspires us to see the world with an open heart. When our hearts are open, we are also open for blessings.

Christopher arrived at his residence and ascended the stairs to his second-floor study with purpose, his movements deliberate and filled with a quiet reverence. As he removed the ruby-colored gem and gold cross talisman from his coat pocket, a sense of serenity washed over him. Placing it carefully into an oak box befitting its size, he felt reassured, knowing it was safely housed. With a satisfied nod, he placed the oak box inside a locked cabinet where he kept other cherished books and antiques secured beneath the bookshelf behind his desk, each a testament to his journey and beliefs. With a contented sigh, he immersed himself in the tranquility of his sanctuary. After changing into more comfortable attire and washing away the traces of the day's endeavors, Christopher descended to the first-floor living area, feeling a sense of relief wash over him as he left the world's cares behind. Soft, ambient lighting bathed the room, casting a warm, welcoming glow that enveloped him like a gentle embrace. The transition from the fading light of day to the gentle illumination of the night brought a sense of calm and tranquility, casting a soothing spell over his tired mind. Settling into his favorite armchair, Christopher allowed himself to unwind completely, sinking into the plush cushions as he savored the night's quietude.

As Christopher's thoughts drifted, he couldn't help but recall the tender moment he shared with Sarah earlier that evening. The memory of her gentle embrace and the soft touch of her lips against his cheek lingered in his mind, filling him with a warmth that transcended the chill of the night air. It was a simple gesture, yet it held a profound significance, stirring something deep within him that he could not quite put into words. In that fleeting moment, he felt a familiar connection between them, a bond forged in shared experiences and mutual understanding. There was something else he could not explain. It was as if they had met somewhere else, some other time, or in a forgotten dream. Her kiss on his cheek was like the flutter of a butterfly's wings against his skin, first sensed and then lost, like a gentle breeze that lingered in his thoughts.

The memory of Sarah's affectionate gesture brought a soft smile to Christopher's lips as he basked in the warmth of the recollection. It was a moment of pure simplicity and sincerity, a testament to their genuine connection. As he sat in the quiet solitude of the living area, surrounded by the gentle glow of the night, Christopher found himself feeling grateful for the unexpected gift of Sarah's presence in his life, knowing that the memory of their shared moment would linger in his heart long after the night had faded into memory. Christopher drifted into a peaceful slumber in the warm embrace of his favorite cushioned chair, his body and mind gratefully surrendering to the tranquility of the night. Outside, the nocturnal symphony of nature unfolded, with crickets chirping rhythmically, night owls hooting in the distance, and the haunting calls of loons echoing across the stillness. Each sound blended seamlessly into the tapestry of the night, creating a soothing melody that lulled Christopher deeper into his restful sleep. As he surrendered to the embrace of slumber, Christopher was immersed in tranquility and serenity, where time seemed to lose its hold and worries melted away into the darkness. The night air carried a sense of peace and renewal, wrapping him in its gentle embrace like a comforting blanket. In that moment, surrounded by the harmonious symphony of nature, Christopher found solace and contentment, allowing himself to drift effortlessly into the realm of dreams. The town of Silver Ridge, nestled amidst the towering peaks and whispering pines, also succumbed to the calm embrace of the night. Streets once bustling with activity now lay quiet, bathed in the soft glow of moonlight filtering through the unseen clouds overhead. As the residents retreated to the comfort of their homes, a calm settled over the town, casting a sense of peace and stillness upon its streets.

The next morning, the sun glowed warmly over the town center square, awakening the sleepy town of Silver Ridge. A serene atmosphere enveloped the square, punctuated by the sound of birds and the distant chatter of townsfolk starting their day. Sarah, her steps light with anticipation, met Christopher at the town center square amidst the tranquil surroundings, their meeting marked by a shared excitement for the journey ahead. As they exchanged smiles and greetings, the grand facade of the Silver Ridge Institute loomed before them, its towering presence a testament to the knowledge and discovery housed within its walls.

With determined strides, Sarah and Christopher crossed the institute's threshold, welcomed by its marble interior's cool embrace. The soft murmur of activity echoed through the halls as they approached the reception desk, where Julie, the ever-gracious receptionist, awaited them with a warm smile. Her eyes sparkled with familiarity as she greeted them, her genuine warmth setting the stage for the day's adventures. Sarah and Christopher exchanged a glance, their anticipation growing as they prepared to embark on a journey of exploration within the halls of the Silver Ridge Institute. Silence lingered between Sarah and Christopher as they traversed the corridors of the Institute, each lost in their own thoughts and anticipation. The weight of their purpose hung in the air, a palpable energy driving them forward until they reached Christopher's office. With a quiet nod, Christopher turned the handle and ushered Sarah inside, closing the door behind them with a soft click.

In the quiet sanctuary of the office, the outside world fell away, leaving only the two of them in a cocoon of focused intent.

"I've been thinking about what we uncovered yesterday," Christopher began, his voice low and thoughtful as he turned to face Sarah. "What we read in Isabella's journal about the Veil of Shadows." Sarah met his gaze, her expression mirroring his seriousness, a silent acknowledgment of the weight of their discovery. Nodding in agreement, Sarah replied softly, "There is still much to learn about the book's contents and origins." Christopher's eyes sparkled with determination as he nodded in affirmation, his mind racing with possibilities and avenues for further exploration. Together, they shared a silent resolve to unravel the secrets hidden within the ancient texts, their partnership fortified by a mutual thirst for knowledge and understanding.

Sarah continued, "Remember when I told you the Angel Ambriel visited me, and he revealed the location of the Veil of Shadows to me? He guided me in my mind toward the heart of the institute, where, just as Isabella described in her journal, the Veil of Shadows is hidden in a chamber behind the walls of the upstairs library." "We should concentrate on locating the chamber undetected and reading what the Veil of Shadow's pages reveal," she added. Christopher listened intently as Sarah recounted her encounter with the angelic visitor, his brow furrowing slightly in deep concentration. "Yes, I remember, and I think that's remarkable," he murmured, his mind already racing with the implications of her revelation. "If the angel guided you to the Veil of Shadows, then perhaps it holds even more significance than we initially realized." Sarah's words sparked a renewed sense of purpose within him, and he nodded in agreement. Christopher's gaze hardened with determination as he met her eyes, a silent vow passing between them to pursue the truth hidden within the institute's hallowed halls, no matter the obstacles they may encounter along the way.

"I have a confession to make," Christopher begins, "After our conversation yesterday, you have confirmed my beliefs about angels. Since I was a child, I have felt a presence around me," he admitted, his voice tinged with a mixture of reverence and uncertainty. "I believe in the existence of good and evil, which is not solely confined to human actions but extends to the presence of otherworldly beings. Not only do I believe in benevolent beings such as angels, guides, spirits, elementals, and inter-dimensional travelers, but there are malevolent beings such as specters, demons, or entities beyond my comprehension. I cannot explain why I do, but I sense they exist.

As Christopher nervously confides in Sarah about his belief in angels, good and bad, he feels a weight removed off his shoulders. Sarah listens intently, her eyes reflecting understanding and acceptance. She nods thoughtfully, her presence offering him a safe space to share his deepest convictions. Christopher's admission strengthens the connection between them, as Sarah's openness and empathy validate his beliefs, affirming that he's not alone in his spiritual journey. Sarah gently grasped his hand, offering silent comfort and solidarity, and in her response, Sarah reassured Christopher that his beliefs were valid and respected. Their conversation becomes a moment of mutual understanding and trust, deepening their bond. Sarah's acknowledgment of Christopher's childhood experiences and throughout his life lends credence to his beliefs, fostering a sense of solidarity between them. As they continue to converse, Christopher finds solace in Sarah's companionship, grateful for her support in embracing his spiritual truths.

Christopher tells Sarah, "I brought the talisman home to my residence yesterday and secured it in a place for safekeeping." Sarah responds, "That's smart thinking,

71

Christopher. Keeping it away from prying eyes is crucial. No one would suspect you have it. However, Isabella's journal also holds valuable information. Let's ensure it's safe, too." Christopher responds, "Absolutely, Sarah. We cannot afford to take any chances. I'll retrieve the journal, and we'll find a secure spot for it alongside the talisman. Our investigation into these artifacts is just beginning, and we must protect every piece of the puzzle." Christopher's revelation about bringing the talisman home elicits a nod of approval from Sarah, who recognizes the importance of safeguarding the artifact. Her acknowledgment reassures Christopher, affirming his decision to take responsibility for protecting the talisman. With Sarah's support, he feels more confident in his ability to keep it hidden from prying eyes, ensuring its safety while he delves deeper into its mysteries. Sarah's suggestion to remove Isabella's journal underscores her pragmatic approach to the situation. By proposing they secure the journal along with the talisman, she demonstrates her foresight and commitment to protecting both items. Christopher appreciates Sarah's practicality and recognizes the importance of preserving any potential clues or insights contained within Isabella's writings.

❧ CHAPTER SEVEN ❧

Christopher and Sarah, their minds brimming with ideas and discussions from their meeting in Christopher's office, decide to adjourn to the second-story library for further exploration into the origin of the Veil of Shadows. With a nod of agreement, they rise from their seats, the weight of their decision palpable in the air. Christopher reaches for the doorknob, his fingers lingering momentarily before turning it decisively, departing and sealing the room behind them. With a soft click, the door locks, ensuring their privacy and undisturbed focus. Together, they ascend the grand staircase, its steps adorned with polished marble and rich mahogany railing. Each footfall echoes in the expansive foyer, a testament to the solemnity of their purpose. As they reach the top, the imposing entrance to the library beckons them forward, its ornate double doors standing as guardians to a realm of boundless knowledge. With synchronized movements, Christopher and Sarah push open the doors, revealing the sanctum of the library beyond. They step into the hallowed space, their footsteps muffled by the plush carpeting that lines the floor.

The second-floor library at the Silver Ridge Institute of Existential Studies exudes an aura of intellectual sanctuary. Rows upon rows of towering bookcases line the walls, their shelves adorned with manuscripts and parchments bearing the weight of centuries of existential thought. Each volume whispers its secrets, inviting seekers to explore the depths of existential inquiry. Amidst this labyrinth of wisdom, study desks and private study spaces provide havens for contemplation. Soft lamplight bathes the room, casting a warm glow upon the worn wooden tables and velvet chairs. A stone-faced fireplace is built into the wall between two large bookcases in the center of the room, A welcome respite on chilly winter nights. Here, scholars and students immerse themselves in the existential musings of philosophers past and present, engaging in discourse transcending the boundaries of time and space. In this hallowed space, the pursuit of understanding takes precedence, fostering an atmosphere of profound introspection and intellectual growth.

Disappointed but undeterred by the presence of students and researchers, Sarah and Christopher resign themselves to postpone their quest for the hidden chamber and the enigmatic Veil of Shadows. With a shared glance filled with determination, they silently agree to return after hours when the library is deserted, ensuring their pursuit remains uninterrupted. For now, they make their way to a secluded corner of the library, where private study spaces await them. Nestled amidst the labyrinth of shelves, they find a haven of solitude, shielded from prying eyes and distractions. They select the historical books and manuscripts they had intended to peruse and settle into their respective chairs, eager to uncover the secrets and insights they contain. They immerse themselves in their research, the soft rustle of pages turning and the faint scratch of pens against paper the only sounds in their secluded enclave. Together, they unravel the threads of history, tracing the origins of civilizations and philosophy through the annals of time. A revealing pattern begins to emerge within the volumes of writings as they explore ancient accounts of the rise and fall of civilizations and human existence, including modern-era nations. Despite the delay in their quest, their spirits remain undimmed, fueled by the promise of discovery that lies beyond their reach.

Sarah discovered a scroll written in Latin titled "Talisma Rubini." "The Ruby Talisman," among the shelves, labeled the "Holy Relics" and excitedly unrolled it before Christopher. Their anticipation and awe at this rare find overcame them with discovery. Both Sarah and Christopher were familiar with the Latin language and could tell this was indeed an authentic scroll, if not an original, then certainly an accurate reproduction. As they carefully examined the intricate calligraphy and faded illustrations adorning the scroll, Sarah and Christopher felt as though they were transported to another era. The words seemed to dance off the parchment, weaving tales of ancient mysticism and forgotten legends. With each passing moment, their excitement grew, fueled by the realization that they were on the cusp of unraveling a mystery centuries in the making. The scroll whispered secrets of a bygone era.

The scroll reveals that deep within the hallowed halls of Rome's holy archives, many years ago, a monk known only as Brother Alessandro held a secret that transcended the boundaries of faith and time. For generations, his ancestors had safeguarded a mysterious Ruby talisman; its origin was shrouded in the mists of antiquity. Legends whispered of its power to channel divine energies and bestow blessings upon the chosen faithful. Yet, as the world changed and faith waned, Brother Alessandro knew that the true purpose of the talisman must be preserved.

In a clandestine ritual cloaked in the dim glow of candlelight, Brother Alessandro carefully embedded the Ruby talisman at the heart of a magnificent golden cross, an emblem of unwavering devotion and sacred symbolism. With each stroke of his quill, he inscribed ancient prayers and blessings upon the cross, infusing it with the sanctity of centuries past. Thus, the cross became more than a mere religious artifact—it became a vessel of divine mystery, concealing the true nature of the Ruby talisman within its hallowed core. As centuries passed, the cross adorned altars and sanctuaries across the globe, revered by countless worshippers who gazed upon its radiant form with awe and reverence. Yet, unbeknownst to all but a select few, the Ruby talisman pulsed silently within, its potent energies veiled by the aura of faith and devotion that surrounded it. And so, under the watchful eye of Brother Alessandro's descendants, the secret of the talisman remained safe, its true purpose obscured by the cloak of religious tradition, awaiting the day when its power would be needed once more.

The scroll continues to reveal a section titled "Aeta's Moderna" in Latin. "Modern Era" in English, which Sarah and Christopher understand, encompasses the period of history from roughly the late 19th century to the present. The scroll reveals whispers of a dark pact forged in the shadows of ambition and greed as Archduke Franz Ferdinand, the heir to the Austro-Hungarian throne, was assassinated. The formation of alliances among the European countries, such as the Triple Entente (Britain, France, and Russia) and the Triple Alliance (Germany, Austria-Hungary, and Italy), created a mutual defense system and increased the risk of a large-scale war. Lured by promises of power, the German Alliance sought to unleash an ancient malevolence upon the world. With the Ruby talisman in their possession, stolen from its sacred guardians, they wielded ancient incantations and energies and used the Ruby Talisman to open a portal between worlds and tear the fabric of reality asunder, plunging Europe into the maelstrom of World War I. The malevolence spread its tendrils of chaos and despair, sowing discord and destruction in its wake.

Amidst the chaos of war, whispers of the talisman's role in opening a portal allowing passage between the celestial and the earthly domain reached the ears of those who dared to confront the encroaching darkness. With courage and determination, they rallied to seal the portal and restore balance to the world. Through acts of valor and sacrifice, they reclaimed the Ruby talisman from the clutches of the German Chancellor. They returned it to its original resting place in the archives beneath the Basilica Sancti Petri in Rome.

Between World War 1 and World War 2, a new threat loomed over war-torn Europe—a sinister power of ancient origin emerged, spreading like a dark plague across the continent and the world from the Atlantic to the Pacific regions. Terrible evil and atrocities were perpetrated, culminating in the use of weapons beyond anything the world had ever seen. At the height of World War 2, with Europe and Asia scarred by devastation and turmoil, looming darkness began to spread across the continents and the world. Sensing an ancient force stirring beneath the surface, the Keepers of the Ruby Talisman, in a bold and secretive move, turned to the power of the Ruby Talisman to safeguard the delicate balance of spiritual energies. High-ranking clergy members convened in solemn council, invoking ancient rites and prayers from secret writings passed down through generations, as they sought to harness the talisman's mystic energies to seal off a burgeoning portal threatening to engulf the world in further chaos.

With the weight of history bearing down upon them, the holy emissaries journeyed to the heart of the European continent, where the portal pulsed with malevolent energy. In a climactic ritual shrouded in secrecy and sacrifice, the Ruby Talisman was brought forth as the benevolent agents worked to channel its power. With a resounding surge of divine energy, the portal was sealed shut, its dark influence banished and contained, leaving Europe and the rest of the world to rebuild amidst the ashes of war, shielded by the unseen guardianship of the Keepers, and the timeless power of the Ruby Talisman. The world emerged, its spirit renewed, and its future safeguarded against the forces of chaos and destruction.

As the gravity of their discovery settled upon them like a heavy cloak, Sarah and Christopher exchanged a solemn glance, their hearts pounding with excitement and trepidation. They knew that they stood on the precipice of something monumental, something that could alter the course of history itself. The "Talisma Rubini" scroll before them was the key to unlocking untold mysteries and the potential to unleash unfathomable darkness upon the world. With determination, they understood that their task was a race against time, a quest to thwart the now-present evil foretold within the "Talisma Rubini" scroll. Their hands still trembling, the weight of their revelation now steadied as they vowed to delve deeper into the secrets hidden within the enigma of the Veil of Shadows and safeguard humanity from its vicious grasp.

Sarah carefully rolls up the "Talisma Rubini" scroll and reties the purple-colored satin ribbon around its outer surface, holding the scroll's secrets within. It is not uncommon for the institute's resident faculty and researchers to remove books, manuscripts, and artifacts from the library for further examination and return them to the library afterward. Christopher informs Sarah that they will take the scroll with them for further examination, and he places it among the other items they intend to examine when they return to his office. As noon approaches, the institute's library begins filling up with students as their morning classes disperse, allowing them to explore the many volumes of material the library offers to pursue their studies. Christopher believes that the chants and rituals accompanying the energies of the Ruby talisman may be linked to the Veil of Shadows pages. He thinks the connection between the two items will be revealed once he and Sarah locate the ancient manuscript. Christopher and Sarah gather up the items they want to examine further, along with the "Talisma Rubini" scroll, and exit the library.

As Christopher and Sarah stepped into the second-floor corridor, they were met by the warm greeting of Dr. Isadora Vale, Professor Thorne's capable assistant. With a smile, Isadora addressed Christopher, acknowledging him with respect due to his position. "Good afternoon, Professor Daniels," Isadora said. "Good afternoon, Dr. Vale,"

Christopher replied. Isadora's attention then turned to Sarah, Christopher's new research assistant. "And this must be your new assistant?' she asks. "Yes, I would like you to meet my new research assistant, Sarah Hope," Christoper replies. Sarah's demeanor was a polite acknowledgment, her smile reflecting genuine interest in meeting Isadora, "Pleased to meet you, Dr. Vale. Dr. Vale, preferring to be addressed by her first name, responds, "Please call me Isadora." she adds, "Such a lovely assistant you are." Her attention lingered on Sarah, captivated by the delicate features that adorned her fair complexion. Sarah's eyes, a striking shade of blue reminiscent of a tranquil morning sky, seemed to hold a depth of secrets and mysteries yet to be unveiled. Isadora couldn't help but be drawn to Sarah's presence, sensing an aura of intrigue surrounding the new assistant. As Sarah exchanged pleasantries with Isadora, she could not help but notice the striking features that defined the professor's assistant. Isadora's dark, almost ebony hair framed her face in cascading waves, adding to her enigmatic allure. But her piercing green eyes captured Sarah's attention the most, radiating a sense of authority and confidence that demanded notice. There was an undeniable magnetism to Isadora's presence, an effortless charm that drew others in, including Sarah, with grace and poise.

Sarah noticed a subtle sense of unease beneath Isadora's calm exterior. Despite her friendly manner, Isadora seemed a little nervous, as if there was something dark and unsettling that she was hiding. Sarah could not shake the feeling that Isadora kept some secrets hidden behind her vibrant eyes, adding an intriguing layer of mystery to her persona. Sarah's intuition warned her not to be deceived by Isadora's charming facade. It reminded her of Isabella Grey's journal entries, which described her and Professor Thorne's ominous encounter with the Veil of Shadows and her retrieval of the Ruby talisman, followed by her hasty departure from the institute. Sarah could not help but feel uneasy about Isadora's role as Professor Thorne's new assistant and what might have happened since that fateful event mentioned in Isabella's journal. With each passing moment, Sarah's curiosity mingled with a growing sense of apprehension, wondering what dark forces might be at play and what part Isadora might have in them.

After exchanging a few more pleasantries, Christopher and Sarah bid Isadora a pleasant afternoon as she made her way to her office across from Professor Thorne's. With a nod of acknowledgment, Isadora disappeared behind the door, leaving Christopher and Sarah to continue their journey down the corridor. As they walked, Sarah could not shake off the lingering unease of her encounter with Isadora, her mind still preoccupied with the mysteries hinted at in Isabella Grey's journal. Turning their attention away from the second-floor corridor, Christopher and Sarah descended the marble staircase, their footsteps echoing softly in the grandeur of the institute's architecture. With each step, they retreated deeper into the familiar comfort of Christopher's office on the first floor, where the weight of intrigue momentarily lifted from their shoulders.

As they settled back into the familiarity of Christopher's office, Sarah felt compelled to share her feelings about the unsettling encounter with Isadora. With a furrowed brow, she recounted the unease she had sensed and the uncomfortable vibes emanating from Isadora during their brief introduction. Christopher listened attentively, nodding in agreement as Sarah voiced her concerns. He admitted that his interactions with Isadora had been limited, primarily confined to the formal exchange of research proposals and papers for Professor Thorne's review. Sarah's disclosure deepened the intrigue surrounding Isadora, adding another layer of uncertainty to their journey of discovery. As they pondered the implications of Isadora's role in the institute's affairs, Christopher and Sarah could not get over the lingering feeling of unease that permeated the air. With renewed determination, they resolved to tread cautiously, mindful of the secrets and shadows lurking within the hallowed halls of the institute.

Christopher suggests to Sarah that they get some fresh air, clear their thoughts, and grab a quick lunch away from the Institute's influence. Sarah agrees. Christopher recommends they stop at Lena's Baker's Dozen Bakery and Cafe on the main street before walking the short distance to his residence. He suggests they bring Isabella Grey's journal and the "Talisma Rubini" Scroll to his residence for safekeeping, away from the Institute. Sarah nods in agreement, knowing that the atmosphere at the Institute is becoming unstable and suspects Isadora and Professor Thorne may be getting suspicious of their research. When the students and faculty, including Isadora, leave early in the evening, Christopher and Sarah plan to return to the institute. Their mission: to locate the hidden chamber where the Veil of Shadows is rumored to be kept. Fully aware of the secrecy and potential consequences, Sarah agrees to this risky endeavor.

———

As they depart the institute and cross the town square, Sarah embraces Christoper's arm, locking her arm in his. They walk arm in arm down Main Street towards Lena's Baker's Dozen Bakery and Cafe, feeling safety and comfort washing over them both. As they step into Lena's, the aroma of freshly baked goods envelops them, momentarily distracting Sarah from the weight of their mission. Christopher's favorite spot by the window is open, offering a view of the main street outside. As they settle into their seats, Sarah carefully places Isabella Grey's journal and the "Talisma Rubini" Scroll on the table, keeping a watchful eye on their surroundings. Despite the cozy ambiance, she cannot shake the feeling of unease lingering from their recent encounters at the Institute. Christopher catches her gaze and offers a reassuring smile, silently acknowledging the gravity of their situation.

Sarah ordered a croissant and fruit cup, while Christopher chose a ham, cheese sandwich, and chips. As they ate their lunches, sipped their coffee, and discussed their next move, Sarah could not help but feel a sense of urgency creeping in. The Institute, once a sanctuary for scholarly pursuit, now feels like a prison of scrutiny and suspicion. Christopher remarks, "Isadora and Professor Thorne, once trusted allies, now seem like potential adversaries; their activities, I fear, are bordering on a dangerous obsession."

Sarah carefully nibbled on her croissant, her mind swirling with thoughts as Christopher voiced his concerns. She could not agree more—the Institute's atmosphere had shifted drastically just in the short time she had been there, and she knew Christopher's fears and recent awareness of the sinister activities taking place at the Institute that they have uncovered, up to this point in their research, is cause for alarm. With each passing day, the weight of their discoveries seemed to grow heavier, burdened by the fear of falling into the wrong hands. Christopher's words echoed her apprehensions, and she nodded in solemn agreement. She sipped her coffee with a sigh, steeling herself for the challenges ahead. They couldn't afford to underestimate the risks posed by those Christopher once trusted implicitly. Their mission to safeguard Isabella Grey's journal, the Ruby talisman, and the "Talisma Rubini" scroll had never felt more critical or precarious. Hopefully, they can better understand how to proceed when they find the Veil of Shadows.

Sarah and Christopher departed Lena's Baker's Dozen Bakery and Cafe, their conversation lingering on the flavors of the meal they had just enjoyed. The quaint establishment now receded behind them as they walked the short distance to Christopher's residence, a path familiar to Sarah in its physicality and ethereal resonance. Memories of visiting Christopher's home in her celestial form flooded Sarah's consciousness, reminding her of her true nature as an angel inhabiting a human body. As they crossed the threshold into Christopher's abode, Sarah felt a surge of emotions overwhelm her, the dichotomy of her existence as both a celestial being and a mortal human pressing upon her mind. It was a moment of revelation for her, a realization that she had been underutilizing the divine powers bestowed upon her by the ascended ones, relying instead on her human faculties and limitations. This epiphany propelled Sarah to confront the purpose of her transformation head-on, acknowledging the peculiar sensation of inhabiting a physical vessel while retaining the essence of her angelic nature.

Urgency pressed against Sarah's consciousness like a relentless tide, each moment slipping away inexorably. Time was running out. Deep within, she knew the veil hiding her celestial identity from Christopher could no longer endure. The urgency of their mission to restore the delicate equilibrium of reality weighed heavily upon her heart. As they embarked on this challenging journey to safeguard humanity from the encroaching darkness, Sarah understood that she must draw upon her intuition and celestial powers in unison with Christopher if they were to have any hope of success. It was time to cast aside the cloak of secrecy, to reveal the truth to Christopher, and to unite their strengths against the looming threat that loomed over their world. With resolve burning in her eyes, Sarah prepared to unveil her celestial essence to Christopher, contemplating how she would approach the subject and when would be the right time to embrace her destiny and confront the shadows that threatened to engulf them all.

Sarah decided to wait for Christopher to fall asleep, and then she would enter his dream in celestial form. She would manifest herself as an ethereal entity in his mind's eye, planting a seed of recognition within his subconscious. Her presence would instill a profound sense of peace and connectedness, a silent assurance that he was not alone. Revealing her true angelic nature and the reasons for her arrival would wait for another time, allowing him to slowly come to understand the extraordinary bond they shared.

As Christopher led Sarah up to his second-floor study, the anticipation of their shared mission filled the air. He deftly unlocked a panel hidden at the base of the bookcase, revealing a concealed cabinet. Sarah's eyes widened as she recognized the Ruby gem and gold cross talisman nestled among other ancient artifacts and tomes. With relief, Christopher carefully placed the Talisma Rubini scroll and Isabella's journal in the cabinet, securing them alongside the other items before locking it shut. Turning to Sarah with a reassuring smile, he remarked, "There, much safer now. I feel better already." Sarah mirrored his smile; her anxiety eased seeing their precious finds safely stowed away. "I do, too! So much better knowing they are locked up secure away from the institute and prying eyes," she agreed, her voice tinged with gratitude. With a shared sense of accomplishment, they exchanged a knowing glance, their partnership strengthened by their shared mission to protect these invaluable relics from those who sought to exploit their power.

❧ CHAPTER EIGHT ❧

After returning downstairs to the living room area, Christopher and Sarah settled into plush cushioned chairs opposite each other. The room's soothing ambiance enveloped them, inviting relaxation after their recent endeavors. As Sarah stretched out her legs, placing them on a soft fabric ottoman, she leaned back, allowing the chair's comforting embrace to cradle her. With a contented sigh, she closed her eyes, surrendering to the moment's tranquility. Christopher, reflecting her sense of calm, let out a sigh of his own. With a tone of ease, he suggested, "Let's rest and relax for a while before we return to the Institute." Sarah's smile conveyed her gratitude as she replied reassuringly, "Thank you, Christopher." She continues, "Christopher," Sarah said, her voice echoing softly in the warmth of the living space, "there is something very important I need to share with you. But first, we must get to the Veil of Shadows and decipher what's hidden within its pages. Everything will become clear to us when we have cracked its secrets."

Christopher nodded, "I trust your intuition, Sarah," he said, his voice filled with compassion and conviction. "If you believe that the key to our future success lies within the Veil, I will honor your request and be patient. When you are ready and the time is right, you will tell me what you want to share with me. I am certain it is essential and look forward to discussing and hearing it." Christopher could sense something was on Sarah's mind, and she seemed troubled about it. Perhaps she is feeling the same fear and apprehension that he is feeling. After what has been revealed so far in our research and the mystery and uneasiness that permeates the institute, he is confident it must be affecting her, as gentle and compassionate as she is. Christopher thinks to himself, I will keep her safe and protect her with all my heart. In a reassuring voice, as if she could read his mind, Sarah replied, "Thank you, Christopher." In this shared space of serenity, they found solace in each other's company, appreciating the respite before the next chapter of their journey unfolded.

Sarah had observed Christopher from her cushioned chair as she watched relaxation wash over him. Sarah listened as his breathing became steady as he fell into a restful slumber. At that moment, she decided to use her intuitive celestial power to enter Christopher's dreams. With the grace and ease of her angelic presence, she projected her image across his mind's eyes. Christopher stirred in his dream state as he heard a soft rustle of feathers, and an angelic being appeared, bathed in a shimmering aura of light, standing before him. As his gaze focused on the being, he recognized a female form familiar to him from a previous dream. She is a vision of divine grace, adorned in flowing white silk robes. Her golden hair cascades over her shoulders, while her eyes, a radiant blue, shine with an inner light. Around her head is a soft white glow resembling a halo. A delicate fragrance of lilacs and lavender filled the air. This time, he recognized her features! "Sarah!" he exclaims as she comes into full view, standing within arm's reach.

With a gentle touch, she reaches out and takes Christopher's hand. Sarah's celestial essence enveloped Christopher like a comforting embrace in the ethereal realm of dreams. His heart skipped a beat as he gazed upon her, his mind instantly recognizing her presence. The soft radiance emanating from her figure bathed the dream world in a soothing glow, casting away any lingering shadows of doubt or fear. As she moved closer, her aura filled the void within him, whispering of a profound connection that transcended mortal understanding. As their hands intertwined, a surge of warmth flooded Christopher's being, igniting a sense of familiarity that transcended the confines of time and space. With a calm celestial voice, Sarah spoke,

"We are the ones we've been waiting for." Christopher felt a lump form in his throat as he listened to Sarah's words. He could not speak, and a profound sense of awe washed over him. It was unclear to him what her words meant; however, in Sarah's gaze, he found solace and understanding, as if every question he had ever harbored found its answer in the depths of her azure eyes. In this shared dream, they weaved a tapestry of memories and emotions that bound their souls together across the vast expanse of the cosmos. As the afternoon's slumber and the dream began to fade, Christopher clung to Sarah's presence, knowing that even in the waking world, her essence would linger as a guiding light in the depths of his heart.

The late afternoon sun shed its golden rays through the room, as Christopher slowly opened his eyes, the remnants of the dream still vivid in his mind. The soft light illuminated Sarah, sitting across from him in the cushioned chair she had settled into earlier. Both comforting and perplexing, her presence mirrored the ethereal vision he had just experienced. The dream felt so real, so tangible, that he could not shake the feeling it was more than a mere figment of his subconscious. The sight of her in the waking world, so serene and radiant, only deepened his sense of an unspoken bond between them. Christopher's thoughts swirled with a mix of wonder and confusion. The dream had been a welcome respite, where his connection with Sarah felt undeniably profound and almost otherworldly. Yet, the line between dream and reality blurred, leaving him to ponder the true nature of their relationship. He secretly watched her quietly, contemplating the possibility that their connection transcended ordinary boundaries. The vividness of the dream and the calm assurance of her presence suggested that their souls were intertwined in ways he had yet to understand fully.

Sarah slowly opened her eyes with a serene smile and met Christopher's gaze. Her expression was warm and comforting, a gentle reminder of their shared connection. "It was nice to have a small nap," she said softly. "We should be getting ready to return to the institute before the sun goes down." Christopher nodded in agreement, feeling a sense of calm wash over him. As they both rose from their seats, they steadied each other with outstretched arms, a silent testament to their mutual support and understanding. As Sarah embraced Christopher, he felt a profound sense of reassurance. She held him for a moment, the warmth of her body grounding him in the present. Then, tenderly, she brushed his cheek with the tips of her fingers. The touch was delicate, yet it sent a wave of emotions through him. The soft fragrance of lilacs and lavender that clung to her enveloped him, stirring memories of the dream he had just awakened from. The scent, so reminiscent of the dream's ethereal quality, deepened his belief in their deeper connection, making him feel the boundary between dream and reality had momentarily dissolved.

Bringing his thoughts back to the present, Christopher suggested they freshen up before heading to the institute. Sarah nodded in agreement and went to the first-floor bathroom while Christopher climbed the stairs to the second-floor bathroom. Sarah found soap, washcloths, and all the amenities she needed in the cozy confines of the bathroom. She washed her hands and splashed cool water on her face, relishing the refreshing sensation. Glancing at her reflection in the mirror, Sarah noticed a subtle, ethereal glow still emanating around her, reminiscent of the dream. She wondered if Christopher also saw it as a sign of the connection that bridged their dream world and reality.

Sarah combed through her hair, smoothing out tangles, and straightened her clothes, preparing herself for whatever lay ahead at the institute. The reflection staring back at her was serene, yet there was a hint of curiosity and determination in her eyes. She knew their journey was far from over and that the institute held answers and challenges they had yet to face. With a final glance in the mirror, she took a deep breath, feeling a renewed sense of purpose. Ready to rejoin Christopher, she stepped out of the bathroom and focused on the tasks ahead and their unwavering bond. Christopher met Sarah in the first-floor dining room and kitchen entrance, holding two cold, refreshing water glasses. They drank together, savoring the moment of refreshment and replenishing their thirsts. The cool water provided a brief respite, invigorating them for the journey ahead. Christopher grabbed a vintage over-the-shoulder leather-type messenger bag, consisting of a digital camera, several flash drives and cables, and a spiral notebook, including blank paper for transcribing. With a shared sense of readiness, they left Christopher's residence, united in purpose as they made their way to the institute.

Strolling up Silver Ridge's main street towards the town square, Christopher and Sarah observed vendors and shopkeepers wrapping up their day, closing their stalls and shops. The air was filled with the murmur of evening conversations and the clatter of shutters being drawn. Students from the Institute strode past them, heading towards their homes and apartments, exchanging farewells and making plans for the evening. The last remnants of sunlight cast long shadows across their paths, stretching over the town's center square and giving the scene a tranquil, almost nostalgic feel. The bustle of the day gradually gave way to the calm of the evening, creating a serene ambiance as they continued toward their destination.

Christopher and Sarah arrive at the Institute, stepping through the main doors into the quiet lobby. The usually bustling area is serene, with the staff and students already departed for the day. Even Julie, the receptionist, had also left, leaving the space calm and undisturbed. The lobby and hallways are bathed in a warm glow, as the main lights have been dimmed to 30 percent, creating a tranquil atmosphere. Taking the main stairway to the second floor,

Sarah and Christopher glance down the hallway. They notice that both Isadora's and Professor Thorne's office doors are propped open by janitorial carts, indicating their departure. The hum of a vacuum cleaner fills the air, accompanied by the soft murmur of the evening janitorial crew as they chat and go about their tasks, adding a quiet yet lively backdrop to the Institute's otherwise still environment.

As they entered the library, Christopher whispered to Sarah, "Use your intuition. Sarah." They both nodded in silent agreement with the unspoken plan. The grand, dimly lit room was filled with towering bookcases, each shelf brimming with ancient tomes and mysterious volumes. Sarah felt a rush of determination as she began to methodically canvass the rows, her fingers lightly brushing the spines of the books. The air was thick with the scent of aged paper and ink, and the faint echo of their footsteps added to the library's mystical ambiance. Sarah's mind flashed back to her vision, a vivid encounter with Guardian Angel Ambriel. In the vision, Ambriel revealed the location of the Veil of Shadows manuscript, a legendary book that was said to hold the keys to unlocking profound truths. The manuscript was hidden in a secret chamber, concealed behind one of the many bookcases lining the walls. Guided by this ethereal knowledge, Sarah's eyes scanned the room with renewed focus, seeking any sign of the hidden entrance.

Sarah felt an energy emanating from one bookcase as she moved along the rows of books. Intrigued, she followed the sensation, her fingers trailing along the spines until she reached a spot where the energy seemed strongest. Carefully removing several books, she uncovered a hidden lever. Excitement surged through her as she exclaimed, "I've found it; this is it, Christopher!" Christopher quickly approached as Sarah pulled the lever. With a soft creak, the bookcase began to pivot on a center axis, slowly revealing a hidden chamber behind it. The entryway, now open, beckoned them into the inner sanctum. Sarah looked back at Christopher, their eyes meeting in a moment of shared triumph before they both stepped into the secret room. The chamber was dark, save for the sliver of light seeping in from the library. As their eyes adjusted, they made out the faint outline of a pedestal at the center of the room, upon which lay an oversized book. Candle holders with long, tapered candles stood on either side, casting ghostly shadows in the dim light.

Christopher ran his hand along the chamber's entranceway wall, feeling for a switch. His fingers soon found an electric light switch, and the room was illuminated with a flick, revealing the mysterious and ancient artifacts in more detail. The sudden light exposed the walls with dust. Cobweb-laden shelves, some had artifacts, some with manuscripts and tomes, and the full grandeur of the pedestal's centerpiece: the Veil of Shadows manuscript they had been seeking. Sarah reached up and pulled the inside lever as the library bookshelf returned to its former position, closing the chamber off from the library and allowing them the privacy they needed.

Sarah and Christopher made their way over to the pedestal in the center of the chamber as the Veil of Shadows came into view—a weathered tome bound in leather, shimmering with an otherworldly glow. The air around it seemed to hum with latent power. "The Veil of Shadows," Sarah murmured, her voice barely above a whisper. It has been waiting for us." Christopher's eyes widened as he took in the sight of the mystical book. "This is it," he said, his voice filled with awe. It is the key to understanding and closing the portal." They carefully opened the tome with reverence, revealing pages filled with intricate Latin incantations and diagrams. The ancient symbols seemed to pulse with their own life, drawing them deeper into the manuscript's secrets. Sarah traced her fingers over a passage, her brow furrowing in concentration. "Here," she said, pointing to a set of incantations. "These are the rituals we need to close the Veil of Shadows and banish the darkness."

Christopher leaned in closer, reading the Latin text aloud: "Angelorum custodes et magistri ascensi, adiuvate nos in pugna contra malos et claudendum portam umbrae." Translation: "Guardian Angels and Ascended Masters, assist us in the battle against evil and in closing the door to the shadows." As he spoke, the air around them grew charged with energy, and they felt a presence as if unseen beings were gathering to lend their strength. Sarah read aloud, her voice strong and unwavering: "Per potentiam rubini, claudatur velum umbrae." Translation: "By the power of the ruby, let the Veil of Shadows be closed." Sarah exclaimed, "There is the connection, Christopher!" As Sarah and Christopher delved deeper into the ancient tome, their eyes fell upon pages adorned with intricate Latin incantations and descriptions of powerful rituals. Each word seemed to pulse with latent energy, hinting at the arcane power contained within. As they pored over the ancient text, Sarah's intuition guiding their search, they began unraveling the mysteries within its pages. They discovered prophecies of a great darkness looming on the horizon, threatening to consume the world in chaos and despair. But woven amidst the tales of doom and destruction were threads of hope, whispers of one who would rise against the darkness and restore balance to the cosmos. Sarah and Christopher exchanged a knowing glance, their hearts pounding with purpose.

"We are the ones we've been waiting for," Sarah said, her voice tinged with certainty. "Together, we will confront the malevolent darkness that hangs over Silver Ridge and the rest of the world. And we will emerge victorious with the Veil of Shadows as our guide." Christopher's heart dropped. These were the words she spoke to him in his dream. How could this be possible, he asked himself. His mind was racing, thoughts swirling in a chaotic storm. He had to pull himself together. With a deep breath, he composed himself. "Sarah," he began, his voice steadying as he met her gaze, "I need to know... how did you know to say that? I heard those exact words in a dream earlier today before we found this book." Sarah's eyes softened, and she touched his shoulder reassuringly. "Christopher, our connection goes deeper than you realize. The dream messages you received were meant to prepare you for this moment. There will be time to tell you more later, but we must decipher the texts. Christopher felt a wave of awe and understanding wash over him. The fragments of his past dreams and experiences started to fall into place, forming a clearer picture of his destiny. "So, this has all been leading to this point," he said, his voice filled with newfound determination. "We were meant to find the Veil of Shadows and use it to end this threat."

Sarah nodded, her eyes shining with conviction. "Exactly," she said, "we have the power to close the portal and banish the darkness." Christopher nodded, a fire burning in his eyes as he gazed at Sarah. At that moment, he knew their destiny was intertwined, bound by a common purpose that transcended the boundaries of mortal understanding. As Sarah and Christopher delved deeper into the ancient tome, their eyes fell upon pages adorned with intricate Latin incantations and descriptions of powerful rituals. Each word seemed to pulse with latent energy, hinting at the arcane power contained within. "It's more than just a book," Sarah murmured, her voice filled with wonder. "The Veil of Shadows isn't just the title of this manuscript—it's the portal's name itself." Christopher's eyes widened in astonishment as he realized the significance of Sarah's words. The Veil of Shadows was a metaphorical concept and a tangible gateway to realms beyond normal comprehension. "We have to be careful," he said, his voice tinged with caution.

Sarah solemnly nodded; her gaze fixed on the ancient text before them. She could sense the immense power pulsating within the incantations, a power that could be harnessed for both good and ill. "But we may not have a choice," she replied, her voice tinged with urgency. "The darkness looming over Silver Ridge grows stronger each day. If we are to stand any chance of defeating it, we must be willing to take risks." Christopher nodded in agreement, his resolve hardening as he gazed at Sarah. With trembling hands, they began deciphering the incantations, their voices echoing through the chamber as they spoke the ancient words.

The air crackled with energy as the very fabric of reality bent and warped around them. Sarah said, "We should not speak these incantations or perform these rituals out loud here. This is not the place, and we could start a chain reaction that we are unprepared to face. I am certain the portal is not here at the institute but somewhere else." As Sarah and Christopher continued to study the pages of the Veil of Shadows, a realization dawned upon them: Professor Thorne had already opened the portal named the Veil of Shadows. "Without the ruby talisman, we could open the portal even wider, which would be bad," Sarah added. The gravity of their task weighed heavily upon them as they understood that their mission was not only to confront the darkness but also to close the portal once and for all. "We can't let this portal remain open," Christopher said, his voice filled with determination. "If we don't close it, who knows what kind of havoc it could wreak upon the world." The urgency in his tone was matched by the steely resolve in his eyes. They both knew the stakes were unimaginably high. The malevolent forces already slipping through the rift threatened to consume everything they held dear. With each passing moment, the risk of more entities crossing over grew exponentially, making their mission even more critical. Sarah nodded in agreement, her eyes scanning the ancient text for clues on how to seal the portal. "We need to act swiftly," she said, her voice tinged with urgency. "But we must also ensure that the knowledge contained within these pages is preserved." The ancient tome they held was a double-edged sword, filled with both the knowledge to banish the darkness and the potential to unleash it. As they deciphered the cryptic passages, the weight of their responsibility became clearer. They had to find a way to harness the power of the ruby talisman and perform the sealing ritual correctly or risk an apocalypse unlike any the world had ever seen.

With a shared sense of purpose, they set about copying the incantations and rituals onto the spiral-bound notebook's pages and photographing the remaining pages, capturing every detail to take with them on their journey. They worked quickly and methodically; their minds focused on the task at hand. Once they had documented everything they could, they carefully closed the Veil of Shadows cover, leaving it within its hidden chamber in the library, concealing it from prying eyes. It was a risk to leave such powerful knowledge unguarded, but they knew that it was necessary to keep it safe until they could return to retrieve it. "We'll come back for you," Sarah whispered to the ancient tome, her voice filled with determination. "But for now, our priority is to close the portal and protect the world from the darkness that threatens to consume it." Christopher noticed a manuscript on one of the dusty shelves titled in Latin "Per Aetates: Umbrae Temporis," translated, "Through the Ages; Shadows of Time," written by Archbishop Alejandro Patrici. Christopher decided to take the manuscript with them.

Christopher glanced at his watch, noting the time was 10:30 p.m. Almost five hours had passed since they entered the library and explored the hidden chamber. He ensured everything within the chamber appeared undisturbed, assuring the "Per Aetates: Umbrae Temporis" manuscript would not be discovered missing by Professor Thorne or Isadora. With the notes, photos, copies, and the manuscript securely placed in his over-the-shoulder bag, he nodded to Sarah. Sarah activated the exit lever, causing the bookshelf barrier to open and allowing them to step back into the library. Christopher, careful to leave no trace of their presence, flicked the wall light switch to the off position, plunging the chamber into darkness. Now silent and concealed, the room guarded its secrets once more.

As they emerged into the library, Sarah quickly pulled the access lever, closing the bookshelf barrier seamlessly against the wall. The hidden chamber was once again out of sight, its existence known only to those who sought its secret knowledge. Satisfied with their covert operation, Christopher and Sarah exchanged a knowing glance before approaching the library exit. Once in the upstairs corridor, they headed for the stairs. The corridor was empty and quiet, with the second-floor office doors closed, adding to the stillness. Christopher felt relieved, knowing they could slip out of the library and down the stairs without being detected. Their footsteps echoed softly as they made their way towards the exit, the weight of the materials and manuscript in Christopher's bag a constant reminder of their clandestine mission.

❧ CHAPTER NINE ❧

Stepping out of the Institute into the chilly, starlit night, Sarah and Christopher found the town square silent except for the sound of crickets and nighttime bird calls. The streets were devoid of pedestrians and automobiles, as most residents of Silver Ridge were tucked away in their homes well before 10:00 p.m. The empty square, bathed in the soft glow of streetlights, felt like a sanctuary of calm, contrasting sharply with the tense moments they had spent inside the hidden chamber. They walked briskly, eager to disappear into the night and return home before anyone could notice their absence.

Christopher and Sarah made their way down Main Street to Sarah's residence. They agreed to meet at Christopher's house in the morning. In the safety of his home, they could further study the notes and photographs they had taken of the Veil of Shadows and explore the "Per Aetates: Umbrae Temporis" manuscript. They needed to carefully formulate a plan of action to proceed with their newfound knowledge and the secrets they had uncovered. Sarah agreed, mentally preparing herself for the next day's revelations. She knew she must reveal her true nature to Christopher, a truth she had kept hidden until now. There was much to discuss, and the gravity of their discovery weighed heavily on her mind. As they parted ways for the night, Sarah felt a mix of anticipation and apprehension, knowing that tomorrow would bring significant changes to their quest and their relationship.

As they arrived outside Sarah's residence, Christopher gently embraced her, reassuring her with a soft kiss on her cheek. After a tender moment, their lips met in a kiss that was as tender and sweet as any loving kiss that two souls could ever share. Sarah felt a warm sensation spread through her soul and body, thinking how much she loved this mortal man. She had been his guardian through the years, watching him transition from a young boy to adulthood. It was in her nature as an angel to love deeply, and she knew that her love for Christopher was nurturing and eternal—a love that transcended time itself.

As their lips parted and they stepped back from each other, Sarah smiled, reassuring Christopher. Christopher felt tremendous relief and a sense of familiarity as if the kiss had healed something deep within him that had been troubling him for years. It was a sensation he was not used to, but it brought him comfort and peace. Sarah's smile and calm demeanor reassured him further, and he felt a connection beyond ordinary human experience, though he could not yet fully comprehend its depth. Sarah reached up and touched Christopher's cheek, bidding him goodnight before turning to climb the porch to her residence entrance. Christopher watched her enter the house, feeling thankful for their companionship and the reassurance that he did not have to face his challenges alone. He turned towards his home, his heart feeling lighter and his mind at ease, comforted by the knowledge that Sarah would be by his side, guiding and protecting him through whatever trials lay ahead.

From the second-floor window of the Silver Ridge Institute, Professor Thorne stood as a shadowy figure gazing down through the veil of night. The town square below was dimly lit, bathed in the soft glow of streetlights, casting a serene ambiance over the quiet scene. Thorne's corner office provided a vantage point that allowed him to observe the square closely, where he noticed the silhouettes of two individuals exiting the Institute and crossing the square. As they moved under the streetlights, he recognized one of them as Professor Daniels. The other, a woman with light blond hair that shimmered under the streetlights, he thought, must be the new assistant Daniels had mentioned, described in detail by Isadora. The radiant halo around her head and the cascade of light over her shoulders momentarily distracted Thorne from his troubles, stirring a long-dormant part of him. A genuine smile of hope softened his features as he watched them disappear from his view, a fleeting moment of brightness piercing his usual gloom. However, the pleasant distraction quickly gave way to suspicion and unease. Why were they leaving so late? Thorne's thoughts darkened, contemplating whether they had stayed for a late-night research session or something more clandestine. The creeping fear that they might have stumbled upon his secrets gnawed at him, although he tried to dismiss it as paranoia, a symptom of the curse that clouded his judgment. Resolving to inquire about Daniel's latest research project, Thorne could not shake the dread lingering in the corners of his mind.

Professor Thorne knew that madness had overtaken him since his obsession with the Veil of Shadows and the now-missing Ruby Talisman had consumed his every thought. These artifacts tempted him with the promise of immense power, allowing a veil to be lifted and a portal between realms to open. This dark quest drove him to the brink, costing him the loyalty and presence of his first assistant, Isabella. She fled, terrified not only by Thorne's growing insanity but by the fear that the same madness would consume her. He thought that perhaps Isabella had taken the Ruby Talisman with her when she fled so abruptly, intending to protect him from further madness or prevent him from opening the portal. Unbeknownst to her, the portal had already been opened, and the worst was yet to come. His attempts to track her whereabouts were unsuccessful, and through intervention from the dark ones, he realized that the Ruby Talisman could not be far. Perhaps she had hidden it somewhere within the Institute or the town of Silver Ridge.

Determined to find the talisman, Thorne and Isadora searched Isabella's office on the first floor and scoured every corner of the Institute, but to no avail. They even combed through her empty apartment, yet nothing surfaced. Somewhere in Silver Ridge or the surrounding area, the Ruby Talisman must be hidden. This question—where could it be? continuously haunted Thorne's thoughts, consuming him as he wrestled with the fear that without the talisman, he could never close the portal and reclaim his sanity. Professor Thorne also thought about his current assistant, Isadora Vale. Initially, her eagerness to explore the origins and intricacies of the Veil of Shadows and how to reverse the portal's power had been a source of hope for his salvation. She shared his passion for discovery, and they fervently delved into the mysteries. However, her curiosity soon morphed into a dangerous lust for power, and the malevolent spirits that traversed through the portal quickly overtook her just as they had trapped him.

Thorne and Isadora had become slaves to the dark side, their wills subjugated by the malevolent entities they had unleashed. They were no longer merely researchers; they were now physical hosts, compelled to execute the commands of the dark ones. This shared fate deepened Thorne's despair as he realized they were both lost to the same malevolent forces, their lives, and souls entwined in a sinister dance orchestrated by the very evil they had sought to control. Thorne realized too late that his soul was lost to the darkness. Haunted by his actions and the malevolent entities he had unleashed, Thorne felt hopeless, a mere puppet to their will. The only glimmer of hope lay in finding the lost Ruby Talisman, a chance to close the portal and regain his sanity. Yet, the talisman remained elusive, and with each passing day, Thorne sank deeper into despair. The weight of his mistakes and the overpowering influence of the dark forces left him feeling like a broken man, trapped in a web of his own making.

Turning away from the window, Professor Thorne returned to his office couch, where he had spent countless sleepless nights. There, on his office couch, he had often

100

contemplated his profound loneliness and the evil he had unleashed upon the world. The couch had become a refuge of sorts, though it provided little comfort from the turmoil within his mind. As he lay down, the weight of his actions pressed heavily on him, and he could only hope for a reprieve from the relentless nightmares that haunted his every moment. His only prayer was that the nightmares would not overtake him tonight, allowing him a brief respite from the horrors that plagued his thoughts. The darkness seemed to seep into his very soul, but the promise of a single peaceful night offered a sliver of solace. As he closed his eyes, he yearned for the escape that sleep could bring, however fleeting, from the madness that had become his existence.

———

Sarah entered her resident studio apartment, her body heavy with exhaustion from the day's relentless pace. The dim lighting of the cozy space embraced her as she kicked off her shoes and let out a deep sigh. The thought of a hot shower and a cup of chamomile tea called out to her like a welcome sanctuary. Shedding her clothes, she stepped into the bathroom shower, the steam rising to meet her. As the hot water cascaded over her tired muscles, it felt like each droplet was washing away the physical strains of the day. The lather of the soap against her skin brought a refreshing sensation, grounding her in the present moment and soothing her weary spirit. Sarah felt peace return after toweling off and slipping into soft cotton pajamas. She moved to the kitchenette, where she prepared a steaming cup of chamomile tea, the gentle aroma filling the room with a sense of calm. With the tea in hand, she sank into her favorite side chair, the plush cushions cradling her as she sipped the warm, floral brew. Each sip was a small comfort, the flavors unfolding and inviting her to savor the quiet of the evening. In this tranquil moment, Sarah felt the day's tensions dissolve, replaced by a deep sense of relaxation and contentment. As sleep began to take over, Sarah retired to her bed, her body sinking into the soft mattress, enveloping her in blissful cushions. The day's activities dissolved from her mind, replaced by a serene, drifting sensation. The comfort of her bed cradled her, soothing away the last remnants of fatigue. With each breath, she felt herself slipping further into a peaceful slumber, the gentle hum of the night lulling her into a deep, restorative sleep.

Christopher arrived at his residence and glanced over his shoulder; the walkway and streets were clear of activity, which calmed his nerves as he entered his home. The familiar creak of the front door and the comforting stillness of the house welcomed him back. He went to his downstairs study, a sanctuary filled with books and mementos. He placed his shoulder bag on the floor next to his desk and noticed the amber light on his combination phone and answering machine blinking steadily. Despite the ubiquity of modern communication tools, Christopher held onto this relic from the past. He had a landline phone at home and the institute, and though he owned a cell phone, he rarely used it. Computer and smartphone proficient, for him, the answering machine's gentle blinking was a nostalgic comfort, a link to simpler times. Because of the late hour, Christopher left the message unchecked until morning. The quiet of the night deepened as he powered down his computer and turned off the lights in his study. He felt a sense of calm, knowing he could deal with whatever awaited him on the answering machine after a good night's sleep. His home, with its blend of old and new, was his haven, and as he showered and prepared for bed, he appreciated the quietude that allowed him to unwind. The unanswered messages could wait; for now, the tranquility of his surroundings was all he needed.

Christopher's last thoughts before surrendering to slumber were of Sarah, his assistant, companion, and muse. He marveled at her uniqueness and otherworldly wisdom, qualities that set her apart from anyone he had ever known. Her intuition was uncanny, and she accepted him wholly as he was, without judgment. Sarah's gentle naivete contrasted beautifully with her profound knowledge and foresight, a combination that continually impressed and intrigued him. He remembered the kiss they had shared, a tender and nurturing moment. Her lips had been warm, soft, and ethereal, conveying not sexual or erotic passion but a sense of familiarity and upliftment. It was as if something deep within him had awakened, opening his awareness to realms beyond his understanding. The experience felt almost celestial, a gentle touch transcending the physical. Christopher's mind lingered on this ethereal connection as his breaths became shallower and further apart. With its celestial quality, the memory of Sarah's kiss enveloped him in a soothing embrace. The day's stresses and concerns melted, replaced by a profound sense of peace. He felt as if he were drifting on a gentle current, guided by the memory of Sarah and the inexplicable bond they shared. With each passing moment, he slipped further into a peaceful slumber, comforted by the thought of Sarah's otherworldly presence in his life.

After midnight, deep within the misty expanse of Mount Hood National Forest, ethereal energy begins to flicker, intertwining with the symphony of nocturnal creatures. The rhythmic chirping of crickets creates a steady undertone while the haunting hoot of a forest owl echoes through the trees. A distant howl of wolves occasionally punctuates the night, adding a layer of wild mystery to the darkened woods. The atmosphere is charged as if the forest is alive with an ancient power awakened by the night events. Earlier in the evening, Sarah and Christopher's incantations had stirred something profound within the forest's heart.

Their voices, chanting in unison, had built to a crescendo that seemed to resonate with the very soul of Mount Hood. As the final words of their incantations were spoken, a palpable wave of energy swept through the trees, causing the mist to thicken and swirl with a life of its own. An ethereal energy pulsed through the forest, reaching a peak before gradually subsiding, leaving behind an eerie, lingering mist that draped over the landscape like a ghostly shroud. Occasional sparks of energy crackle in the air, their brief flashes reflecting off the streams and creeks that flow from a hidden wellspring deep within Mount Hood's Forest wilderness. These sparks illuminate the water with a fleeting, mystical glow, creating a scene of otherworldly beauty. Amidst this charged atmosphere, a hidden vortex begins to stir; its presence felt more than seen. It beckons an enigmatic force calling to those who are brave enough to venture closer, promising secrets and power to those who dare to answer its lure. The forest, now alive with the remnants of the incantation, waits in breathless anticipation for what might come next.

Morning arrives at Cascadia Maple Drive. The sun's warm glow cascades through the windows of Christopher's residence, casting a golden hue across the room and gently nudging him awake. There is a crisp freshness in the air as he gets dressed and prepares a steaming cup of coffee, the rich aroma filling the kitchen. As he takes his first sip, he reflects on yesterday's discoveries, a mix of excitement and curiosity stirring within him. He knows there is still a substantial amount of material for him and Sarah to review, and the prospect of delving deeper into their findings energizes him. The day ahead promises to be filled with exploration and analysis. Christopher's thoughts drift to Sarah, an invaluable partner in their research journey. Together, they have unearthed fascinating insights, but the puzzle is far from complete. With purpose, he finishes his coffee and gathers his thoughts, focusing on the tasks ahead. The tranquil ambiance of Cascadia Maple Drive contrasts with the fervent activity that awaits in his study, where he and Sarah will piece together the intricate details they copied from the Veil of Shadows manuscript, pushing the boundaries of their knowledge and understanding.

Christopher went to his downstairs study, remembering he had a voice message to review on his message machine. Sitting at his desk, Christopher pushes the listen button on his message machine. The device clicks and whirs for a moment before a voice begins to speak, professional yet edged with urgency. "Hello, my name is Elias Crossford. I am the Deacon at Forest Haven Parish. I am calling on behalf of Father Aidan Green, our Pastor. I was given your name by someone you have never met but have much in common with: Dr. Isabella Grey." Christopher pauses the playback and leans back in his chair, a wave of shock washing over him. They must know or suspect something, but how could they have known to contact him? He asked himself, grappling with the sudden onslaught of questions and implications.

Christopher's mind races as he tries to piece together the puzzle. He had arrived at the institute only after Isabella had left, their paths never crossing directly. But mentioning her name in the message brought a cascade of memories and associations—her journal, her research, Professor Thorne, and her enigmatic encounter with the elusive Veil of Shadows. It seemed improbable, yet it was the only logical explanation: Isabella must have divulged details of her work to someone at Forest Haven Parish. Realizing that others knew of his and Sarah's involvement sent him a jolt of fear and apprehension. He could feel his pulse quicken, a deep-seated anxiety taking hold. How much do they know? he asks himself. Taking a deep breath to steady himself, Christopher pushes the listen button once more to continue the message playback. His mind reels, and he tries to focus on the voice coming through the machine. Every word now seems laden with significance, every sentence a potential clue. He listens intently, aware that this call could unravel secrets he and Sarah had only begun to understand or thrust them deeper into the mysterious and dangerous world that Isabella and Professor Thorne had navigated before him.

Deacon Crossford's message continues, "We would very much like to meet with you to discuss matters of great importance that would benefit our interests as well as yours. Perhaps we can set up a meeting at Forest Haven Parish where we can discuss these matters." Christopher feels a sense of urgency in the deacon's voice, a subtle insistence that hints at the gravity of the situation. "Under the circumstances, meeting at the institute or in Silver Ridge would compromise both your and our positions. It is of the utmost importance to keep our meeting confidential and away from certain individuals' watchful eyes or ears." As the message progresses, Christopher's apprehension grows. The deacon's words suggest a network of hidden watchers, a web of intrigue that extends far beyond what Christopher had initially imagined. "I hope that you understand we are your allies and not adversaries. Please get in touch with me at Forest Haven if you agree. Thank you." The message ends with Deacon Crossford leaving his phone number, a lifeline to a potential ally in this unfolding mystery.

Christopher leans back in his chair, staring at the message machine. The implications of the deacon's words swirl in his mind, mixing with his fears and uncertainties. The mention of keeping their meeting away from prying eyes resonates with his and Sarah's actions. The Deacon's offer of alliance was a beacon of hope. He knew he had to respond, seek out the hidden truths, and discover what role he and Sarah were meant to play in this intricate, shadowed game. Christopher decides that he needs to hear Sarah's thoughts before making any decisions. He paces the living room, his mind racing with the possibilities Deacon

Crossford's message has revealed. Every scenario he envisions deepens his resolve that Sarah's insight is crucial. The weight of the situation presses on him, and he knows he cannot shoulder it alone. Her intuition and keen understanding have guided them through difficult situations, and this moment is no different. Christopher's thoughts continue churning as he waits for Sarah's arrival. He recalls their past conversations, her perceptive observations, and how she always seems to see the heart of the matter. The situation's complexity feels overwhelming, but he trusts in her ability to bring clarity. He glances at the clock, feeling a mix of anticipation and anxiety. The decision ahead is significant, and he needs Sarah to navigate the murky waters they now find themselves in.

Christopher couldn't stop thinking about Dr. Isabella Grey's journal and the deacon who mentioned her name. He was curious about what happened to her after she left the Institute. He hoped the Forest Haven Parish clergy could provide information about her whereabouts and well-being. Christopher wished Isabella Grey was doing well and hoped to meet her someday. He deeply empathized with her and greatly respected her bravery in escaping the Institute. In his heart, he fervently wished for her safety and peace, hoping that she had found a haven far from the darkness that once threatened to consume her.

Christopher leans over the side of his desk. He retrieves from his shoulder bag the "Per Aetates: Umbrae Temporis" manuscript, along with the handwritten copies, notes, and photographs of the Veil of Shadows manuscript. He places them carefully on the desk before him. As he waits for Sarah, Christopher's mind races with thoughts of the night before at the institute. The manuscripts and copies they had obtained were filled with cryptic symbols and passages, each a key to unlocking the secrets of the Veil of Shadows. He knows that understanding these texts is crucial before they can even consider meeting with the clergy at Forest

Haven Parish. The message from Deacon Crossford had been clear: discretion was paramount, and there were eyes and ears they needed to avoid.

Christopher sat in contemplation, waiting for Sarah to arrive. His thoughts lingered again on the kiss they had shared the night before at her doorstep, the way her soft, gentle touch on his cheek had sent a wave of calm and healing through his entire body. Her smile was reassuring, and her eyes, hypnotic, seemed to penetrate his very soul. The memory of her presence filled his senses with how she smelled to him, a soft aroma of lilacs and lavender. What was it about her that drew him to her so completely? There was a gentle yet strong presence about her, a gracefulness he had never encountered. He felt they had known each other for much longer than they truly had.

As he waited, Christopher found himself reflecting on these feelings. He tried to piece together fragments of dreams that danced just beyond his reach, fleeting like the wind. It was as if the answers he sought were hidden within these dreams, but they remained elusive no matter how hard he tried. He knew, though, that Sarah's intuition would guide them. There was something about her that made him trust in the path they were on, even if he couldn't quite see where it led.

❧ CHAPTER TEN ❧

Sarah awakened from a restful sleep, her body feeling refreshed and rejuvenated. She had showered the night before, so after dressing, she went to the kitchenette to prepare a cup of Jasmine tea and a croissant with a dab of honey. As she savored the delicate flavors and buttery textures, she felt a sense of calm and readiness for the day ahead. The tea's floral aroma mingled with the sweet honey, creating a comforting start to her morning. Eager to start the day, Sarah walked to Christopher's residence. The town was waking up, with shops opening their doors and locals beginning their daily routines. She passed students heading in the opposite direction toward the institute, their laughter and chatter adding to the vibrant morning atmosphere. The crisp morning air carried the scents of freshly baked bread and blooming flowers, enveloping her senses and adding to her anticipation. As she neared Christopher's home, the familiar sights and sounds of the town filled her with a sense of purpose and readiness for the mysteries they were about to unravel.

When Sarah arrives, Christopher greets her with relief and anticipation. "Good morning, Sarah. I am so glad you are here. I have much to share with you," he says. Sarah Smiles and replies, "Good morning, Christopher, I hope you slept well?" she inquires. "Yes, thank you. he replies. "I received a voice message on my answering machine that you need to hear right away," he adds. They both enter the first-floor study. Once they are settled in his study, Christopher replays the message from Deacon Crossford. As the Deacon's voice fills the room, Sarah listens intently, her brow furrowing in concentration. When the message ends, a heavy silence hangs in the air, punctuated only by the soft ticking of the clock on the wall. Christopher watches her, waiting for her reaction, hoping she might see something he had missed or offer a perspective to help them navigate this unexpected development.

Sarah takes a deep breath, her eyes meeting Christopher's, with a mix of determination, understanding, and caution. "This may be what we need," she says slowly. "If they know about Isabella and Professor Thorne, they are deeply involved in the same mysteries we've been unraveling. We should meet with them, but we must be careful what we divulge. The Deacon's message could allow us to gather more information from them. Maybe Deacon Crossford is right; we may all benefit. My intuition tells me we must follow the clues to where they lead us. "What can you tell me about Forest Haven Parish?" She asks. "Let's not respond just yet. Instead, let's gather as much information as possible and then decide on our next move." Christopher nods, appreciating her pragmatic approach. Christopher shares his thoughts on the matter and his concerns with her. Sarah listens carefully, her expression thoughtful and serious. "We need more knowledge," she agrees. "Our manuscripts could hold crucial information about the Veil of Shadows and its significance. We need to understand as much as possible about them before we step into this meeting."

Christopher shared with Sarah his recollections about Forest Haven Parish, nestled among the ancient trees of the Mount Hood National Forest, east of Silver Ridge. He described its picturesque setting as a place where nature and spirituality blend seamlessly. The parish is home to St. Sylvan's Church, a beautiful structure adorned with stained glass windows that depict woodland landscapes, forest scenes, and the changing seasons. Parishioners, seminarians, and students gather for mass, prayer, and reflection. In addition to the church, the Forest Haven Parish is home to Sacred Cedars Seminary and an abbey, which are integral parts of the parish's spiritual life. The seminary provides theological education and training for future clergy, while the abbey offers a place for monastic living and contemplative prayer. He shared with her that he had visited the parish only once. While there, he felt comfortable and sensed the serene environment that the seminary and abbey offer; surrounded by the beauty of the forest, it fostered a deep sense of reflection and spiritual growth within himself and those who reside and study there. Sarah smiled and nodded her approval of his description.

Christopher spread out the copies and research material they had gathered from the institute the night before on a table in the center of his study. He uploaded photographs of the pages of the Veil of Shadows from a flash drive to a desktop computer and monitor on the same table. He also carefully placed the "Per Aetates: Umbrae Temporis" manuscript on the desk, keeping the delicate parchment pages intact. Sarah and Christopher began to piece together the story of the Veil of Shadows using the materials spread out in front of them. As they read the ancient passages from the manuscript, an understanding of its contents begins to unfold.

The Veil of Shadows, shrouded in mystery and whispered about throughout the ages in hushed tones among scholars and seekers of esoteric knowledge, chronicles cataclysmic wars between the forces of good and evil. Written in cryptic language and adorned with illustrations that seem to shift and dance when observed, the manuscript tells of a time when the boundaries between dimensions were porous, and reality trembled under the weight of cosmic conflict. Legends speak of celestial beings locked in eternal struggle, their battles echoing through the ages and leaving indelible marks upon the fabric of existence. At the heart of the manuscript lies the enigmatic tale of a portal known as the Veil of Shadows—a gateway between worlds that blurred the line between the mortal realm and the celestial planes. It is said that through

111

this portal, the forces of darkness sought to infiltrate and corrupt the very essence of creation while the champions of light stood vigilant, guarding against the encroaching tide of chaos.

The Veil of Shadows became a focal point in the war, a battleground where cosmic powers clashed, and the ebb and flow of celestial forces shaped mortal destinies. Its existence heralded hope and despair, for within its depths lay the potential for salvation or annihilation, depending on whose hand wielded its power. It is described as both a doorway and a barrier, capable of sealing away the malevolent forces that seek to breach the mortal realm or unleash them upon unsuspecting worlds. Forged in the crucible of celestial craftsmanship, its true nature remains elusive, known only to those who dare to seek its secrets. According to the legends preserved within the manuscript, the Veil of Shadows incantations and prayers can open or close the portal between dimensions, depending on whose hand wields its formidable might. It also speaks of an artifact known as the Ruby Talisman that, in conjunction with the prayers uttered from the pages of the Veil of Shadows, has the power to open or close the gateway between realms.

In the hands of the righteous, it is a beacon of hope, a tool to safeguard the realms from the encroachment of darkness. However, in the grasp of the malevolent, it becomes a weapon of unparalleled destruction, capable of unleashing chaos and devastation upon all that stands in its path. Its significance in the cosmic struggle between good and evil cannot be overstated, for the fate of worlds hangs precariously in the balance, swayed by the intentions of those who seek to control its power. Sarah and Christopher continued to read over the manuscript they had copied. The incantations they read within the pages that they dared not repeat out loud from the night before reached out to them in detail.

Spread out in Latin phrases, rituals, and ancient symbols, the manuscript's words weaved a sequence of ritual incantations with variations that could be spoken to open the Veil of Shadows portal:

"Ad per fringendum tenebras, aperiatur velum umbrae."
Translation: "To break through the darkness, let the Veil of Shadows be opened."

"Per virtutem rubini, aperiatur velum umbrae."
Translation: "By the power of the ruby, let the Veil of Shadows be opened."

"In nomine lucis et umbrae, aperiatur porta ad aeternitatem."
Translation: "In the name of light and shadow, let the door to eternity be opened."

"In nomine rubri lapidis, aperiatur porta ad umbras."
Translation: "In the name of the ruby stone, let the door to the shadows be opened."

"Aperi, aperi, porta ad abyssum tenebrarum."
Translation: "Open, open, the door to the abyss of darkness."

"Rubinus, claudite oculos nostrum et aperite viam ad tenebras."
Translation: "Ruby, close our eyes and open the way to darkness."

As Sarah and Christopher continued reading the Latin phrases, rituals, and ancient symbols, the counterparts of these incantations are revealed for closing the Veil of Shadows portal in the same manner:

"Per angelorum potentiam, claudatur porta ad umbras."
Translation: "By the power of angels, let the door to the shadows be closed."

"Per potentiam rubini, claudatur velum umbrae."
Translation: "By the power of the ruby, let the Veil of Shadows be closed."

"In nomine angelorum bonorum, concludatur velum tenebrarum."
Translation: "In the name of good angels, let the Veil of Shadows be sealed."

"In nomine rubri lapidis, concludatur porta ad umbras."
Translation: "In the name of the ruby stone, let the door to the shadows be sealed."

"Spiritus celestes, auxilium nobis ferant, ut claudamus portam umbrae."
Translation: "Celestial spirits aid us in closing the door to the shadows."

"Hic rubinus portam claudat, ut umbrae recedant."
Translation: "Let this ruby close the door so the shadows may retreat."

Sarah, already aware of the dark forces that plagued both the celestial realm and the earthly world, felt a surge of purpose as she spoke to Christopher. "We have finally deciphered the Veil of Shadows manuscript and have discovered its secrets and purpose," she declared, her voice steady with resolve. The manuscript's revelations were crucial, offering insights to help them confront and defeat the malevolent forces threatening their existence. Despite the gravity of their discovery, Sarah felt a sense of calm; her hidden identity as an angel gave her a unique

114

perspective and strength, though Christopher remained unaware of her true nature.

Christopher looked into Sarah's deep blue eyes and nodded, gratitude and determination shining in his eyes. "Thank you, Sarah, for being so diligent and staying by my side through this journey of discovery," he said earnestly. "I believe our task ahead will be one of extreme trial, but ultimately, we will triumph as we face the forces of evil and close the Veil of Shadows portal." His confidence and hope were palpable, yet Sarah knew the truth about her angelic heritage would soon become known. This revelation would change everything, fortifying their mission with divine power and ensuring they were prepared for the trials ahead. Sarah knew that together, they stood on the brink of a monumental battle, their bond and newfound knowledge being their greatest weapons against the encroaching darkness.

Christopher spoke, "Shall we delve into the "Per Aetates: Umbrae Temporis" manuscript while we have the time before we make that call to Deacon Crossford? I am eager to find out what it will reveal to us." "Yes, I am equally eager to see what you have discovered hidden in the dusty shelves of the library's hidden chamber," she replies. Christopher opened the manuscript written by Archbishop Alejandro Patrici. The "Per Aetates: Umbrae Temporis," which translated means; "Through the Ages; Shadows of Time," Among the myriad tales spun within its aged parchment, references to the two powerful artifacts captured their attention: the Ruby Talisman and the Veil of Shadows. According to Patrici's writings, these artifacts held immense power, capable of shaping the course of history itself.

As they had already discovered, Patrici mentions the Ruby Talisman, which was said to have been forged by an ancient civilization known for its mastery of gem craft. Legend whispered of its ability to harness the very essence of life, granting its wielder unimaginable strength and vitality. Conversely, the Veil of Shadows was also mentioned as a relic steeped in mystery, its origins shrouded in darkness. Patrici's manuscript spoke of a time when the Veil was used to cloak entire civilizations from prying eyes, granting them sanctuary in the depths of the shadows. However, the darkness spread throughout nations, becoming a malevolent force that could not be controlled. These portals also became known as the Veil of Shadows to open gateways between worlds. As Sarah and Christopher pieced together the fragmented accounts within the manuscript, they realized that the Ruby Talisman and the Veil of Shadows were inexorably linked. Throughout history, those who sought to control one artifact inevitably crossed paths with the other, their fates intertwined in a dance of light and darkness.

Across civilizations and epochs, the Veil of Shadows represented the constant struggle between good and evil, its mysteries veiled in allegory and symbolism. From the hallowed libraries of ancient Sumeria to the sacred scrolls of biblical prophets, its presence reminds us of the quest for enlightenment and the timeless battle for humanity's soul. As the pages of history turn and new chapters unfold, the Veil of Shadows casts its shadow over the hearts and minds of those seeking to unravel its secrets and unlock the true nature of existence.

In ancient Sumeria and throughout biblical lore, the enigmatic tome known as the Veil of Shadows has held a profound significance, its pages whispering secrets that bridge the realms of mortals and the divine. From the earliest civilizations to the hallowed texts of the Hebrew Bible, its presence, referred to by other names, looms large, a testament to the eternal struggle between forces of light and darkness. Among its most notable appearances is in the Book of Enoch, an ancient text excluded from most canons but revered for its vivid depiction of the Watchers' descent and the ensuing cosmic conflict. According to Enochian lore, the Veil of Shadows served as a conduit through which the fallen angels, led by the rebellious archangel Lucifer, sought to corrupt and ensnare humanity. Through its arcane teachings, they whispered promises of forbidden knowledge and power, tempting mortals to stray from the path of righteousness. Yet, amidst the chaos and strife, a remnant of righteous souls, guided by the wisdom contained within the texts, rose to confront the forces of darkness, forging a legacy of courage and redemption that echoed through the ages.

In the annals of ancient China, the tome known as the 魔影之幕 (Mó yǐng zhī Mù), or "Veil of Shadows," held a revered place in the esoteric traditions of the Middle Kingdom. Within its pages were inscribed the secrets of manipulating cosmic energies and navigating the ethereal realms that intersected with the mortal plane. Guided by the wisdom contained within the Veil of Shadows, adepts of the arcane arts utilized the 宝石护身符 (Bǎoshí hùshēnfú), or "Talisman of Gems," known in legend as the Ruby Talisman, to open and close the portals that bridged the divide between worlds. With each passing dynasty, the guardians of ancient China entrusted the Veil of Shadows' secrets and the Ruby Talisman's power to those deemed worthy of safeguarding the celestial balance.

In the history of ancient Egypt, the sacred text known as بردي الظلال (Bardī al-Zalāl), or the "Veil of Shadows," became part of the mystical traditions of the Nile. The secrets of harnessing powers to the underworld and traversing the ethereal dimensions that intersected with mortal existence were inscribed within its hieroglyph-laden pages. Across the epochs of dynastic transitions, practitioners of the mystery arts harnessed the power of the الياقوت الأحمر التميمة (Al-Yaqut al-Ahmar at-Tamīma), or "Ruby Talisman," a revered artifact believed to embody the harmonizing forces of the cosmos, to open and seal the portals that bridged the chasm between worlds. As pharaohs rose and fell, ancient Egyptian custodians became the guardians of the Veil of Shadows and the mastery of the Ruby Talisman, those deemed worthy of safeguarding the universe's equilibrium.

In the ancient realms of Persia and India, the mystical text known as پردهٔ سایه‌ها (Pardé-ye Sāyeh-hā), or the "Veil of Shadows," Held within its illuminated pages the secrets of controlling divine energies and transcending the levels of the heavens that intertwined with mortal existence. Across the epochs of dynastic cycles, high priests, sheiks, and sages wielded the power of the طلسم روبی (Talism-e Ruby), or "Ruby Talisman," to harness the primal forces of creation, to unlock and seal the portals that connected the realms of existence. Thus, throughout the epochs of Persian history, the Veil of Shadows remained a silent sentinel.

Archbishop Alejandro Patrici writes of other legends tied to the Veil of Shadows. Deep within the enchanted forests of Europe, amidst the mist-shrouded glades and ancient ruins, whispers abound of an ancient portal where the forces of good and evil converge, and the heavens and other realms intertwine with the mortal world. This mystical gateway, hidden from the eyes of ordinary mortals, is said to hold the key to unlocking the universe's secrets. According to legends, the portal was created by celestial beings of ethereal beauty and boundless magic to traverse the realms and maintain the delicate balance of existence.

Legends speak of the portal's guardians, ancient and powerful beings tasked with safeguarding its secrets from those seeking to misuse its power for their nefarious ends. It is said that only those pure of heart and steadfast of spirit may pass through its shimmering veil unscathed, while those tainted by darkness risk being consumed by the very forces they seek to harness. Yet, tales of brave adventurers and intrepid seekers abound, drawn by the promise of untold treasures and forbidden knowledge that lie beyond the threshold of the ancient portal. And so, the legend endured, weaving its threads through the tapestry of history as a testament to the eternal struggle between light and shadow that shapes the destiny of worlds.

Archbishop Patrici also writes; In the heart of the lush Amazon rainforest, amidst the vibrant foliage and echoing calls of exotic creatures, lies a hidden secret known only to the ancient tribes who call this land home. It is whispered among the elders that deep within the dense jungle exists an ancient portal where the forces of good and evil, the heavens and the other realms, converge to touch the mortal world. This mystical gateway, veiled by tangled vines and towering trees, is said to hold the key to unlocking the mysteries of the cosmos and the spirits that dwell beyond mortal perception.

According to the oral traditions passed down through generations, the portal was created by the divine serpent, guardian of the rainforest and keeper of its secrets, to maintain the delicate balance between the realms. It is said that those who possess the courage to seek out the portal may glimpse into the infinite expanse of the heavens or venture into the depths of the underworld, their fate guided by the whims of the spirits that dwell within. Yet, the path to the ancient portal is dangerous, for the jungle teems with unseen dangers and ancient guardians who fiercely protect its sanctity. And so, the legend of the ancient portal in South America endures, a testament to the timeless struggle between light and darkness that shapes the destiny of all who dare to tread its hallowed ground.

The archbishop spoke of a new kingdom across the great waters, a land where lush forests, vast prairies, towering mountains, and expansive deserts stretch from sea to sea. In this distant realm, ancient energy vortexes form where ley lines intersect, and dormant portals lie sealed, awaiting their inevitable reopening. He warned that someday, driven

119

by the lust for enlightenment, wisdom, and power, individuals would seek to unseal these portals, believing they could unlock the secrets of immortality. However, the archbishop cautioned that such ambitions would not lead to the promised enlightenment but instead to chaos and despair. In their pursuit, these individuals would unwittingly unleash malevolent forces upon the land, corrupting the hearts of men and sowing turmoil across the kingdom. The ancient warnings inscribed in the Veil of Shadows spoke of this dire fate, a grim reminder that the thirst for power can lead to the downfall of even the greatest civilizations.

Christopher and Sarah believe that in this final passage, Archbishop Alejandro Patrici refers to the North American continent and specifically to the United States of America, which had not been formed as a nation when he wrote about it and was unknown to the people of Europe other than the "land beyond the waters." The United States falls primarily within the category of Western civilization. Historically and culturally, the United States has been deeply influenced by European traditions, mainly Western European ones. The foundations of American society, including its democratic governance, legal systems, and cultural norms, can be traced back to European roots, particularly those of England, France, and other Western European nations. Additionally, the United States has been shaped by Judeo-Christian values and traditions, central to Western civilization. Furthermore, the United States has significantly shaped Western civilization through its contributions to art, literature, philosophy, science, and technology. While the United States is diverse and multicultural, its cultural and historical ties align closely with Western European civilization.

✎ CHAPTER ELEVEN ✎

With reverence, Christopher closed the leather-bound manuscript, "Per Aetates: Umbrae Temporis," with the weight of its ancient pages pressing down on him. He and Sarah stepped back from the table, the morning light casting long shadows across the room. They both took a deep breath, exhaling slowly, their sighs a mixture of relief and awe. The air around them seemed charged with the gravity of their discovery, the culmination of their relentless search for the truth. "What an amazing manuscript," Christopher began, his voice tinged with excitement and respect. "This manuscript ties everything together. The Veil of Shadows, the Ruby Talisman, the 'Talisma Rubini' scroll describing Brother Alessandro's quest, and how the Ruby Talisman came into the possession of the Holy Roman Church, and how they directed its influence to close the portal." He paused, running a hand through his hair, the reality of their situation sinking in. "We still don't know how it wound up here in Silver Ridge, but the facts are that it is here, and we have it in our possession."

Sarah nodded, her eyes still fixed on the closed manuscript, the mysteries it contained echoing in her mind. "I guess that is not as important as how we will use it and the knowledge of the Veil of Shadows to close the portal that has been opened up somewhere in our vicinity," she said softly. The enormity of their task loomed large, but the knowledge they had uncovered gave them a good understanding of what was ahead of them and prepared them to meet with Deacon Crossford. Sarah turned to Christopher; her brow furrowed in thought. "Maybe if we find out the whereabouts of Isabella Grey from Deacon Crossford, she may be able to shed some light on how the Ruby Talisman made its way into the Silver Ridge

Institute," she suggested, her voice filled with a determined resolve. "Or perhaps Deacon Crossford knows something," she added, her eyes searching Christopher's for agreement.

Christopher nodded slowly, clasping his hands together in a prayer configuration, a gesture that grounded him amid their turbulent discoveries. "You're right, Sarah," he said, his voice calm yet resolute. "Isabella Grey might hold the key to understanding this mystery. And Deacon Crossford...he's been around long enough to have seen things we haven't even considered." They stood silently for a moment, the weight of their next steps pressing down on them. The manuscript, now closed, had given them the knowledge they needed, but it was up to them to follow the leads and piece together the remaining puzzle.

Christopher carefully transported the "Per Aetates: Umbrae Temporis" manuscript and the copied material from the "Veil of Shadows" document to the study on the second floor. He meticulously placed these precious items into the locked cabinet, ensuring they were secure alongside other significant artifacts and documents he had previously stored there. Satisfied with the safety of the collection, he returned downstairs to the study, where Sarah awaited him. Once back in the downstairs study, Christopher suggested to Sarah that they contact Deacon Crossford at Forest Haven Parish to arrange a meeting, as the Deacon had requested. Recognizing the importance of this connection, Sarah promptly agreed to the suggestion, understanding that the Deacon might provide crucial insights or assistance related to their ongoing research.

Christopher picked up the telephone, feeling a slight tremor of anticipation as he dialed the number for Forest Haven Parish. Each press of the buttons seemed to echo with a sense of urgency, the gravity of their situation pressing upon him. The number had been provided by Deacon Crossford himself, a beacon of hope in their labyrinthine quest. He glanced at Sarah, who watched him intently, the shared weight of their mission clear in her eyes. The phone began to ring on the other end, each tone heightening the moment's suspense.

After a few rings, the line clicked, and a male voice greeted him: "Hello, Forest Haven Parish. This is Deacon Elias Crossford speaking; how can I help you?" The Deacon's voice was calm and steady, imbued with a reassuring authority that immediately put Christopher at ease. Collecting his thoughts and taking a deep breath, he conveyed their purpose and urgency. The connection to the Deacon felt like a lifeline, a bridge to the answers they so desperately needed. Christopher straightened his posture, ready to articulate their request. "Good afternoon, Deacon Crossford," Christopher began, his voice steady but urgent. "This is Professor Christopher Daniels. I received your voice message and must admit, I am intrigued by your message and request for a meeting." He paused briefly, ensuring his words were clear and direct, emphasizing the importance of the matter. Christopher continued, "My colleague and assistant, Ms. Sarah Hope, and I are agreeable to a meeting with you and Father Aidan Green at Forest Haven Parish." He glanced at Sarah, who gave him an encouraging nod, both recognizing the potential significance of this meeting. The mention of Father Green indicates that the Deacon is involved with other key figures, which only heightens Christopher's anticipation.

On the other end, Deacon Crossford's response was immediate and accommodating. "Thank you, Professor Daniels. I am pleased to hear that you and Ms. Hope are available. We look forward to discussing these matters in detail. Let us coordinate a time that works for all parties involved." Christopher responded, "Shall we say 11:00 a.m. tomorrow at your location? Would that be convenient for you and Father Green?" He added, hoping to finalize the details swiftly.

Deacon Crossford replied, "Yes, that would be perfect. We also have a visiting emissary from Rome, Father Luciano Rossi, who would like to meet you. If it's okay with you, it would be to our benefit if he attends the meeting as well."

Christopher felt a surge of anticipation. "Of course, that would be fine," he replied. "We'll see you tomorrow at 11:00 a.m. Thank you, Deacon Crossford." "Thank you, Professor Daniels. We look forward to it," Deacon Crossford said before the call ended. Christopher hung up and turned to Sarah, who was watching him intently. "We're set for tomorrow at 11:00 a.m.," he said. "And it seems we have another key figure joining us—a visiting emissary from Rome, Father Luciano Rossi. We need to be thoroughly prepared." Sarah nodded, her expression serious yet hopeful. "Then tomorrow it is. Let's take the rest of the afternoon off, have an early dinner, and prepare ourselves for the meeting tomorrow," she suggested. "This could be the breakthrough we've been waiting for."

"Agreed," Christopher said, feeling a renewed sense of purpose. "Let's make sure we're ready for anything." He appreciated Sarah's practical approach, knowing that a clear mind and being well-prepared would be crucial for the success of their meeting. They spent the rest of the day relaxing and mentally gearing up for the next day's critical engagement. They decided to have an early dinner at Hawthorne's Cafe and were pleased to find the available table they had sat at the last time. Tucked away in a quiet corner, the table offered a perfect blend of privacy and a view of the bustling cafe. It was an ideal spot for them to converse and enjoy the ambiance and activities around them. The familiar surroundings provided comfort and continuity as they settled into their seats. They ordered their meals and began to outline their plans for the meeting, their conversation punctuated by moments of reflection and anticipation.

Over dinner, they discussed the key points they wanted to address with Deacon Crossford, Father Green, and Father Luciano Rossi. The quiet corner allowed them to speak freely without distractions, reinforcing their focus and determination. The early evening at Hawthorne's Cafe provided a much-needed break and strengthened their resolve as they prepared for the significant day ahead. Christopher told Sarah they would drive to Forest Haven Parish from his residence. He mentioned that his Sport Utility Vehicle (SUV) would be ideal for the drive, ensuring comfort and ample space for their journey. Sarah smiled at the thought, feeling a tinge of excitement. It would be her first time riding in a vehicle, and she couldn't help but imagine what the experience would feel like—the prospect of this new experience added to her anticipation for the next day.

Sarah's excitement grew as they continued their dinner at Hawthorne's Cafe. The cozy corner of the cafe provided the perfect setting for her to express her curiosity and enthusiasm about the upcoming drive. Christopher assured her that the journey would be smooth and enjoyable. As they finished their meal, Sarah's mind was filled with thoughts of revealing her angelic nature to Christopher. She determined it was necessary before they met with Deacon Crossford, Father Green, and Father Rossi. The weight of her secret pressed heavily on her, knowing that understanding the truth would be crucial for the battles ahead. She suggested they walk together because she had something very important to tell him that couldn't wait any longer. Christopher agreed, his curiosity piqued. He paid the bill, and together, they departed Hawthorne's Cafe. The evening air was cool and filled with the scent of pine tree bristles and cedar.

Walking side by side through the quiet streets, Sarah gathered her courage. The moment felt surreal, but she knew it was the right time. She gazed at Christopher with a soft smile, her eyes shimmering with a depth that held the mysteries of the universe. "Christopher," she began, her voice soft yet resolute, "there's something you need to know about me before we face what's coming. I've been keeping it a secret, but it's time you knew the truth." Christopher turned to her, sensing the solemnity in her tone. "What is it, Sarah?" he asked, his eyes searching hers for answers. Taking a deep breath, Sarah closed her eyes briefly, summoning the courage to reveal her celestial nature. A radiant aura enveloped her as she did, casting a warm glow around her form. Christopher's breath caught in his throat as he witnessed the ethereal light surrounding her. "Christopher," Sarah continued, her voice infused with a celestial resonance, "I am not like other humans. I am an angel, sent to you in human form."

She paused, taking another deep breath, then continued, "I am an angel in human form, your guardian angel. I have been watching over you, guiding you, even in your dreams. The sensation you felt of not being alone was my presence." She looked into his eyes, willing him to believe her. "We have a mission, and it's far greater than either of us can handle alone. I've come to you in human form to work together to close the Veil of Shadows and dispel the malevolent darkness threatening Silver Ridge and the world." Christopher's eyes widened in astonishment, but Sarah reached out and gently touched his hand before he could utter a word. At that moment, a wave of reassurance washed over him as if Sarah were speaking directly into his mind. "I know this may be overwhelming," Sarah said, her words echoing within Christopher's consciousness, "but I assure you, it is the truth. I have watched over you, guided you, and now I must reveal my true self to you."

Christopher felt a sense of awe and wonder coursing through him, mingled with a profound sense of peace. He looked into Sarah's eyes, now glowing with a divine light, and knew in his heart that she spoke the truth. They came

126

upon a bench on a grassy area off the main street and sat side by side. As they sat together in the embrace of the celestial night, Christopher felt a bond between them that transcended mortal understanding. In Sarah's presence, he found solace, acceptance, and a love he knew was not bound by earthly constraints. A flood of memories rushed through his mind. Moments of despair, joy, moments when he felt a comforting presence surrounding him, even when he was utterly alone.

"How..." he began, his voice barely a whisper, "how is this possible?" Sarah smiled gently, her eyes glowing with a celestial light. "I know things, Christopher. Things that only you would know. I know about the dreams you have held close to your heart, the fears that have kept you awake at night, and the moments of triumph and defeat that have shaped your soul. I've been there through it all, guiding you, protecting you because you are special." Christopher felt a lump form in his throat as he listened to Sarah's words, a profound sense of awe washing over him. It was as if she could see into the deepest recesses of his being, unraveling the mysteries of his soul with a single glance.

"And now," Sarah continued, her voice tinged with urgency, "we face a new challenge that threatens not just you or me but all of humanity. The Veil of Shadows has revealed a darkness lurking on the horizon, an evil that seeks to sow chaos and destruction." Christopher's heart quickened at her words, a sense of dread creeping over him. He had always sensed that there was darkness in the world, but to hear Sarah speak of it so directly sent a shiver down his spine. "But why me?" he asked, his voice trembling with uncertainty. "Because you have a role to play in this battle," Sarah replied, her gaze unwavering. "You have a light within you, Christopher, that can pierce even the deepest shadows. Together, we can confront this evil, vanquish it from the world, and restore balance to the cosmos."

Christopher looked into Sarah's eyes, seeing the truth reflected in their depths. He knew then, without a doubt, that she spoke the truth. And as they sat together beneath the watchful gaze of the moon, he felt a newfound sense of purpose stirring within him. Together, as guardian and charge, angel and mortal, they would face whatever trials lay ahead, united in their mission to protect humanity from the darkness that threatened to consume it. Christopher accepted what Sarah shared with him even though it seemed impossible. He just knew it was true. Too many strange things were happening around him lately, and Sarah's radiance was otherworldly and intoxicating. From the moment he met her, something seemed too familiar to him. She was indeed his guardian angel, but how could this be possible? A myriad of questions raced through his mind. Would she remain by his side in her human form? In angelic form? Of all the existential studies and research, he had done in the past, nothing compared to this revelation. As they sat there, a wave of emotions swept over him. One moment, he felt sad; the next, joyful, then lonely, and confusion set in.

Sensing his turmoil, Sarah embraced Christopher, pulling him close. He felt her heart beating and absorbed the softness and comfort of her embrace. Smelling the scent of lilacs and lavender in her hair and on her person, he felt the warmth of her celestial aura, and at that moment, all his doubts disappeared. Sarah gently whispered, "Christopher, I am here, my love, always. All will be revealed." The calm certainty in her voice reassured him, anchoring him in the storm of his emotions. For now, it was enough to know that they were together, ready to face whatever challenges lay ahead.

Christopher felt unsteady as they arose from the bench, his head spinning with Sarah's revelations. Sarah sensed his imbalance and steadied him, grounding him as they reached their feet. Together, they strolled arm in arm down the street to Sarah's residence. Once they arrived at the entrance, Sarah embraced Christopher, kissing him gently and encouraging him to accept that she would always be by his side. As she turned to enter her residence, Sarah said, "Sleep well, Christopher. Tomorrow will be an important day for us. I will be at your home early tomorrow morning for our journey to Forest Haven Parish." "Goodnight, Christopher," she added. Christopher replied, "Goodnight, Sarah, and pleasant dreams." Christopher watched Sarah enter her residence and then turned to walk the rest of the distance to his home. He wondered to himself, do angels dream? And if they do, what do they dream about? The night air was cool, and the weight of Sarah's words lingered with him. The streetlights cast long shadows, mirroring the thoughts that danced in his mind. As he approached his front door, he could not shake the feeling that tomorrow would indeed be significant, a turning point in their intertwined destinies.

––––––––

As the evening ended, Sarah decided to shower and retire to her bed. Sarah stepped into the shower, hoping the warm water would ease her mind. As the steam enveloped her, she could not help but worry about Christopher's mental well-being after sharing her celestial nature. The gentle cascade of water over her skin provided a momentary distraction, but her thoughts remained with Christopher. She knew how deeply he was affected by her words, and she hoped her revelation would not overwhelm him. The shower, a sanctuary of warmth and comfort, allowed Sarah to gather her thoughts and draw strength. Wrapped in a soft, comforting robe, Sarah dried her hair and slipped into her nightgown, the familiar fabric bringing peace.

As she climbed into bed, she could not shake the concern for Christopher that lingered in her heart. Once again, her room was her haven, infused with a lingering sense of ethereal light and peace. Sarah settled under the covers, her mind still racing with thoughts of Christopher and his reaction to the divine revelation she had shared. In bed, Sarah's thoughts turned to a moment of deep reflection. Suddenly, the room filled with soft, ethereal light, and Guardian Angel Nanael appeared, his divine aura radiating a comforting and enlightening presence. Guardian Angel Nanael is known as the angel of spiritual communication. His name means; "God Who Humiliates the Proud". In Judaism, Guardian Angel Nanael is an Elohim, and his superior is Archangel Raphael. But in Christianity, Nanael is one of the Principalities. Therefore, his superior is Archangel Haniel. As the angel of spiritual communication, Nanael conveyed a message filled with inspiration and guidance. Nanael assured Sarah that her quest was supported and divinely guided. He informed her of his intention to visit Christopher to provide him with reassurance, strength, and encouragement regarding Sarah's revelation.

Nanael's visit to Christopher would serve as divine confirmation, strengthening their interconnectedness and easing any doubts he may have. His promise left Sarah with a profound sense of peace and purpose, knowing that Nanael's guidance would not only aid her but also extend to Christopher's connection to her and his spiritual journey, reinforcing his enlightenment and understanding. With this comforting thought, Sarah allowed herself to relax fully. As sleep gently claimed her, she felt a deep-seated peace, knowing that she and Christopher were under divine protection.

Christopher arrived at his home, and after showering, he retired for the night. His mind racing with thoughts. As he tossed and turned in his bed, unable to fall asleep, the room filled with an ethereal glow. Guardian Angel Nanael, revered as the angel of spiritual communication, appeared to Christopher with large, resplendent wings that shimmered with a soft, iridescent glow, signifying his divine connection and purity. Nanael filled the room with a calming light, symbolizing his role in bridging the celestial and earthly realms. Nanael's appearance was otherworldly, his presence both comforting and awe-inspiring. He wore flowing, ethereal robes of white and gold that accentuated his grace and authority, emphasizing his divine nature. The gentle rustling of his robes added to the serene atmosphere, making Christopher feel an immediate sense of peace and reassurance.

Nanael's eyes were deep and serene, reflecting boundless wisdom and compassion. As he looked into Christopher's eyes, Christopher felt an overwhelming sense of understanding and empathy. It was as if Nanael could see into the depths of his soul, recognizing his fears and doubts. Nanael's posture exuded a gentle yet commanding presence, his every movement deliberate and purposeful. This combination of gentleness and strength made Christopher feel protected and inspired, knowing he was in the presence of a powerful yet benevolent being. Angel Nanael holds sacred knowledge of mysticism. Therefore, he brings secret and hidden knowledge about the spiritual world. Also, he brings the spiritual teachings of enlightened masters. Nanael inspires you to contemplate spiritual topics, such as The Divine, higher dimensions, and planes of existence.

At that moment, Nanael conveyed his message to Christopher with a soothing and authoritative voice. He reassured Christopher of the significance of Sarah's revelation and encouraged him to embrace what Sarah revealed as the truth. Nanael's visit was to provide reassurance and offer guidance and support, ensuring that Christopher understood his place in the grand tapestry of existence. Christopher felt his worries dissolve with each word, replaced by a profound sense of purpose and clarity.

Nanael's presence left an indelible mark on his heart, reminding him of his divine connection with Sarah and the spiritual path they were destined to explore together. He taught Christopher to understand the spiritual meaning of love. Nanael also imparted a deep passion for the spiritual realms and their mystery to Christopher.

No doubts remained as Christopher realized that he was in the presence of a true angel, "Nanael," and that Sarah was indeed his guardian angel who had come to him in human form. As Nanael's presence faded from his room, the soft, iridescent glow slowly dimmed, and Christopher felt an overwhelming sense of fulfillment and tranquility. The revelation that angels were real and that his wish to see and feel them had been fulfilled brought him immense comfort. The realization washed over him like a soothing wave, dispelling years of doubt and longing. He felt a profound sense of peace and connection, knowing that the divine presence he had always hoped for was not just a dream but a beautiful reality.

This newfound understanding gave him a sense of purpose and reassurance as if he had finally found the missing piece to his spiritual puzzle. With his heart now light and his mind at ease, Christopher fell into a deep, restful sleep, knowing he was divinely protected and guided. The worries and fears that had once plagued his thoughts melted away, replaced by a profound sense of security and peace. Wrapped in the comforting embrace of this newfound assurance, he surrendered to sleep, his dreams filled with serene visions and the gentle presence of his celestial guardians.

❧ CHAPTER TWELVE ❧

Sarah woke early as the morning sun rose in the east, casting a warm glow across her room, bathing her in light as mourning doves filled the air with a peaceful rhythmic sound. She dressed in comfortable slacks and a cream-colored blouse and chose attractive yet comfortable shoes for the day's journey. Excitedly, she hurriedly prepared a cup of jasmine tea and a croissant for breakfast, placing fruit and a bottle of spring water in her woven handbag. She neatly tied a lavender and cream-colored scarf in her hair. After departing her residence, Sarah walked a short distance to Christopher's home. The streets were quiet, and the early morning air was crisp and fresh. She felt a sense of anticipation and joy with each step, eager for the day ahead. The familiar path brought back fond memories of previous visits, adding to her excitement. As she approached Christopher's house, she saw him waiting by the door, his smile mirroring hers.

Christopher greeted her, "Good morning, Sarah." "Good morning, Christopher," she replied as they entered his residence. Christopher said, "The drive to Forest Haven will not take long. We will take Mount Hood Highway 26 east and exit at Forest Haven Road. The road to the parish is a scenic route through pine-lined wooded areas until we reach our destination. I think you will enjoy the scenery." Sarah smiled in anticipation of this new experience she was about to embark on. She appreciated the detailed directions and the promise of a picturesque drive. Traveling through such beautiful landscapes filled her with adventure and tranquility. The morning seemed perfect for a journey through nature, and she could not wait to see the majestic pine trees and serene woodland that Christopher described. As they prepared to leave, the excitement in the air was palpable, marking the beginning of what promised to be a delightful day.

Christopher gathered some items for the trip and turned to Sarah, saying, "Thank you, Sarah, for revealing your angelic nature to me last night. After arriving home, I was visited by an angel who appeared to me, spoke about your revelation, and encouraged me to embrace what you revealed as the truth. I believe with all my heart that angels are real and what you told me is the truth. I still have many questions, but I understand our divine connection and the love we share. I am blessed to always have you by my side as a guardian or companion. I wanted you to know I place my fate in your divine hands."

Christopher's words deeply moved Sarah. She could see the sincerity in his eyes and felt profound gratitude for his acceptance and trust. "Thank you, Christopher," she said softly, "Your faith means everything to me. Together, we will navigate the questions and uncertainties. Our bond is strong, and our journey is just beginning. I promise to guide and support you with all my love and care." With that, they both felt a renewed sense of purpose and unity, ready to embark on their journey to Forest Haven, knowing their connection was blessed and guided by a higher power. They stepped out of Christopher's residence, closed the door, and walked across the front yard to the driveway where Christopher's Sports Utility Vehicle (SUV) was parked. Christopher helped Sarah into the vehicle's passenger seat, closed the door behind her, and then entered and settled into the driver's side. He fastened his seat belt and showed Sarah how to attach hers. Tucked into her seat and strapped in, Sarah felt excitement building as Christopher turned the key in the ignition, and the engine came alive with a whirring musical pitch and a rhythmic vibration that she could feel with her whole body.

As they pulled out of the driveway and onto the quiet morning streets, Sarah gazed out the window, her mind racing with anticipation. The gentle hum of the SUV's engine seemed to harmonize with the serene landscape around them, creating a sense of calm and adventure. Christopher glanced over at her, smiling reassuringly, and she felt a surge of warmth and confidence. The feeling of moving forward and the sound of the wheels on the road felt exhilarating to Sarah. Each turn and stretch of highway amplified her sense of adventure, making her pulse quicken with excitement. "This is what traveling in a vehicle feels like," she thought. "I like this." The journey ahead was filled with promise, and as they navigated through the winding roads toward Forest Haven, Sarah couldn't help but feel that this trip would be a defining moment in their shared path, guided by love and faith.

Sarah noticed a sign along the highway saying, "The Inn of Whispers—just one mile ahead." Christopher noticed her looking and explained, "The Inn of Whispers is a unique shop and reading room serving travelers seeking answers and information about the area's legends. The proprietor, Madame Elara, possesses ancient knowledge about the Mount Hood area. "Sarah felt drawn to the sign and mentioned to Christopher, "I would like to visit the Inn on our way back to Silver Ridge. Something tells me Madame Elara has information that may help us." Christopher nodded in agreement, "We can definitely stop on the return trip," he replied.

The route east along the Mount Hood corridor was a scenic wonderland, lined with towering pine and cedar trees that stood as majestic sentinels on either side of the road. Their lush green branches swayed gently in the breeze, creating a soothing, natural symphony. Sunlight filtered through the branches, casting dancing light patterns on the pavement. Along the way, sparkling lakes and streams came into view, their clear waters reflecting the sky. Some lakes had small rowboats drifting lazily, with anglers patiently waiting for a bite, adding a tranquil charm to the picturesque landscape. Campsite and tour signs dotted the highway, hinting at adventures waiting just off the main road. Roadside turnouts featured quaint supply stores, fruit stands, and souvenir shops, each inviting travelers to pull over for refreshments and provisions. The vibrant colors of fresh fruit and handmade crafts contrasted beautifully with the natural greens and blues of the surrounding scenery. The aroma of ripe berries and freshly baked goods wafted through the air, tempting passersby to stop and indulge. Every mile of the journey offered a new delight, making the drive a feast for the senses.

Turning off Highway 26 onto Forest Haven Road, the ride became bumpier as the road narrowed and the surface transitioned from asphalt to gravel. The change in terrain added a rustic charm to their journey, making the adventure feel even more authentic. Through the trees, views of the Zigzag River running westward from the glacier on Mount Hood came into view. The mid-morning sunlight glistened off the river's flowing water, creating a dazzling light display. In some places, the river transformed into rapids, careening over rocks and outcroppings, adding a dynamic and exhilarating element to the serene landscape. The sight was breathtaking, a harmonious blend of tranquility and power. The sound of the rushing water added to the symphony of nature, complementing the chirping birds and rustling leaves. Sarah couldn't help but marvel at the beauty surrounding them, feeling a deep connection to the natural world. Christopher, too, seemed captivated by the scenery. Forest Haven Parish came into view as they continued along the bumpy road.

Entering the grounds of Forest Haven Parish is a serene and enchanting experience where faith and nature beautifully converge. As you drive through the ornate wrought iron gates, you are immediately welcomed by the harmonious blend of spirituality and the natural world. The pebbled driveway, gently crunching beneath your tires, meanders gracefully through the lush landscape, leading you toward the heart of the parish. The driveway curves elegantly around a stunning fountain and a meticulously maintained garden centerpiece, creating a picturesque scene that calms the soul. Vibrant flowers in a riot of colors and majestic tall cedars line both sides of the driveway, adding to the tranquility and reverence that pervades the atmosphere.

To the right of the driveway, a spacious parking area provides a convenient spot for visitors to park their vehicles before they explore the parish grounds. This well-thought-out arrangement ensures that the natural beauty and peaceful ambiance remain undisturbed. With its welcoming facade, the administrative building stands at the end of the driveway, inviting visitors to enter and begin their journey through this sanctuary, where faith and nature intertwine. The entire setting, from the entrance gates to the garden centerpiece, speaks of a place designed for reflection, peace, and a deep connection with both the divine and the natural world. Christopher parks their vehicle in the guest parking area and helps Sarah step out; they both feel excitement and reverence for the serene surroundings. The natural beauty of Forest Haven Parish, with its colorful flowers and towering cedars, sets a tranquil tone for their visit.

As they walk towards the entrance of the administration building, the purpose of their visit—to meet with Deacon Crossford and the others—fills their minds, adding a sense of solemnity to their anticipation. Flanked by nature's splendor, the pathway seems to guide them gently toward their destination, heightening their sense of connection to the sacred space they are about to enter. Upon entering the administration building, Christopher and Sarah are immediately struck by its breathtaking interior. The wide-open beam ceilings and intricate stained-glass windows create a majestic atmosphere, while the polished wooden floors gleam underfoot. Statues of saints in the corners of the lobby and painted portraits of angels adorning the walls

137

add to the spiritual ambiance. The scent of cedar permeates the air, evoking memories of the forest and the natural surroundings just outside, reinforcing the harmony between the spiritual and natural elements of the parish. This sensory experience deepens their reverence and reminds them of the unique blend of faith and nature that defines Forest Haven Parish.

Waiting to greet them in the lobby is Deacon Elias Crossford, his slightly greying brown hair and welcoming green eyes portraying a soft yet professional demeanor. His tall, steady stance exudes grace and warmth, inviting comfort and trust. "Welcome to Forest Haven, Professor Daniels and Ms. Hope," he says, extending a hand with a sincere smile. Christopher accepts the handshake with a friendly, "Thank you, Deacon Crossford." Sarah follows suit, offering her hand, which Elias accepts with a formal yet gentle grasp. "Please call me by my first name, Elias," he requests warmly. Christopher quickly responds, "Thank you. You can also refer to me by my first name, Christopher." Sarah also acknowledges this, "And you can call me Sarah."

As Elias greets Sarah, he senses something ethereal about her. Her softness and grace immediately put him at ease, and there is a subtle glow about her that catches his attention. The soft scent of lilacs and lavender from her fills his senses, evoking calmness and a feeling of familiarity. This serene aura makes their interaction feel almost otherworldly, creating a moment of quiet connection. However, Elias quickly refocuses on the present task and is keen to maintain his established professional and welcoming atmosphere. "Shall we join the others in the parish meeting room to have our most important discussions undisturbed?" Elias suggests his tone is both inviting and purposeful. "Afterward, I would love to give you both a tour of our parish grounds." Christopher enthusiastically responds, "Yes, we would like that very much." Sarah smiles and nods in agreement, feeling a growing anticipation for the discussions and the tour. The trio then proceeds towards the meeting room, each step resonating with the promise of meaningful dialogue and a deeper connection to Forest Haven Parish's serene and spiritual environment.

As they enter the meeting room, Christopher and Sarah see a long conference table surrounded by comfortable high-back chairs at the center. Stained glass windows line the walls, allowing the sun's rays to cascade into the room in prismatic colors, creating a warm and inviting atmosphere. Seated at the table are three figures who immediately stand to greet the trio. "Welcome, Professor and Ms. Hope. My name is Father Aidan Green. I am the pastor here at Forest Haven," says a tall, kind-faced man. "I would like to introduce you to Father Luciano Rossi, our visiting emissary from Rome, and Dr. Isabella Grey, formerly a research assistant at the Silver Ridge Institute and currently residing in Forest Haven's visitor's quarters while teaching at our Sacred Cedars Seminary."

Christopher and Sarah exchange glances, their curiosity about Isabella's whereabouts now resolved. Smiling, Christopher turns to face the three individuals, "Thank you, Father Green; it's our pleasure to make your acquaintance and an honor to meet with all of you here at Forest Haven." Sarah nods in agreement, feeling a sense of relief and excitement about the meeting ahead. As the group returns to their seated positions, Sarah, Christopher, and Elias take their places at the conference table among the others, ready to engage in what promises to be a meaningful and enlightening discussion. The room, filled with the interplay of light from the stained glass and the presence of these distinguished individuals, is the perfect setting for the important conversations to come.

Father Green addresses the group solemnly, "We have asked Professor Daniels and Ms. Hope here to discuss a very important and impending matter and share the knowledge we all possess. This knowledge would benefit all present; perhaps we can form an alliance. These are very perilous times, and the balance of both the celestial and earthly realms is in jeopardy of collapsing if we don't combine forces to combat a malevolence that threatens to devour all of humanity." He pauses, allowing the gravity of his words to sink in, before continuing, "I believe that you, Professor Daniels, and you, Ms. Hope, know what I am referring to, and, as all of us present here also believe, this is true."

Christopher looks Father Green directly in the eyes, a newfound fortitude evident in his demeanor that Sarah had not witnessed before. "Tell us more, Father; tell Ms. Hope and me what you know," he says, his voice steady and unwavering. Before Father Green can speak, he looks around the room, noting the silent nods of agreement from Father Rossi, Deacon Crossford, and Dr. Grey. With a lump in his throat and a slight quiver in his voice, he utters the words, "The Veil of Shadows." The room falls silent, the weight of the revelation hanging heavily in the air as the enormity of the threat and the importance of their alliance becomes unmistakably clear to everyone present.

After a few minutes of silence, allowing everyone to gather their thoughts and composure, Christopher glances at Sarah. With a knowing wink from her, he responds, "Yes, Father Green, we do have something in common." He continues, "It appears to me that we are all on the same path, and our destinies have brought us to this place for your purpose. Ms. Hope and I are on the same quest. If we share all that we know about these matters up to this point, we can establish a clear direction to thwart the evil that has taken hold of not only Silver Ridge but the whole of the Mount Hood Wilderness and the Pacific Northwest.

Christopher's voice grows more persistent as he continues, "There is an evil that grows stronger as we speak, and with the tools and knowledge we possess, we can close the portal known as the Veil of Shadows once and for all. We must trust each other and remain steadfast in our secrecy and commitment. We must commit to keeping our alliance strong and protected, allowing only those we trust into this holy alliance." The others nod in agreement, their faces reflecting determination and solemnity.

Father Green replies, "You have my pledge that what we discuss and the actions we take as allies moving forward will be strictly confidential, and we will protect the secrecy, sanctity, and well-being of our alliance, with the backing of the Holy Roman Church and the Angels above as our protectors. I give you my solemn word." Christopher smiles at Father Green as both men rise from their seats and take each other's hands in a binding handshake. Father Green signs the cross across his chest. Then he repeats the gesture to the others present, blessing the members of the alliance and speaking the Trinitarian invocation in Latin, "In nomine Patris, et Filii, et Spiritus Sancti." Translated, "In the name of the Father and the Son and the Holy Spirit." The group responds in unison, "Amen," their voices united in a shared commitment to their sacred mission.

Father Luciano Rossi, speaking with a distinct Italian accent in remarkably precise English, addresses the group. "I am here as an emissary of the Holy Roman Church. My assistant, Brother Marco De Luca, a monk of the highest order, and I have been sent here on a quest to return the sacred artifact known as the Talisma Rubini to its rightful place among the ancient artifacts held sacred within the archives of the Basilica Sancti Petri in Rome. The artifact, originally recovered and placed there by Brother Alessandro of the older order, was removed by The Triple Entente and used to open a portal over Europe, essentially releasing malevolent forces that resulted in the conflicts of World War I and World War II. The church sent emissaries to recover the Talisma Rubini. Through acts of valor and sacrifice, they reclaimed the artifact from the clutches of the German Alliance. They returned it to its original resting place in the archives beneath the Basilica Sancti Petri in Rome." The weight of history hangs heavy in the air as he speaks.

Father Rossi continues, his voice filled with reverence and urgency. "As war raged across Europe and the Pacific, and sensing an ancient force stirring beneath the surface, the Keepers of the Talisma Rubini convened in solemn council, invoking ancient rites and prayers from secret writings. They journeyed to the heart of the European continent and, with prayer and a resounding surge of divine energy, sealed the portal shut, its dark influence banished, leaving Europe and the rest of the world safe from the evil forces unleashed. The Talisma Rubini was returned to the archives beneath the Basilica Sancti Petri, where it remained until several years ago when the Keepers discovered it was missing along with other sacred scrolls and manuscripts." He pauses, letting the gravity of the situation sink in, the room filled with a palpable sense of shared determination and purpose.

Sarah and Christopher recalled reading about this history in the "Talisma Rubini" scroll and the "Aeta's Moderna" section, so they knew Father Rossi's tale to be true. Father Rossi continued, "It has been discovered through investigation that the journey of the Talisma Rubini to the Silver Ridge Institute, although steeped in mystery and intrigue and woven with threads of ancient prophecy and modern discovery, found its way to Silver Ridge. As the years passed, whispers of the talisman's hidden power spread like tendrils across continents, drawing the attention of scholars and seekers alike. Among them was Professor Gabriel Sinclair, a renowned archaeologist and expert in esoteric artifacts, whose tireless quest for knowledge led him to the fabled Talisma.

142

Driven by a thirst for understanding and a sense of destiny, Professor Sinclair followed a trail of cryptic clues and obscure references that eventually led him to the Basilica Sancti Petri archives. There, in the dim recesses of forgotten tomes and dusty scrolls, he uncovered the long-guarded secret of the Talisma Rubini and its enigmatic connection to the golden cross of Brother Alessandro. Sensing the weight of responsibility upon his shoulders, Professor Sinclair resolved to bring the Talisma Rubini to a place where its power could be studied and understood without the confines of religious dogma. Thus, under cover of night, Professor Sinclair embarked on a clandestine journey to transport the Talisma Rubini to the Silver Ridge Institute, nestled amidst the rugged peaks of the Cascade Mountains. Guided by ancient maps and whispered legends, he removed the artifact from the archives of the Basilica Sancti Petri in Rome and eluded those who sought to thwart his quest.

Professor Sinclair's journey began with a transatlantic flight as he crossed the ocean. Upon landing on the East Coast, his journey continued by train and automobile, moving from bustling cities to vast plains and towering mountains, each step meticulously planned according to his research. Finally, he arrived in the Pacific Northwest, where the Mount Hood wilderness awaited. Amidst the ancient trees and hidden trails, Sinclair felt the convergence of energies he had long sought, knowing his quest had brought him to the threshold of discovery. Finally, Professor Sinclair arrived at the Institute's gates, carrying the key to unlocking the "Talisma Rubini's" hidden mysteries and ushering in a new era of understanding. This began a quest by specific individuals at the institute to attempt to unlock its secrets, thus placing all of us in the grasp of the evil peril we face today."

Father Green says, "Thank you, Father Rossi. We are at your service to help ensure the safe return of the Ruby

Talisman artifact to its rightful place in the archives beneath the Basilica Sancti Petri. There is a shadowy alliance of government agencies and world leaders, driven by insatiable ambition and a thirst for control, who see the Ruby Talisman and the Veil of Shadows as a strategic asset of immeasurable value. They envision exploiting its power to manipulate reality, furthering their agendas, and cementing their grip on power. For them, the Veil of Shadows and Ruby Talisman represent the opportunity to transcend the limitations of conventional authority and a means to wield influence on a cosmic scale, reshaping the very course of history to suit their whims. We cannot allow that to happen." He then turns to Christopher, asking, "What do you think about this, Professor Daniels?"

Christopher takes a moment to gather his thoughts before responding to the group. "I agree that since the keepers of the Ruby Talisman have kept it safe from these malevolent government agencies and world leaders through most of the modern era, it would be best if it were returned to its rightful place of safekeeping. However, I hope the Holy Roman Church would secure such an artifact within a locked, impenetrable safe to prevent it from falling again into the wrong hands of individuals seeking to harm." As he speaks, Christopher shoots a quick glance at Father Rossi, who responds by making the sign of the cross upon his forehead and kissing the tip of a cross at the end of a pair of rosary beads he holds in his other hand. Nodding in agreement, Father Rossi replies, "And so it shall be."

❧ CHAPTER THIRTEEN ❧

Sarah looks at Christopher with pride in her eyes. She is proud of him for his command of thoughts and words, recognizing how much he has grown. Her revelation and Guardian Angel Nanael's visit have given him the courage and divine wisdom to rise to the occasion and lead the group to victory against the forces of evil. Christopher's resolute demeanor and thoughtful words inspire confidence, which is precisely what is needed to lead the alliance to a shared commitment to protect humanity from the malevolent forces seeking to exploit the Ruby Talisman and the Veil of Shadows.

Dr. Isabella Grey then addresses the group, her voice steady yet tinged with emotion. "My journey to Forest Haven has been fraught with danger, emotional turmoil, and mental distress; however, I am glad that my path led me here and grateful for the support and unselfish healing that the members of the parish have given me. I will always be in your debt. My faith has grown; through this, my inner demons have been banished with the prayers and support you generously offered me." She continues, "I came to the Silver Ridge Institute as a research assistant to Professor Edmund Thorne. Soon after arriving, I became aware of the Veil of Shadows manuscript he had in his possession, and shortly after that, he revealed the Ruby Talisman artifact to me during a clandestine ritual he was attempting to perform. I could tell he was becoming obsessed with unlocking its power as his demeanor began to change and his mind began to deteriorate. Fearing for my life and mental well-being, I started a journal in case I became incapacitated. As I sensed an evil presence descending on the Institute and the Silver Ridge area, it became apparent that malevolent forces were at play. I felt my mental health deteriorating, and after one particularly harrowing night of rituals performed by the Professor, I decided to hide the

Ruby Talisman where he could not find it and depart the institute, determined never to return to that dreadful place."

Isabella continues, "I hid my journal among the artifacts and books on my office bookcase behind my desk, hoping someone, sometime, would find it and be forewarned of the dangers lurking within the institute's walls. The journal and the hidden Ruby Talisman were all I dared to leave behind, hidden in my office for fear that the Professor would discover anything else missing. I drove to the Portland area, rented an apartment, and found employment as a research assistant for local news agencies and several magazine publications. It was all I could do for my sustenance. Still, I was unable to shake the fear and nightmares that plagued me about the malevolent forces the Professor and I had unwittingly let loose. However, I do fear that the Professor's obsession beckoned him to join the forces of evil that we unleashed. Fear and my mental instability prevented me from moving on and kept me frozen in Portland."

"Finally, I could not stay silent or in fear any longer, so I packed up and headed east on Highway 26 towards the Mount Hood National Forest. Seeking rest and redemption, I turned off the main highway at Forest Haven Road and found myself at the gates of Forest Haven Parish. Here, I found the support and healing I so desperately needed. The parish clergy welcomed me with unconditional love and encouragement, and here is where I revealed my story to them. I felt safe and secure within the arms of the church. Father Green offered me a position teaching at the Sacred Cedars Seminary, which included residence at the visitor's quarters. Destiny has brought us all together at this place to right the wrongs that I played a role in creating."

Noticing tears welling up in the corners of Isabella's eyes, Sarah reached across the table, took Isabella's hands in hers, and gently spoke, "You are not to blame, my dear. The powers that Professor Thorne unleashed are far more powerful than either of you had control over. You were just his research assistant and had no clue what would happen. The fact that you realized the significance of your discovery and escaped, leaving a trail of clues to be found, is a testament to your faith and consciousness to do the right thing and save yourself and others from the evil unleashed. You must always believe you did the right thing, and your destiny has brought you here, as has ours. You are in good company, Isabella, and well protected. Let go of your fears, for we are at your side to protect you."

Isabella looked into Sarah's eyes and saw pure love looking back at her. She could see a warm glow around Sarah's face and sensed a celestial beauty she had never seen in someone before. She felt a wave of calmness and assurance come over her, and a heavy burden lifted off her chest. "Thank you, Ms. Hope," she replied. "Please call me Sarah," Sarah responded. Isabella smiled, feeling a deep sense of connection and relief, knowing she was among friends who would stand by her side in the days ahead. Isabella asked Christopher, "Did you find my journal, Professor Daniels?" "Yes, I did, Isabella, and something else as well. We have the Ruby Gem embedded in the Golden Cross. We have the Ruby Talisman, and it is safe."

Sounds of relief echoed around the conference table. Hands rose in jubilation at the news that the artifact had been recovered. Praise sang out from the others in the group as Sarah and Christopher met each other's gaze, knowing that the mention of the recovery of the Ruby Talisman had consummated the holy alliance. Still, Sarah and Christopher knew there was much to be done in preparation for the final conflict between the forces of good and the forces of evil. Once the fervor had receded, Christopher reassured them that the Ruby Talisman was safe, though he did not have it with him today. They understood that Christopher did not know the whole nature of the meeting invitation. He hid it securely until he felt confident enough to return it to the church for safekeeping. Christopher had not considered returning it to its rightful place until today's meeting, as well as Father Rossi's revelations and his quest to return the artifact to Rome. Now, it had become clear what he must do. He would convey to the others the urgent need to close the Veil of Shadows portal and use the Ruby Talisman as a divine tool to accomplish this task.

Father Green suggested they break for lunch and reconvene around 1:00 pm to continue their discussions. All agreed. The group rose from their seats, the atmosphere charged with relief and resolve. As they moved toward the dining area, conversations buzzed with newfound hope and determination. Christopher and Sarah walked side by side, sharing a moment of silent understanding of the immense responsibility ahead. They knew that the coming hours and days would be crucial in shaping the fate of their mission, and they were ready to face the challenges together, fortified by the strength of their alliance and the faith that bound them all. The dining area was a warm and inviting space, filled with natural light streaming through large windows and decorated with simple yet elegant wooden furnishings. Lunch consisted of sandwiches, fresh fruit, and various pastries, providing a satisfying and comforting meal for everyone.

After lunch, the group reconvened. Christopher began the conversation, picking up where he had left off earlier. "You all have many questions; perhaps I can answer a few. What Isabella has told you is true. There is a malevolence hanging over the Silver Ridge Institute, and yes, Professor Thorne and his assistant, Dr. Isadora Vale, have been swept up in it and have become conduits and pawns through which this malevolence works. I am unsure to what extent their participation is, but I know they are involved. Dr. Thorne has the Veil of Shadows manuscript hidden at the institute, but Sarah and I have deciphered its pages, decrypting its symbols, incantations, and writings. We have made copies of its contents and secured them in a safe place."

Father Rossi said, "The one at the institute is a copy that church scribes have translated. The original is still in the Basilica Sancti Petri archives. Then, the one at the institute must be one of the manuscripts taken from the archives." "I believe you are correct, Father," Christopher continued. "Sarah and I have another titled 'Talisma Rubini,' with a section named 'Modernitas.' We also recovered the 'Per Aetates: Umbrae Temporis' manuscript written by Archbishop Alejandro Patrici, which no doubt was removed from the archives by Professor Sinclair."

Christopher conveys to the group, "Our task as a team will be to locate the open portal, which Sarah and I believe to be somewhere in the vicinity of Mount Hood, perhaps not far from here, and with all the tools and spiritual power we have amongst us, close the Veil of Shadows portal permanently. Our goal will be to banish the evil unleashed and return it to where it came from. We must work swiftly to prevent nefarious individuals and corrupt government agencies from obtaining the power and location of the portal to exploit it for their desires." Father Green responds, "The spread of evil through this portal must be stopped. Many portals remain dormant throughout the world, closed by divine intervention. There will always be an evil present. The veil between the heavens and earth is thin, and since the descent of the fallen angels, humankind has witnessed many atrocities, encountering evil in many places. But when a portal such as this has been opened, the balance of nature and humanity is in jeopardy."

Christopher and the others in the group nod, and he replies, "Yes, Father, you are correct. Sarah and I have been working hard to solve this puzzle, yet much remains to do. We must follow the remaining clues that lead us to the exact location of the Veil of Shadows portal. I suggest

Sarah and I return to Silver Ridge and gather as much information as possible before returning to Forest Haven with our findings and the remaining artifacts in our possession." Father Green adds, "We will also gather information and prepare a summary and strategy to share upon your return." Father Luciano Rossi adds, "I will contact the Church in Rome and inform them that we have recovered the Talisma Rubini and the other artifacts you mentioned. They will be incredibly pleased. Thank you, Professor Daniels and Ms. Hope. "Christopher replies, and Sarah nods, "You are welcome, Father Rossi." With that, the group adjourns, agreeing to meet back at Forest Haven on Saturday to continue their quest.

As Sarah and Christopher exit the administration building, Deacon Crossford bids them farewell, saying, "Thank you both. I still owe you that tour, perhaps when you return." Christopher replies, "Yes, we would like that. See you then." As they turn toward the parking area, Isabella calls after them and catches up to them. Dr. Isabella Grey has short shoulder-length brown hair and brown eyes, her slender figure conveying a sense of elegance. Her eyes, reflecting intelligence and compassion, catch the afternoon sun, which bathes her face in a soft, graceful glow. She has smooth, beautiful features, and her face reflects a lovely innocence. However, as she approaches Sarah and Christopher, there's a subtle hint of nervousness in her demeanor, suggesting she may have secrets yet to be revealed. She says, "Thank you, Sarah and Professor Daniels; perhaps we can talk when you return. There is much I would like to share with you both." Sarah responds, "Yes, Isabella, there is much to share with you. You are a very special and important partner in our quest. Our destinies are intertwined, and our futures are bright."

Bidding farewell to Isabella, Christopher assists Sarah into the SUV passenger seat, opening the door and closing it once she settles into her seat. He gets in on the driver's side and starts the engine. Pulling out of the parking area and exiting through the gates of Forest Haven Parish, the afternoon sun sheds its rays through the pine and cedar trees that line the road, reminding them of the splendor of nature even as shadows loom over their impending quest. Turning onto the main highway, Sarah reminds Christopher of the Inn of Whispers and Madame Elara, whom she feels compelled to visit. Christopher smiles in agreement and makes a mental note to pull off the highway at the Inn's location. Sarah closes her eyes as they continue in silence. The sound of the wheels on the road, wind whooshing by the slightly opened side window, and the occasional bird song from the trees that line the road send her into a transcendental state of mind, realizing her soul as an entity that exists entirely apart from her body. In this meditative state, she is at one with her celestial being, a refreshing respite from her physical form.

Christopher glances at Sarah and sees a warm, ethereal glow around her, reminding him of her angelic revelation. A calm comes over him. The smell of lilacs and lavender fills the air, touching his heart and pulling at his soul. Sarah's beauty draws him in, his love for her fills his whole being. Tears form around his eyes, blurring his sight for a moment, yet they are tears of joy. His own guardian angel sitting next to him in half-human, half-celestial form is more than his heart can bear. At this moment, time stands still. Nothing else matters. Gathering his composure, he sets his eyes on the road up ahead as the sign for the Inn of Whispers comes into view. Pulling off the road, Sarah is stirred into the present by the change in motion and the feel of the wheels touching the gravel turnoff. "We have arrived," Christopher announces with a grin.

The Inn of Whispers is a curious and intriguing sight for any traveler on the highway. Its architecture combines rustic charm with an esoteric flair, drawing the eye and inviting curiosity. The Inn's exterior is constructed from

151

dark, weathered timber, giving it a timeless and foreboding appearance. Large, arched windows framed in wrought iron line the front of the Inn; their glass panes stained in deep emerald and sapphire hues cast a mystical glow on the interior. Above the entrance, a wooden sign swings gently in the breeze, creaking softly. The sign bears the name "Inn of Whispers" in an elegant, flowing script. A cobblestone path leads to the Inn's front door. Lanterns hang on either side of the door, their flames flickering with an otherworldly light, casting shadows that dance and shift mysteriously. The Inn's roof is steep and shingled, with chimneys puffing out tendrils of smoke that carry the scent of burning wood and exotic herbs.

As Sarah and Christopher step into the Inn of Whispers, they are enveloped by an atmosphere that feels timeless and mystical. The interior is dimly lit by flickering candles, oil lamps, and the warm glow of a grand fireplace, creating an inviting ambiance. The spacious yet cozy main room is filled with the evocative scents of old books, burning incense, and ancient herbs, blending to form a rich and intriguing aroma. The floor, adorned with intricately patterned rugs featuring arcane symbols and natural motifs, cushions their footsteps and enhances the room's mystical allure. In one corner stands a counter fashioned from polished dark oak, where Madame Elara welcomes them with a genuine smile. Behind her, shelves are stocked with jars of rare herbs, potions, and other alchemical ingredients, their labels hinting at their potent and mysterious properties. Every so often, a faint, melodic chime echoes through the room, a subtle reminder of the enchantments and secrets that reside within the Inn. "Welcome to the Inn of Whispers," Madame Elara says warmly to Sarah and Christopher. "I have been expecting your arrival. Through visions granted to me, I recognize both of you. You are the chosen ones."

"And you, my dear," Madame Elara's voice carries a hint of mystery as she addresses Sarah, "are not of this world." Sarah's eyes twinkle with curiosity and recognition as she smiles at the enigmatic woman and says, "You are quite intuitive and wise. You know who I am and why I am here. Yes, we are the ones who have been chosen, and our paths have not crossed with yours by coincidence. There is a higher power at work here. Perhaps you can enlighten us and provide information to help us on our journey." Madame Elara, a figure of elegance and wisdom, does a curtsey and replies, "I think you are the one who can bring enlightenment into my world. Yes, of course, I am at your service. How can I help?" Sarah introduces herself and Christopher to Madame Elara and then asks her what she can tell them about the Mount Hood area and portals.

Madame Elara's eyes gleam with otherworldly light like two pools of ancient wisdom as she listens to Sarah's words. "Indeed, my dear," she begins, her voice confident. Your presence here is not a mere chance. There are forces beyond our understanding, guiding us towards the delicate balance of light and shadow." With a graceful gesture, Madame Elara invites Sarah and Christopher to sit at a nearby table, where the Inn's ambiance seems to deepen, the air heavy with the weight of ancient knowledge. "Mount Hood," she continues, "is a place of great power, where the natural world intertwines with mystical energies. Legends speak of a gateway hidden in the depths of its forests, connecting our realm with others beyond." Her eyes glint with a mixture of reverence and caution. "This portal or gateway is not to be trifled with. It holds the potential to bridge our world with realms of both light and darkness.

Madame Elara pauses, her gaze shifting between Sarah and Christopher as if weighing the gravity of their quest. "In your hands," she continues, "lies the fate of this delicate balance. There is an artifact in your possession, and the knowledge you seek is the key to understanding and closing this portal. But beware, for some would misuse such power for their ends." Madame Elara leans forward slightly, her expression earnest. "I will share with you what I know, what whispers have reached my ears through the ages. But remember, the journey ahead is fraught with peril and mystery. You must tread carefully, guided by your intuition and the wisdom of those who came before." Sarah nods, her eyes alight with determination. "Thank you, Madame Elara," she says sincerely. "Your insights are invaluable to us. With your guidance, we hope to unravel the mysteries of Mount Hood and protect our world from the darkness that threatens it." Madame Elara smiles knowingly. "The threads of fate have woven us together for a reason," she replies cryptically. "Now, let us begin."

"In the depths of Mount Hood National Forest lies a legend as old as time itself—a tale of a portal that I just mentioned connects the celestial realms of heaven and the earth, where light and darkness converge. According to the ancient lore whispered among the trees, the portal was crafted by celestial beings and born from the clash of opposing forces—the meeting point between good and evil. It is said that when the world was young, a great battle raged between the forces of light and darkness, and in the aftermath of this cosmic conflict, the portal was formed as a rift in the fabric of reality itself."

"Another legend passed down from the indigenous Kaskali people of the region states that the guardians of the forest, ancient spirits bound to the land since immemorial, watch over the portal with unwavering vigilance. These guardians, known as the Wardens of the Veil, are beings of elemental power, embodying the very essence of the forest itself. The first warden is the Guardian of the Oak, a towering figure whose roots spread deep into the earth, anchoring the portal to the physical realm. With gnarled branches outstretched like protective arms, the Guardian of the Oak stands sentinel. The second warden is the Guardian of the Mist, a spectral entity whose form shimmers like the morning fog. It is said that this warden can manipulate the mists of the forest, obscuring the path to the portal. The third warden is the Guardian of the Flame, a creature of living fire whose flickering light dances upon the forest floor. With a gaze as fierce as the blaze it embodies, the Guardian of the Flame wards off any who would seek to misuse the portal's power. And finally, there is the Guardian of the Waters, a serene being whose form ripples like the surface of a tranquil lake. It is said that this warden holds sway over the rivers and streams of the forest."

Madam Elara continues, "Unlike other legends, this portal does not discriminate—it allows passage for both virtuous angels and malevolent demons alike. It is a gateway through which beings from both realms can traverse, their intentions shaping the course of their journey. The promise of power and knowledge draws those who seek the portal, for it is said that on the other side lies secrets beyond mortal comprehension—ancient wisdom whispered by the celestial beings of heaven and forbidden sorcery whispered by the sinister denizens of the underworld. For every soul that emerges from the other side enlightened and empowered, countless others are lost to the darkness, their minds twisted, and their hearts corrupted by the malevolent energies that permeate the realm beyond." She adds, "The portal is located at the base of Mount Hood, hidden deep within the thick forest greenery and towering pines, accessible only by an old timberline trail that winds its way through streams and gulleys, becoming steeper. Following the trail, you will see a secluded lake shrouded by mist. Following the trail past the hidden lake, you continue climbing. Several miles past the lake, the trail becomes overgrown and more complex, cutting through thick forest. The portal manifests as a circle of ancient stones overgrown with moss and surrounded by a halo of ethereal light. When the conditions are just right—when the moon is complete and the stars align—the portal becomes visible to those who seek it, appearing as a glowing archway in a perpetual veil of mist. This is where you will find the portal you seek.

Madam Elara reaches under the display case and produces an old, folded map. "I have acquired this old lumberjack map showing the route to the portal area, and I shall entrust it to you for your quest." She hands the map to Sarah and then reaches her hand out to Christopher. "May I read your palm, young man?" she asks. "Yes," Christopher answers, placing his hand face up on hers. "I see something very special about you—a strength and connection to the other side. Madame Elara gazed deeply into Christopher's eyes and said, "I see danger ahead, but you shall overcome it, and your life will never be the same. After a period of grief, you will find peace and understanding. I also see your lifeline splitting in two directions, indicating a rebirth at a crucial point soon. The signs show me that your life will change, and your purpose will take on new meaning and direction." Christopher and Sarah thank Madame Elara for her assistance as they turn toward the Inn of Whisper's exit. Madame Elana calls out to them, "May the angels and ascended masters guide you and protect you both."

Christopher and Sarah depart the Inn of Whispers, return to the SUV, and merge onto Highway 26, continuing west to Silver Ridge. Arriving at Christopher's residence, they enter and settle into the plush chairs in the downstairs living quarters after freshening up and enjoying a cold glass of iced tea. The room is cozy, and the soft hum of a ceiling fan adds to the relaxing atmosphere. They unfold the old lumberjack map on the coffee table, tracing the route to the portal area; their minds and conversation focused on the meeting at Forest Haven Parish, their visit, and reading with Madame Elara, as well as the journey ahead.

❧ CHAPTER FOURTEEN ❧

A knock sounds at the front door. Christopher reacts, saying, "Now, who could that be? I rarely get visitors at my residence." With a curious look, Sarah glances at him and then at the front door as Christopher rises to respond to the knock. Sarah remains seated and folds up the map, her eyes following him as he walks across the room. The atmosphere shifts, a subtle tension filling the air. Christopher opens the door to reveal a male and a female, both dressed in casual business attire, standing on the doorstep, shrouded in the soft evening light, holding an air of mystery about them.

"May I help you?" Christopher asks. "Good evening, Professor Daniels. I am Detective Karen Hayes with the Silver Ridge Police Department, and this is my partner, Detective Brian Mitchell. May we ask you a few questions about the Silver Ridge Institute as part of an ongoing missing persons investigation?" she asks. Christopher hesitates as she continues, "May we come in? Coming to your residence seems odd and suspicious, but I assure you it is in our best interests that we meet away from the Institute." Christopher nods in agreement and invites them into his residence. "Please have a seat, detectives," he says, gesturing towards the couch. As they settle on the couch, Christopher introduces them to Sarah, his assistant. "Pleased to meet you," Sarah greets them with a smile. Sarah's intuition tells her that these two individuals possess high levels of integrity. They are seekers of the truth, and she senses they can be trusted. Detective Hayes speaks first, "I'm sure you've heard of the recent disappearances of students and others who have gone missing without a trace around Silver Ridge. Our investigations have led us to look closer at the Silver Ridge Institute. Through information obtained from past faculty and students, we suspect that Professor Thorne and his assistant, Dr. Vale, may have been involved in the students' disappearances.

I assure you that everyone we have interviewed regards you in the highest esteem, and you are in no way a suspect in our investigation. We do fear, however, that you and Ms. Hope could be in danger. We have concluded that Professor Thorne and Dr. Vale are engaged in nefarious activities, and we hoped you could provide any clues that could assist us in getting to the bottom of this activity." Detective Mitchell stated, "We understand this may put you in an awkward position, but surely you have also noticed a tension and a sense of malevolence hanging over the Institute. There is something amiss with the professor's state of mind and wickedness in Dr. Vale's personality and behavior. This may sound like I've lost touch with reality, but I don't know how to describe my feelings after interacting with them both."

Christopher and Sarah exchange glances, their faces reflecting the gravity of the situation. Christopher thinks, "Detective Hayes and Mitchell have uncovered clues that led them to suspect Professor Thorne and Dr. Vale. And they are correct in their assumption that the professor and Dr. Vale are involved in the disappearances. But, of course, the detectives do not know the full extent of the evil hanging over the Institute and Silver Ridge. They would not believe us if we told them what we know." After a moment's pause, Christopher responds, "Yes, we have heard of the disappearances. I have been told hikers regularly come up missing in the Mount Hood National Forest. However, I am sure you investigated these disappearances, and on many occasions, they are found safe yet weary. This is something different. The implication is that students and citizens of Silver Ridge have vanished without a trace, and somehow, the Professor and Dr. Vale are responsible."

Christopher continues, "Yes, I've sensed the unease at the Institute, especially in recent months. Professor Thorne has become increasingly secretive, and Dr. Vale's behavior has been troubling. I've had my suspicions also." Sarah picks up on where Christopher is going with his response and, not wanting to divulge all she knew, nods in agreement and adds, "We've noticed things that don't add up. It is as if they're hiding something dark and dangerous. We will help you in any way we can." Detective Hayes leans forward, her expression earnest, "Thank you. Any information you can provide, no matter how small, could be crucial. We need to stop whatever is happening before more people go missing." Christopher replies, "I'll return to the Institute tomorrow, and if there is anything else I can provide, I'll be in touch." Detective Hayes responds, "Thank you, Professor, but please be careful. You may be in danger." She gives Christopher her personal phone number as she and Detective Mitchell rise from the couch and walk towards the door. Exiting, they bid Sarah and Christopher goodnight as Christopher closes the door behind them. The night air swooshes through the opening as it closes, adding a freshness to the room.

Once the detectives have left, Christopher and Sarah exchange a look of concern and determination. They know that revealing the truth about Professor Thorne and Dr. Vale to the detectives would hamper their efforts to complete their quest to close the portal. Sarah says, "We need to be cautious, Christopher. The detectives' suspicions align with what we've observed, but there's so much more they don't know. We'll have to tread carefully until our task is complete. It is better to withhold all we know than to endanger their lives. It is better that they do not know what they do not know. Do you agree?" Christopher nods in agreement, the weight of their mission pressing heavily on his shoulders. "We'll proceed carefully," he says. "Eventually, the truth will come to light once we complete

159

our mission, for the sake of those who have already vanished and for those who might be next."

Christopher suggests that Sarah stay the night at his residence, offering her a guest bedroom with a private bathroom and shower. He believes she will be safer there for the night, and in the morning, he will escort her to her residence on his way to the Institute. Sarah agrees, tired from the day's activities, and appreciates the added security and comfort of staying under Christopher's roof. Besides, her stay will also give Christopher peace of mind, knowing she is safe under his watchful eyes. They prepare a light dinner, dine, and then retire to the upstairs area. Before entering the guest bedroom, Sarah kisses Christopher gently on his cheek, bidding him goodnight. Christopher replies, "Goodnight, Sarah, sleep well," before he enters his master bedroom, closing the door behind him. Sleep comes easily to them both.

Morning arrives in Silver Ridge, a slight chill in the air drifting down from the distant slopes of Mount Hood, spreading across the national forest. A thin veil of mist lingers, wrapping the landscape in a delicate embrace. As the sun rises, its rays pierce through the towering pines, casting a rainbow of colors as they filter through the morning dew drops clinging to the leaves. The approach of the Autumnal Equinox, less than a month away, is evident in the shifting weather, marking the transition from summer to fall. The crisp air carries the faint scent of pine and earth, mingling with the freshness of the new day. The town of Silver Ridge begins to stir, with the promise of a busy Labor Day weekend ahead. Residents bustle about, preparing for the influx of tourists and visitors who return each year to partake in the local festivals, boating adventures, and camping escapades among the scenic trees and serene lakes of the Mount Hood National Forest.

Christopher and Sarah rise early, refreshed from a good night's sleep. The inviting smell of a fresh pot of coffee fills the air, its rich aroma mingling with the faint scent of mint from a canister of tea bags nearby. A water kettle hisses softly on the stove as steam rises from its spout, curling into the air. Christopher pours himself a cup of coffee, savoring the warmth of the mug in his hands. The dark liquid swirls, releasing a comforting, earthy scent. Equally relaxed, Sarah steeps a bag of green tea with mint in a delicate cup and saucer, and the vibrant green tea bag unfurls slowly in the hot water. Christopher has laid out a simple yet inviting breakfast on the kitchen table. Flaky and warm golden croissants sit beside a small fruit platter arranged carefully. The colorful medley of berries, apple slices, and orange segments adds a cheerful touch to the morning meal. Sarah smiles, warmly touched by Christopher's thoughtfulness. She reaches for a croissant, appreciating the crisp outer surface that gives way to a soft, buttery inside. They sit together, enjoying the quiet intimacy of the early morning, their warm beverages in hand.

Little words need to be spoken between them, as Christopher and Sarah are acutely aware of the events unfolding, and the tasks they must complete to prepare for closing the Veil of Shadows portal. Their recent visit from Detectives Hale and Mitchell has added an extra layer of urgency to their quest. Christopher plans to return to the Institute this morning to avoid attracting suspicion, while Sarah will head back to her residence. She intends to browse the marketplace and the quaint shops along the main street, hoping to discreetly gather any information from the townsfolk that might aid them and the parish alliance in their mission. After breakfast, they leave Christopher's home and head up Main Street towards Sarah's residence. As they pass by, shopkeepers begin to open their doors, and the enticing aroma of freshly baked goods and brewed coffee fills the air. Families and friends gather supplies for picnics and outdoor activities, and their laughter and chatter create a lively atmosphere. The town, nestled in its picturesque setting, exudes a welcoming charm that draws people back year after year. Silver Ridge, alive with anticipation and the timeless beauty of nature, is ready to embrace the seasonal change and the joyful festivities of the long weekend ahead. Arriving in front of Sarah's residence, they exchange a casual hug. Christopher says, "After I am done at the Institute, I will meet you at Hawthorne's Cafe around noon. Will that work for you?" Sarah responds, "Yes, that works for me. Please be careful, Christopher." Christopher nods, offering a reassuring smile. "Thank you, I will. See you around noon."

With a final wave, he continues down the street, heading towards the Institute. The morning sun casts long shadows on the sidewalk, and the sounds of the bustling town fade as Christopher approaches the imposing building. The Institute looms ahead, its facade a stark contrast to the cheerful atmosphere of the town, reminding Christopher of the gravity of their mission. Entering the Institute, Christopher is greeted by Julie, the receptionist. "Good morning, Professor Daniels," she says warmly. "Good morning, Julie," Christopher replies, returning the smile. "Any messages?" he asks. "Yes, I have one from Professor Thorne, who would like a meeting with you this morning. And I have a phone message for you from Senator Eleanor Caldwell. She says she must speak to you about a matter of extreme importance. She has left her number for you to call her back," Julie responds, her face reflecting a mix of curiosity and concern." Thank you, Julie. I am sure it's nothing major. It probably has something to do with fundraising for the Institute. I will return her call. I will also meet with Professor Thorne after I get settled in," Christopher says reassuringly.

He smiles and then heads down the hall to his office, the echo of his footsteps mingling with the quiet hum of the building. Entering his office, he closes the door behind him, ready to tackle the day's unexpected challenges. Wondering about Senator Caldwell's message, Christopher picks up the phone on his desk and dials the number Julie gave him. After several rings, a female voice answers. "Hello, this is Senator Eleanor Caldwell. How may I help you?" she asks. "Hello, Senator. I am Professor Daniels from the Silver Ridge Institute. I am returning your call," Christopher replies. "Oh, I'm so glad I could get a hold of you, Professor. Please call me 'Ellie.' You may not be aware, but a colleague of mine, Senator Richard Hastings, is meeting with Professor Thorne at the Silver Ridge Institute this morning. Professor Thorne, Dr. Vale, and Senator Hastings are planning something unspeakable. I have information that I dare not share with anyone. However, I am told you can be trusted, so I have contacted you, hoping you can help me. I cannot tell you my sources now, but I am telling the truth. I fear you are in danger at the Institute, so please be careful."

Christopher takes a deep breath, exhales, and then responds, "Professor Thorne has requested a meeting with me this morning; no doubt Senator Hastings and Dr. Vale will be present, from what you are telling me. Thank you for the warning. I will meet with them, but I assure you I will not share any information I have with them. From the tone of your voice and the words you speak, I believe you are sincere and can be trusted." Senator Caldwell responds, "I am relieved we are talking before you meet them. Please be careful that they do not manipulate you into revealing what you know. Now that we have talked, I will travel to Silver Ridge and should arrive this evening around eight. I will contact you when I arrive. I will be traveling alone. What I have to share with you is of the utmost secrecy, and I rely on your discretion." "Will you meet with me, Professor?" she adds. Christopher thinks momentarily, then replies, "I need a little more to go on before I can trust meeting with you. Perhaps there is something you can share with me to convince me that you are sincere and can be trusted?" Senator Caldwell responds, "The Veil of Shadows." Christopher's mouth drops, and shivers travel down his spine. "Yes, it seems we have something in common. I will meet you, Ellie. See you tonight around eight." "Thank you, Professor," she replies. "Call me Christopher," he responds as they end the call. Christopher sits back, the weight of the conversation settling in. He can't wait to tell Sarah about the call from Senator Eleanor "Ellie" Caldwell.

Christopher logs onto his desktop computer and begins an internet search on Senator Caldwell. His search quickly leads him to her professional profile as a well-known United States Senator. He finds numerous articles and endorsements that paint a picture of a highly respected and influential political figure. Senator Caldwell is highly regarded on several sites, with glowing endorsements emphasizing her character and accomplishments. Some of the endorsements read: "Senator Caldwell is known for her unwavering commitment to justice, integrity, and the well-being of her constituents. Her principled approach to policymaking has earned her respect from colleagues across the aisle. Whether championing environmental protection or advocating for affordable healthcare, Senator Caldwell remains steadfast in pursuing a better future for all." Another endorsement highlights, "Ellie Caldwell's dedication to transparency and ethical governance is unparalleled. She consistently puts the needs of the people first and fights tirelessly for policies that promote vital equality and sustainability." Reading these endorsements, Christopher feels reassured. The Senator's reputation aligns with the sincerity he sensed during their conversation. With a renewed sense of purpose, he prepares himself for the meeting with Professor Thorne and the challenges, knowing that Senator Caldwell, someone of such integrity, believes in him and shares the same concerns.

Christopher searches the internet for information on Senator Richard "Rick" Hastings. He quickly discovers many articles and reports detailing Hastings' notorious reputation for cunning and self-serving politics. His actions often prioritize personal gain over the welfare of the people he represents. Senator Hastings embodies the darker side of political ambition, whether accepting bribes, manipulating legislation to benefit wealthy donors, or engaging in ruthless smear campaigns against his opponents. His name is frequently associated with scandals and corruption, contrasting Senator Caldwell's ethical and principled image. Logging off his computer, Christopher feels a growing sense of unease. The information he has uncovered sheds light on why Senator Caldwell warned him about the potential dangers of his upcoming meeting with Professor Thorne, Dr. Vale, and Senator Hastings. The knowledge of Hastings' unscrupulous tactics adds a layer of gravity to the situation, making Christopher acutely aware of the need to remain vigilant and cautious. He now understands the importance of not being manipulated and the risks of navigating this treacherous political landscape. Determined to stay true to his mission, Christopher approaches the meeting with a clear mind and a guarded heart.

Christopher offers a warm smile and a nod to Julie as he heads to the stairs leading up to the second-floor meeting room. As he ascends the stairs, the familiar scent of aged books from the nearby library mixes with the faint aroma of polished wood. Once he reaches the second-floor area, he glances down the hallway, noting the entrances to the library, Professor Thorne and Dr. Vale's offices, and the executive meeting room. Steeling himself, he knocks on the meeting room door and steps inside. Professor Edmund Thorne is seated at the head of the table, exuding an air of authority, while Dr. Isadora Vale sits to his left, her demeanor as enigmatic as ever. Directly across from her,

Senator Richard Hastings lounges with an air of casual confidence. As Christopher enters, Professor Thorne and Senator Hastings rise to greet him while Dr. Vale remains seated, her gaze sharp and observant. "Welcome, Professor Daniels; great to see you. I appreciate you meeting with us on such short notice," Thorne says with a cordial smile. "I would like to introduce you to our special visitor, Senator Hastings."

Christopher smiles, stepping forward to shake the Senator's hand. "It's an honor to meet you, Senator," he says, feeling the firm grip of Hastings' handshake. "Call me Rick," the Senator responds smoothly. Christopher nods and takes the chair opposite Professor Thorne at the other end of the table. Dr. Vale's lips curl into a forbidding smile as the two other men resume their seats. "Hello, Professor Daniels. Where is your lovely assistant, Ms. Sarah Hope? Will she be joining us?" she inquires, her tone laced with suspicion. Christopher senses the underlying tension and responds evenly, "She will not join us today." His calm reply is met with a slight narrowing of Dr. Vale's eyes, but he remains resolute, ready to face whatever this meeting might bring.

Professor Thorne addresses those present with a measured tone, "Senator Hastings has traveled here from our nation's capital on a fact-finding mission. He has shared with me that he has obtained information that somewhere around Silver Ridge lies an ancient artifact brought here from Europe. This artifact is of great interest to our government. He tells me he has come to the Institute because, who better to know of such an item than us, here at the Institute, since we study and research these sorts of things." Senator Hastings glances first at Dr. Vale and then at Christopher, his face showing a slyness as he smiles and squints his eyes as if expecting Professor Thorne's words to elicit a nervous response from Christopher. Senator Hastings's expression turns to disappointment when he does not receive one. "Interesting," Christopher responds, maintaining his composure.

Professor Thorne asks Christopher, "Have you heard of such an artifact or discovered anything that points to its existence through your research?" Christopher knows that Professor Thorne is on a fishing expedition, trying to bait him into revealing any clues to its whereabouts. He senses that Professor Thorne knows about the missing Ruby Talisman, and suspects Christopher knows where it is. He realizes that Professor Thorne, Dr. Vale, and Senator Hastings are working together in a diabolical plan to recover the Ruby Talisman for nefarious purposes. Even though Senator Caldwell warned him about Senator Hastings's involvement, Christopher and Sarah already suspected Professor Thorne and Dr. Vale. Christopher smiles, projecting intrigue and curiosity on his face, and says, "Fascinating. Tell me more. What type of artifact are you looking for? What does it look like? What is its purpose?" Professor Thorne leans forward in his chair and folds his hands. In a quieter voice, as if not to allow others outside of the room to hear his words, he begins to describe the artifact. "It is a cross-shaped artifact with a gem in its center crossbeam. I am told it can reveal ley lines, portals, and hidden vortexes." "Have you heard of such an artifact, Christopher?" he asks. Christopher realizes this is the first time Professor Thorne has referred to him by his first name in the meeting, a tactic no doubt to gain his trust.

Christopher thinks for a moment and then responds, "Although I have an open mind, in my research concerning ley lines, portals, and energy vortexes, I have concluded that while ley lines and energy vortexes may lack empirical validation from mainstream science, they continue to capture the interest and imagination of many people around the world. Whether regarded as spiritual phenomena, geological anomalies, or simply products of human perception, these concepts offer intriguing avenues for further exploration and contemplation. Ultimately, their significance lies in the meanings and experiences individuals attribute to them rather than in any objective scientific reality." Senator Hastings interrupts, "But what about the artifact!" Dr. Vale glares at Christopher with an impatient look on her face. Christopher responds, "Oh, the artifact. I have studied and researched many ancient physical artifacts and ancient scrolls and manuscripts, some of which we scholars refer to as artifacts. Still, I have not come across anything that resembles what you describe. I wonder if I may have overlooked something. My recent research is not on artifacts, ley lines, portals, or vortexes."

Professor Thorne leans forward, his eyes narrowing slightly as he asks, "What is your current research project, Christopher?" Christopher replies smoothly, "Ms. Hope and I are researching the influence of Eastern religions on Western philosophy and society. It is a fascinating topic. While there are differences between the two, in the pursuit of truth and understanding, they share a common ground. Western philosophers often emphasize freedom and independence, while Eastern traditions, like Taoism, focus on unity and interconnectedness. Some argue that Eastern philosophy takes a holistic view, addressing the entirety of human existence, while Western philosophy tends to focus on specific aspects."

Christopher continues, "I hope to gather enough concrete information and history to publish a paper on the subject." His tone remains even, masking the underlying tension of the meeting. The mention of his research momentarily shifts the room's focus away from the artifact. Thorne nods thoughtfully, considering Christopher's words. "An intriguing area of study," he muses. "The cross-cultural influences can offer deep insights into our understanding of human thought and society." Christopher maintains his composed demeanor, aware that the line of questioning may return to the artifact at any moment.

168

✤ CHAPTER FIFTEEN ✤

Senator Hastings shakes his head from side to side and says, "Whew, this conversation is too existential for me. I can see that I have come to the right place; even though you have yet to come across this artifact in your research, Professor Daniels, perhaps others at the institute have? I will leave it to the experts. If you discover something valuable, please bring it to Professor Thorne's or Dr. Vale's attention. Professor Thorne and I have been friends and colleagues for a long time. My donors have been very generous with their support of the institute. They would be pleased to learn that the Institute has discovered such a valuable artifact." Christopher replies, "I certainly will, Senator. They will be the first to know." He feels he has successfully redirected the conversation to a more neutral topic, knowing the game of deception can be played by both sides.

Professor Thorne stands up and, in a formal gesture, says, "Thank you for your time, Professor Daniels. I totally understand you are very busy researching Eastern religions and Western philosophy—a formidable subject. I wish you the best with your studies. Please do not hesitate to ask if you and Ms. Hope need anything. And if you find out anything about this cross-shaped artifact, please let us know." "Thank you, Professor Thorne, I certainly will," Christopher replies as Senator Hastings rises from his chair, and the two men exchange handshakes. Dr. Vale, still seated, turns and nods at Christopher with a sinister smile, thinking she has outsmarted the fox. If only she knew what Christopher knew. For now, Christopher feels he has dodged the bullet. He exits the meeting room, closing the door behind him, confident that he has managed to keep the true nature of his knowledge hidden, at least for now.

Christopher hurriedly departs the institute, giving Julie, the receptionist, a smile and a thumbs-up sign as he passes her on the way to the exit. Julie, sensing his relief, nods back with a knowing smile. Once free of the front steps of the institute, Christopher crosses the town square, taking a deep breath of the fresh autumn air. The crispness fills his lungs, and he exhales, feeling a sense of liberation. Glancing at his watch, he notes that it is close to noon, so he swiftly walks to Hawthorne's Cafe, eager to rendezvous with Sarah and share the details of his phone conversation with Senator "Ellie" Caldwell, as well as the tense meeting he had with Professor Edmund Thorne, Dr. Isadora Vale, and Senator Rick Hastings. It certainly has been a busy morning.

Reaching Hawthorne's Cafe, Christopher feels a mix of anticipation and urgency. The morning's events have left him both anxious and determined. The bell above the door jingles as he steps inside, and the familiar aroma of freshly brewed coffee, home cooking, and baked goods welcomes him. He quickly scans the room and spots Sarah sitting at a cozy corner table, reading papers spread in front of her on the tabletop. She looks up as he approaches, her face lighting up with a warm smile. Christopher feels relief and excitement as he joins her, ready to dive into the intricate web of revelations and suspicions that have defined his morning. The conversations with Senator Caldwell and the encounter with Thorne, Vale, and Hastings weigh heavily on his mind, but now, with Sarah by his side, he feels a renewed sense of resolve.

Clearly frazzled, Christopher greets Sarah with relief and exhaustion, exclaiming about his overwhelming morning. Sarah, perceptive and caring, immediately notes the anxiety written on his face. She gently tells him to take a moment to relax before they delve into the events of their respective mornings and his time at the institute. With a reassuring smile, she also hints at having valuable information to share, adding a touch of intrigue to their upcoming conversation. After gathering his composure,

Christopher sat down with Sarah to recount his call with Senator "Ellie" Caldwell. He described how Ellie had warned him about Senator "Rick" Hastings, hinting at his untrustworthy nature. Sarah listened intently, her eyes never leaving Christopher's as she absorbed every word. Christopher conveyed his belief that Ellie could be trusted. Still, he harbored deep suspicions about Hastings, whose reputation for manipulation preceded him.

Christopher then detailed his tense morning meeting with Professor Thorne, Isadora Vale, and Senator Hastings. The trio had tried to extract information from him regarding the whereabouts of the Ruby Talisman artifact. Christopher played a delicate game of cat and mouse, steering the conversation towards his research on Eastern religions and Western philosophy. Despite their probing questions and evident skepticism, he crafted a narrative that painted him as oblivious to the artifact's existence. By the end of the meeting, Christopher felt he had managed to divert their suspicions temporarily. Although he knew they remained wary, he believed he had secured some precious time for Sarah, himself, and their alliance. The stakes were high, but Christopher was determined to stay one step ahead, using every ounce of his cunning to protect the secret whereabouts of the Ruby Talisman.

"Wow, you certainly had a trying morning, Christopher. I'm so glad you handled it well. I have complete confidence in your quick thinking and wisdom," Sarah said, her voice filled with genuine admiration. Christopher felt a sense of relief wash over him at her words. "Thank you, Sarah," he replied, his tone warm. "Senator Caldwell, 'Ellie,' will arrive at Silver Ridge around eight tonight. I told her we would meet with her. It would be best to meet her at my residence, away from prying eyes." Sarah nodded in agreement, a thoughtful expression crossing her face. "Excellent. I agree," she responded, understanding the need for discretion in their delicate situation.

At that moment, Suzy, the café server, arrived at their table, greeting Christopher with a friendly smile and placing a glass of water and a cup of coffee in front of him. "Will there be anything else, Professor?" she asked politely. "No, thank you, Suzy; coffee will be fine," Christopher nodded. Suzy turned to attend to other patrons, leaving Christopher and Sarah to converse. The café buzzed with clinking dishes and soft chatter, creating a comforting backdrop for their discussion as they prepared for the evening's crucial meeting. Sarah began to recount her morning activities to Christopher. She described how she had leisurely browsed the shops along the main street, taking in the quaint charm of Silver Ridge.

Sarah continued, sharing her visit to the Silver Ridge Gazette newspaper office. "I was greeted by a friendly elderly woman named Sandy who has worked at the paper for many years," she said, a smile playing on her lips as she remembered the encounter. "We discussed the legends around Silver Ridge and hikers who have gone missing over the years. I asked her if she had ever heard of Professor Gabriel Sinclair. Sandy said yes, she recalled a news article they had published almost twelve years ago." Sarah's eyes sparkled with excitement as she spoke, the memory of the conversation vivid in her mind. "We searched the news archives, and she found the article. She made a copy for me, and it is what I have here at the table," Sarah concluded, her voice brimming with a sense of accomplishment. She produced the article and handed it to Christopher. He took the paper from her, his curiosity piqued.

As Christopher unfolded the newspaper article copy, the headline immediately caught his eye: "Local Archaeologist and Team Missing." His brows furrowed as he delved into the article, which detailed the mysterious disappearance of Professor Gabriel Sinclair and his team during an expedition near the base of Mount Hood. The report spoke of a promising archaeological dig that had abruptly gone silent, leaving the community of Silver Ridge in shock and sparking numerous speculations about what might have happened to the group. After several weeks, the search for Professor Sinclair and his team was called off with no trace or clues about what had happened to them.

Sarah watched Christopher intently, gauging his reaction as he absorbed the information. "Sandy was quite helpful," she continued, breaking the silence. "She mentioned that this disappearance caused quite a stir back then, but over time, it faded into one of those unsolved local mysteries. There were whispers of hidden artifacts and ancient secrets, but nothing concrete ever came to light." She paused, allowing Christopher to process the weight of the article's revelations. "This is a significant lead for us. Here is the connection between Sinclair's work and the Ruby Talisman," she added thoughtfully. Christopher nodded slowly, his mind racing with possibilities. "This certainly adds a new dimension to our search," he said, his voice steady despite the whirlwind of thoughts." "It makes sense that Sinclair was experimenting with the Ruby Talisman and the Veil of Shadows, and no doubt opened the same portal we are determined to close. His disappearance is linked to the Ruby Talisman, as are the other missing people who have vanished without a trace. I fear they have been drawn to the other side through the portal." Christopher asked, "Do you think this is possible? That would explain a lot." With an approving nod, Sarah replied," I think you are right about the disappearances and the portal." He looked up at Sarah, appreciation evident in his eyes. "Great work, Sarah. This might be the breakthrough we need."

After finishing their beverages and paying the bill, Christopher and Sarah exited the café and stepped out into the sunny afternoon. They began their walk to Christopher's residence, stopping at Sarah's residence on the way so she could grab an overnight bag and suitcase. She would be staying at Christopher's residence, making it convenient for them to travel to Forest Haven Parish the following day. As they strolled through the charming streets of Silver Ridge, they noticed a police patrol car parked at the corner of Main and Cascadia Maple Drive. Christopher immediately recognized Officer Brandon Shaw seated in the driver's seat. With a friendly wave, Christopher acknowledged Officer Shaw, who returned the gesture with a smile. It was clear that Detective Hayes had stationed Officer Shaw there, perhaps to keep an eye on them for their safety or other reasons. Regardless, the sight of the patrol car provided Christopher and Sarah with a comforting sense of security.

Turning up the path to Christopher's residence, they entered the cozy home and settled into the downstairs living area. The atmosphere was calm and inviting, a welcome change from the morning's tension. Sarah removed her shoes and stretched her legs, placing her feet on a comfortable ottoman. She sighed contentedly, allowing herself a moment to unwind. Meanwhile, Christopher went to the kitchen, preparing two glasses of cold iced tea. Returning to the living area, he handed one to Sarah and sat beside her. They sat silently momentarily, sipping their iced tea and enjoying the room's tranquility. The house was filled with soft, natural light. After a while, Sarah closed her eyes, and her breathing became shallow.

In this meditative state, Guardian Angel Jehoel, the Angel of Presence, appeared to her. As the ruler of the order of Seraphim and a great mentor in conscious raising activities and awareness, Jehoel spoke to Sarah in a gentle yet commanding voice. "Your ascension grows near, my child; you must prepare yourself for this." He added, "I bring to you the celestial gentleness and wisdom to help you prepare Christopher for your ascension. It will be a moment of confusion and emotional pain for him, but with your guidance, he will endure. It is his destiny to do so." Sarah silently replied, "Thank you, Angel Jehoel, for your guidance. Thank you for preparing me for the awakening of the three divine ascension attitudes within me: love, gratitude, and surrender." As Guardian Angel Jehoel's presence faded, Sarah slowly opened her eyes, re-entering the room's presence. Christopher was still beside her, and she gently touched his arm and spoke.

"I must prepare you for something, my love, my sweet Christopher. I will tell you about ascension. As an angel, I will ascend to the celestial realm from where I came. My ascension will transform me from a physical form into a celestial being, not of flesh and blood but of spirit. The time for my ascension draws near. I am telling you this to prepare you for the day I must shed my physical body and ascend to the celestial realm. Christopher, my dear, I will always be by your side. Just call out to me, and I will respond." Christopher's eyes filled with tears as he reacted, "Sarah, I love you and can't lose you. It will break my heart. Please don't tell me this. Is there any other way?"

Sarah continued, her voice steady but filled with emotion, "There is no other way. I have been sent here to aid you in completing this important task for humankind. You have been chosen. We have been connected since you were a child, my sweet man, and we will always be connected for eternity. Your time here as a physical human being is not yet complete. There is much you need to do, much for you to accomplish after I ascend. You can't see it now, but you will. I will be right there with you every step of the way. Please do not worry. There is no death, Christopher, just transformation. The physical body ends, but the soul lives on. So please remain here physically and be my warrior and a mentor to others on the path to enlightenment." With tears in his eyes, Christopher accepted Sarah's explanation yet struggled with his fate. He resolved to do everything in his power to accommodate her request and remain steadfast in his devotion to honor her and live on after her ascension. Together, they will bring the evil and chaos unleashed to its knees through the holy alliance's collective efforts. They will close the Veil of Shadows portal. Sarah leaned in and kissed Christopher warmly, caressing his cheek with her gentle touch. She gently whispered, "Christopher, I am here, my love, always."

As early evening descended upon Silver Ridge, the townsfolk eagerly prepared for the Autumnal Luminous Lantern Festival. Families gathered along the cobblestone streets and grassy lawns, each person holding a delicate paper lantern. With care, they released them into the night sky, each lantern carrying a whispered wish. The lanterns danced among the stars, their gentle glow casting a magical light over the town and illuminating the faces of those below. Sarah and Christopher went to the second-floor balcony, where the view of Silver Ridge and the surrounding areas was unobstructed. They marveled at the night sky filled with beautiful flickering lanterns rising gracefully. The soft glow of the lanterns created a serene and enchanting atmosphere, reflecting the hopes and dreams of the community. The evening breeze carried the townsfolk's faint laughter and joyous chatter, adding to the festival's charm.

As they soaked in the splendor, the upstairs phone extension rang, breaking the tranquility. Christopher excused himself and hurried to the study down the hall, leaving Sarah to enjoy the mesmerizing view. Answering the phone, Christopher was greeted by Senator Ellie Caldwell's voice. "Good evening, Christopher. I have arrived on the outskirts of Silver Ridge. I'll check into an inn off Mount Hood Highway and join you later." Christopher replied, "I would like to invite you to stay at my home with my assistant, Ms. Sarah Hope, and me.

There is plenty of room, and I have an accommodating guest room. After our conversation this morning, I think you would be much safer here and out of sight of curious eyes. I hope you will accept my offer." Ellie responded warmly, "That would be wonderful, Christopher; I would feel much safer in your home since I am traveling from Salem alone. Thank you." Christopher gave her his address and assured her that he and Sarah would wait for her.

After hanging up the phone, Christopher returned to the balcony, where Sarah was still captivated by the glowing lanterns in the sky. He shared his offer to Senator Ellie Caldwell with her. Sarah agreed and expressed her excitement about meeting the senator, feeling that having her stay would be both safer and more convenient for their discussions. Together, they turned their attention back to the beautiful festival, feeling a sense of anticipation for the evening ahead. As the glow of the lanterns faded into the night sky, Christopher and Sarah noticed a car approaching his residence on Cascadia Maple Drive, pulling into the driveway next to Christopher's SUV. They hurried down to greet Senator Ellie Caldwell as she exited the vehicle. Christopher helped Ellie with her suitcase and overnight bag by popping the car's trunk lid and carrying them to his front door. Exchanging pleasant greetings, the three entered the home, ready to engage in conversation, exchange information, and settle in for the evening. In her early fifties, Senator Eleanor "Ellie" Caldwell possesses a well-proportioned yet slender figure that complements her red hair and green eyes. Her beautiful features are framed by an aura of elegance and strength, exuding a natural dignity. With every movement, she carries herself with a grace that commands respect and admiration.

A hush fell over the town of Silver Ridge as the Autumnal Luminous Lantern Festival ended, and a mist from the slopes of Mount Hood spread across the forest pines. The air grew cool and crisp, wrapping the town in a serene blanket of tranquility. Lanterns flickered out one by one, their gentle glow replaced by the soft, ethereal light of the moon, casting a magical aura over the quiet streets. Christopher guided Senator Caldwell to the downstairs guest room, just off the living room area. She returned to the living area after setting out her belongings, hanging her clothes neatly in the accommodating closet, and freshening up in the attached private bathroom.

Sarah had prepared tea and set out a beautiful blue porcelain tea set, including a large teapot with an infuser and matching cups and saucers in an elegant European style on the center coffee table. She offered Senator Ellie Caldwell a cup of chamomile tea and some European cookies that Christopher had arranged. Ellie accepted as Sarah poured the tea. "Thank you, Ms. Hope," Ellie said. "You are welcome; please call me Sarah," she replied. "And please call me Ellie," the Senator responded, smiling.

Christopher said, "We have much to discuss. Please tell us what you know about the Veil of Shadows, Ellie." Ellie gathered her thoughts and replied, "I know about the Veil of Shadows manuscript and an artifact my superiors are trying to obtain. Other interested parties are vying for it, too. I was tasked with finding it before my colleague, Rick Hastings, got his hands on it. He has various groups and individuals bidding for it, and we can't let it fall into their hands." Christopher nodded at Sarah, then turned back to Ellie. "I will tell you the true nature of the Veil of Shadows and the 'Ruby Talisman' artifact you mentioned." He shared everything he and Sarah knew, explaining the critical need to return the artifact to its rightful place for safekeeping. They emphasized that the talisman was more than a mere object of power; it was vital to maintaining the balance between worlds.

Christopher explained the existence of the Veil of Shadows portal and their mission to close it with the help of their holy alliance. They were determined to fight back the malevolent forces that had crossed through the portal, sending them back to their dark realms. The Ruby Talisman was crucial to this quest, serving as a key to sealing the portal and restoring peace. Ellie listened intently, a look of astonishment on her face. She now grasped the gravity of what she had stumbled upon. Realizing that the Ruby Talisman was at the center of a dangerous power struggle filled her with fear for her safety. She understood that the forces vying for the talisman would stop at nothing to obtain it for their dark purposes.

Christopher continued, "We suspect that Professor Thorne and Dr. Grey are involved as conduits through which people have vanished, and these disappearances are likely linked to the Veil of Shadows portal. We believe these people went through the portal and have not returned. Please join us in our quest to close this portal and end the madness once and for all." He added, "Please reconsider your position on obtaining the Ruby Talisman for your superiors at the Government. Join our holy alliance to close the portal and return the artifact to its rightful place, secured in the hands of the Holy Church of Rome."

Ellie closed her eyes for a moment in deep contemplation. Her integrity and keen sense of right and wrong compelled her to consider joining their alliance. She questioned whether her superiors might misuse the Talisman for their own power. In the wrong hands, it could become a tool capable of destroying the fabric of human existence. She sensed no deception in Christopher's voice nor his tales of the portal and the Talisman's connection to world events throughout history. She would willingly sacrifice her Senate seat to stand on the side of goodness and righteousness if forced to choose. Ellie opened her eyes and said, "Yes, I will join you in your quest. I will join your holy alliance for everything I believe in and for the sake of what is right and sacred to my heart." Her declaration brought a sigh of relief and smiles to the faces of

Christopher and Sarah. The weight of her decision felt lighter, knowing she was committing to a cause aligned with her deepest values.

Christopher responded, "There is still much to do. In the morning, we will journey to Forest Haven Parish, and from there, on to victory." Ellie nodded in agreement, adding, "I will contact my assistants at my offices in Salem and inform them of my intentions to go on a private retreat for a few days. They are used to me doing this and will not suspect anything." Sarah said, "Welcome to the alliance, Ellie." Ellie thanked Sarah, saying, "I wasn't sure how I would face my suspicions about Professor Thorne's and Senator Hastings's involvement with this whole Veil of Shadows affair. I felt helpless, but now I know that others like me know the dangers and have formed an alliance through you both. I am grateful you have shared much information I was unaware of."

Christopher remarked, "You must be tired from your drive here, Ellie, and the day's events. I know Sarah and I are." Sarah nodded in agreement, acknowledging the long day they had all experienced. Ellie replied, "Yes, I am. I could use a good night's sleep." Christopher suggested, "Then let's all retire for the night. We will rise early for our drive to Forest Haven. In the morning, we'll put your car in the garage behind closed doors, and all go in my SUV." Ellie agreed, appreciating the practicality of his plan. "Good idea, Christopher," she said.

As they retired to their rooms, sleep quickly overtook them. The darkness of night enveloped Silver Ridge, with stars twinkling through the mist and the moon traveling across the velvet sky. The calm autumn night offered a brief respite from the day's events, allowing them to gather strength for the journey ahead.

✎ CHAPTER SIXTEEN ❧

Rising early, Christopher, Sarah, and Ellie prepared to drive to Forest Ridge Parish. They packed their overnight bags, anticipating an extended stay, and enjoyed a light continental breakfast of coffee, tea, fruit, and pastries. The morning air was crisp, hinting at the day's potential. They chatted quietly, excitement mingling with a hint of apprehension about the journey ahead. In his upstairs study, Christopher unlocked the cabinet. He carefully removed several important items: the Ruby Talisman Artifact, the Per Aetates: Umbrae Temporis manuscript, the Talisma Rubini scroll, the copied material from the Veil of Shadows, and Isabella's Journal. Each item held significance in their quest to close the portal. He placed them in his over-the-shoulder bag alongside other essential tools they had gathered, including the lumberjack map given to them by Madame Elara. Ready and resolute, he knew the adventure awaiting them would test their courage and resolve.

Christopher descended the stairs, his shoulder bag swinging slightly as he carried their luggage and overnight bags to the SUV. After loading everything securely into the vehicle, he parked Ellie's car in the garage and ensured the house was locked tight. Meanwhile, Sarah and Ellie settled into the SUV, with Sarah taking the front passenger seat and Ellie in the back. Christopher joined them, started the engine, and they backed out of the driveway, departing from his residence. They turned onto the main street from Cascadia Maple Drive, crossing a small bridge that marked the town's boundary. As they proceeded towards the onramp to Highway 26, the early morning sun filtered through the trees lining the road. Entering the highway, they headed east towards Forest Haven Parish. Ellie noticed the sunlight reflected off Sarah's hair, creating a glistening aura around her head. She thought about how celestial

Sarah appeared at that moment. Sarah, sensing Ellie's gaze, turned and smiled. If only Ellie knew about Sarah being an angel, she thought. But her true identity had to remain a secret until the day of her ascension. Soon, she told herself.

While driving to Forest Haven, Christopher told Ellie about the other alliance members they would soon meet. He described Deacon Crossford, Father Green, Father Rossi, and Dr. Grey as very committed individuals who would warmly welcome Ellie into the fold. Ellie felt excited about collaborating with these dedicated members and looked forward to the meeting. The camaraderie and purpose invigorated her, making her eager to contribute to their shared mission. Sarah noticed Christopher glancing in the rear-view mirror more than usual, contrasting their previous drives. Concerned, she asked, "Is everything okay, Christopher?" He replied, "Not to alarm you and Ellie, but there's a car following us and pacing our speed for a while now. I see a man and a woman in the front seat. When I change lanes, they do the same, remaining behind our vehicle. For now, we'll keep our eyes on them. It's probably nothing, just me being overly cautious." Both Sarah and Ellie turned to look behind them, then directed their gazes back to Christopher.

Observing the situation closely, Ellie said, "I think you are right; they appear to be following us. They are not from my staff or security team; I would recognize them, and my staff would not send someone to follow me when I'm on a retreat." Christopher nodded, his expression serious but calm. "We are almost at the Forest Haven turnout. We'll see what happens then." The atmosphere in the SUV grew tense, but there was an unspoken agreement to remain vigilant and composed. The early morning sun continued to cast its rays through the trees. Sarah closed her eyes and used her intuition to visualize their present situation. A calm came over her as her mind reassured her that they were not in danger from the individuals following them.

"The individuals following us are no danger to us," she said. "We will be okay. I think they may be Detective Hayes and Mitchell from Silver Ridge. Their features look familiar." Christopher smiled and nodded with a sigh of relief. Ellie looked at them both oddly, unsure what to make of this exchange, but she also found herself calming. Christopher then explained to Ellie about the recent visit from the detectives and their questioning concerning missing person reports. "Officer Brandon Shaw, who had been watching my residence from the end of the street, must have tipped them off about our movements," he said. "They most likely will follow us off the main highway, and I will speak to them when we arrive at the Parish." Ellie's initial anxiety dissipated, replaced by a sense of relief. The tension in the SUV eased as they continued their drive toward Forest Haven, feeling more at ease with the situation.

Turning off Highway 26 onto Forest Haven Road, the pavement changed from smooth asphalt to gravel. Ellie felt the subtle vibration of the uneven road surface beneath the SUV and glanced out the window at the trees that now seemed to close in around them. The serene atmosphere of the forest was calming, a sharp contrast to the tense moments they had just experienced. She noticed the car following them also made the turn, maintaining a discreet distance. Christopher kept his eyes on the road, while Sarah sat quietly, seemingly lost in thought. As they drove through the gates and entered the parking lot for Forest Haven Parish, Christopher slowed down and found a spot to park. The following car did the same, parking a short distance from them. Christopher turned to Sarah and Ellie. "I'll go and talk to them," he said. Sarah nodded, her eyes reassuring, while Ellie, though still a bit unsure, felt a growing sense of confidence in their safety. Christopher stepped out of the SUV and walked towards the other car. The occupants of the trailing vehicle got out, revealing themselves to be Detective Hayes and Mitchell indeed. Christopher greeted them, and after a brief conversation, he motioned for Sarah and Ellie to join them, easing the tension that had built up during their drive.

Christopher introduced Senator Caldwell only as "Ellie" to the detectives, who did not recognize her and were unaware of her position with the government. He explained to Detectives Hayes and Mitchell that they were there for a weekend retreat to enjoy the quiet and solitude. Christopher mentioned they were invited to stay in the guest quarters and tour the grounds, a welcome respite from the tourists and visitors gathering in Silver Ridge for the Labor Day weekend events. "Mount Hood National Forest will be packed with hikers, fishermen, and boaters this weekend," he added. Detective Hayes replied, "Sounds like you made the right choice. I wish I could go on a retreat, but our missing persons cases are building up on us, which brings us here." Detective Mitchell nodded in agreement.

"Any new leads?" Christopher asked. Detective Mitchell replied, " As we mentioned at the last meeting, there is a common link between the institute and the disappearances. Our investigation leads us to believe that something is amiss in the forests surrounding the southern edge of Mount Hood. You should be careful if you plan to hike any trails while on your retreat until we get to the bottom of this mystery. As we do each Labor Day weekend, we have a team of search and rescue personnel standing by, but we have added extra rangers this year." Brian Mitchel is a no-nonsense, thorough detective who follows every clue meticulously. "Have you found any clues since we last met that could help us?" he asked.

Christopher thought momentarily, then scratched his head and replied, "I think you are on the right track about the institute and the connection to the disappearances we discussed the other night. In discussions with colleagues at the institute and additional information Sarah and I have

184

obtained, we became aware of other expeditions sponsored by the institute to the foot of Mount Hood disappearing without a trace, notably that of Professor Sinclair around twelve years ago. I can't say how this is connected, but what you tell me makes me believe and agree with you that there is a connection. That's about all I know. I hope you get to the source of these missing person reports." Detective Hayes said, "Thank you, Professor Daniels. We won't keep you from your retreat. Please be careful if you and Ms. Hope and Ellie wander into the wilderness; there is something in the air, and I fear danger lurking among the dense forests these days." She added that they would check with the administration desk and warn them to be extra careful if planning any hikes for their visitors into the wooded areas. "You have our phone numbers if anything comes up. Enjoy your retreat," she concluded. Christopher thanked her and Detective Mitchell as they smiled at Sarah and Ellie before turning towards the administrative building.

As Sarah, Christopher, and Ellie returned to the SUV to grab their bags, Sarah said, "You handled that well, Christopher. Giving them just enough information to satisfy them for now and preventing them from interfering in our mission." Ellie smiled in agreement, feeling confident in her decision to join them. Gathering their belongings, they walked the short distance to the administrative building. Ellie took in Forest Haven Parish's sights and natural beauty as they strolled up the pathway lined with colorful flowers and cedar trees. The whole scene promoted a feeling of peace and reflection, its serenity washing over her. Although Ellie had not visited the parish before, she felt a deep connection to this sacred place. The tranquil environment welcomed her, giving her a sense of belonging. The vibrant flowers and towering trees added to the idyllic setting, their presence both grounding and uplifting.

As they approached the entrance to the administration building, Detective Mitchell exited and held the door open for them, bidding them a pleasant stay as he and Detective Hayes departed. Deacon Crossford and Isabella Grey were there to greet them in the lobby. "Welcome, Christopher and Sarah. It's been a busy morning already," Deacon Crossford said, smiling and nodding with curiosity at Ellie. Christopher replied, "Thank you, Elias; yes, it has. Hello Isabella, great to see you. I would like you both to meet Senator Eleanor Caldwell." Ellie reached out and offered her hand to the confused pair. Isabella took her hand, followed by Elias, and they greeted her with a warm handshake. "Please call me 'Ellie,'" she said to them. Christopher said, "Not to worry, she is one of us. I trust her completely. However, we shall keep her title to ourselves." They all agreed, and Deacon Elias Crossford escorted them to the parish meeting room. Ellie marveled at the interior of the meeting room, which mirrored the natural beauty outside, with floor-to-ceiling length windows allowing sunlight to stream in and illuminate the space. The peaceful environment seemed perfect for the discussions that lay ahead.

Father Aidan Green, Father Luciano Rossi, and another person dressed in the robes of a monk were seated at the table. As the group entered, the seated individuals rose to greet them. Father Green said, "Welcome back, Professor, Ms. Hope, and your guest, I presume." He looked at Ellie and spoke. "I am Father Aidan Green. You have met Deacon Crossford and Dr. Grey, I assume. Meet our esteemed emissary from Rome, Father Luciano Rossi, and his assistant, Brother Marco De Luca." Ellie smiled warmly and replied, "I am Senator Eleanor Caldwell, but please call me Ellie. Christopher and Sarah have brought me here to join your alliance with your blessings." Ellie continued, "We have much in common, and I assure you, I am here for the same benevolent reasons that all of you are. Christopher

186

and Sarah have filled me in on many details, and I am at your service. There are forces within the government and private sector that would exploit the power of the Veil of Shadows for their own nefarious reasons, and I am here to prevent that from occurring." Father Green and Father Rossi exchanged approving glances and nodded. "Welcome to our holy alliance, Ellie," Father Green said. "Please, everyone, take a seat."

They all took seats at the conference table, the room filled with an air of solemn purpose. The natural light streaming through the stained-glass windows cast a divine glow over the assembly. Father Green began the meeting, "We have gathered here to discuss our next steps in closing the Veil of Shadows portal and to ensure it remains closed and protected from those who would misuse its power. With Ellie joining us, we have a stronger front to face these challenges." Ellie felt a deepening sense of responsibility and commitment to their cause as the discussion progressed. The collaboration and unity among the members fortified her resolve to protect the sacred knowledge they were entrusted with.

Christopher placed his over-the-shoulder bag brimming with items on the table before him. Reaching into the bag, he produced a scroll and laid it on the table for all to see. Brother Marco De Luca's eyes widened with recognition. "Ahh, the Talisma Rubini scroll. You have recovered it. Excellent!" he exclaimed. The room was excitedly buzzing as everyone leaned in to get a better look. "Yes, we have, and something else," Christopher said, reaching back into the bag. With a sense of ceremony, he brought out the Ruby Talisman artifact and displayed it before the group. Father Green crossed himself, repeating the gesture from their first meeting, while Father Rossi followed suit. Brother Marco De Luca brought his hands to his forehead in a prayerful manner. Senator Ellie Caldwell was astonished that Christopher had the Ruby Talisman in his possession, the reality of their mission crystallizing before her eyes. Isabella Grey smiled, her expression a mix of new hope and underlying fear at the sight of the powerful artifact. Sarah, too, smiled at Christopher, a light shining in her eyes as he handed the artifact around for everyone at the table to see.

The Ruby Talisman shone brightly like a beacon of hope, its golden cross reflecting the sun's rays streaming through the room's tall windows. The ruby itself pulsed with a bright red luminescence, captivating everyone present. The atmosphere in the room shifted, a palpable sense of purpose and unity enveloping them. As the talisman was passed around the table, each alliance member felt a renewed commitment to their shared mission. The artifact's brilliance seemed to infuse them with strength, reinforcing their resolve to protect the Ruby Talisman artifact and their quest to close the Veil of Shadows portal, preventing those who would seek to exploit the power of both anomalies.

Once the excitement in the room calmed, Christopher said, "There is still much to do and discuss. Sarah and I have discovered additional information to help us on our quest. Sarah has uncovered details about the disappearance of Professor Gabriel Sinclair shortly after he arrived at Silver Ridge. About twelve years ago, he and his team of explorers went missing during an expedition near the base of Mount Hood. An archived news report spoke of a promising archaeological dig that had abruptly gone silent. After several weeks, the search for Professor Sinclair and his team was called off. They were never found. We suspect that they entered the portal that Professor Sinclair opened, never to return. We also suspect that all the missing person reports point us to the same conclusion: the portal swallowed them up."

Christopher continued, "Two Silver Ridge detectives following missing person clues suspect something is amiss at the base of Mount Hood. At the same time, I had an impromptu meeting at the institute with Professor Thorne, Dr. Grey, and Senator Hastings, which leads me to believe they are exchanging unsuspecting humans for evil entities by luring them into the portal with promises of wealth, power, or whatever desires they wish for. This is why I suspect so many people have gone missing." Pausing, he allowed the gravity of his words to sink in. The room was silent, the weight of the revelations pressing on everyone present. "You all must think I've lost my mind, but these are crazy times," Christopher said, looking around the table. "The meeting with them and our collective research is compelling. This would explain a lot of things. A soul for a soul, unleashing demons and other evil beings into our world through this open portal. Our time is running out, and it has become a race for our alliance to get there before more damage is done." The urgency in his voice was unmistakable. The group exchanged solemn glances, realizing the magnitude of their mission. The peaceful surroundings of Forest Haven Parish seemed a stark contrast to the impending danger they faced. Still, it also strengthened their resolve to protect their world from the encroaching darkness.

Again, Christopher reaches into his bag and removes another item. With a sense of finality, he places the "Per Aetates: Umbrae Temporis" manuscript on the table and hands it to Brother Marco De Luca, who accepts it with a solemn nod. "This must be returned along with the 'Talisma Rubini' scroll and the 'Talisma Rubini' itself," Christopher says. Brother Marco De Luca, with a bow, agrees, understanding the weight of the responsibility. Christopher withdraws one more item from his bag, then unfurls the lumberjack map given to them by Madame Elara, laying it in the middle of the table for all to see. "And this," he declares, "is the final piece of the puzzle. A map of the location of the Veil of Shadows Portal." The group leans in, examining the map with a mix of astonishment and excitement. Father Green exclaims, "You two have really done your homework, Christopher and Sarah! Job well done." The group erupts into unified clapping, their hands a chorus of appreciation and admiration for Christopher and Sarah. Senator "Ellie" Caldwell is momentarily speechless, while Isabella Grey beams from ear to ear, her heart swelling with the redemption she so desperately needed finally within reach.

Father Green addresses the group, "How quickly can we all be ready to embark on our mission to the location of the Veil of Shadows Portal? What preparations must be made before we face these demons head-on?" Brother Marco De Luca responds, "There must be prayer and contemplation to strengthen our hearts and to invoke the protection of the saints and archangels. We must ask them to bless our pathway through the wilderness." Christopher adds, "Time is of the essence; the trails on the map will be difficult to navigate, so I suggest we pack plenty of provisions, water, supplies, and survival gear for the trip. We will travel by car to the trailhead and then on foot to our destination. It may take us several hours of hiking to reach the base of Mount Hood and at least the biggest part of a day to return. We should be prepared for what we will find there when we arrive. I suggest we leave tomorrow if the alliance is in agreement." The group nods in consensus.

Deacon Crossford chimes in, "Well, that's it then, we will leave tomorrow after Sunday morning mass. Today, let's rest and prepare for tomorrow's adventure." Turning to Christopher, Sarah, and Ellie, he offers, "How about that tour of Forest Haven I promised you? Would you be up to it this afternoon? Sarah responds, "Yes, that would be wonderful, but only if Isabella joined us." Isabella, smiling with shy innocence, agrees, "Yes, I would like that very much." Deacon Crossford adds, "Afterwards, you can retrieve your luggage and bring it to the guest quarters so you can freshen up before dinner, and then you can settle in for the night." Father Green interjects, "I will place these artifacts and the Ruby Talisman in the parish safe until morning. Is that acceptable to you, Professor Daniels?" Christopher replies, "Yes, please keep it safe; it is our tool to push back the forces of evil. I entrust it in your hands, Father." With that, they all rise, exchanging pleasantries, and depart the meeting room. Each goes their separate ways until later, when they plan to meet in the parish dining room for the evening meal. Sarah, Christopher, and Ellie follow Elias and Isabella out into the parish courtyard, ready to explore and prepare for the journey ahead.

As they tour the grounds of Forest Haven Parish, they stroll through flowered gardens adorned with statues depicting saints and angels and topiaries shaped like forest animals. Beyond the gardens stands St. Sylvan's Church, blending in with the natural surroundings: the exterior features locally sourced timber, hand-carved wooden details, and a steeply pitched roof. The Deacon explains that the altar changes with the seasons: in spring, it's adorned with fresh wildflowers; during winter, it's draped in evergreen branches. He reminds them that tomorrow, as the sun rises, they will gather with the congregation for a peaceful morning Mass, where sunbeams filter through the trees and stained-glass windows, creating a natural cathedral.

Strolling past the church, Elias tells them about Saint Sylvan's incorruptible body, which lies on display within the Church of St. Blaise in Dubrovnik, Croatia. Though not entirely human, his face appears neither as wax nor stone. It bears the marks of time yet defies decay. Saint Sylvan's story is veiled in mist, much like the morning fog that blankets the forest. Legends whisper of his martyrdom in the 4th century, but the details remain elusive. Some say he was a humble priest, others a wandering mystic. His neck bears a gruesome wound—a testament to his sacrifice. Perhaps he was Saint Silvanus, Bishop of Emesa, Phoenicia, martyred around 311. But it is not the manner of his death that elevates him to sainthood; it is the inexplicable grace that surrounds him. Miracles attributed to his intercession abound: the blind see, the sick recover, and lost souls find their way.

Arriving at Sacred Cedars Seminary, a stone building comes into view with ivy-covered walls. The seminary overlooks a babbling brook, its arched windows surrounded by towering cedars, their branches swaying in reverence. Within its hallowed halls, seminarians study theology, philosophy, and the mystical traditions of the forest. Sacred Cedars Seminary is dedicated to forming priests who will serve the Church with humility, wisdom, and compassion. The Seminary also prepares lay leaders for ecclesial ministry, equipping them to serve in pastoral roles, education, and evangelization. Just past the seminary lies the rectory, where the clergy resides. Adjacent to the rectory are the guest quarters, where Christopher, Sarah, and Ellie will stay the night and where Isabella resides. This building mirrors the rectory's rustic charm and tranquility, with cozy rooms designed to offer comfort and respite to travelers and visiting clergy.

Between the rectory and the guest quarters is an open-air courtyard surrounded by stately cedar columns. The courtyard is a peaceful oasis, with benches lining the perimeter. It is said that those who sit in contemplation within this courtyard can hear the wind carrying whispers of forgotten legends to those who listen.

❧ CHAPTER SEVENTEEN ❧

Passing the guest quarters, the tour leads them to Our Lady of the Pines Abbey, a stone abbey nestled on a hill overlooking the parish—a place where the sacred and the earthly intertwine, offering a haven of contemplation, beauty, and the whisper of ancient vines. The abbey's bell tower chimes softly, echoing through the pines, while a tranquil courtyard features a labyrinth made of river stones amidst rows of colorful roses and vibrant flowers. Sister Helena, a gentle nun, tends to the flower-filled courtyard, nurturing roses and souls with her ancient wisdom. A small stone chapel stands with arched windows framed by climbing roses. At dawn, the sisters gather to chant psalms. Their voices blend harmoniously with the rustling leaves of the nearby pine and cedar trees, creating a sacred symphony.

Beyond the chapel lies a labyrinth of gardens. The Rose Garden blooms with deep crimson, blush pink, and ivory roses, their fragrance lingering like sweet incense. The Herb Garden thrives with lavender, thyme, and basil, tended by the sisters who craft healing balms and teas. Sister Seraphina, the abbey's herbalist, is said to converse with forest spirits and brew teas that ease sorrow and mend broken bones. Finally, a vineyard covers the hillside with rows of grapevines stretching toward the horizon. The leaves rustle secrets, whispering the wisdom of the ages. Sister Miriam tends the vineyard, her hands gnarled like ancient roots cradling clusters of grapes. She prays as she works, invoking blessings upon the harvest. Legend says that her tears, shed during a drought, revived the withered vines, and since then, the wine has flowed abundantly. The sight of the abbey with its flowering gardens and grapevines, coupled with the gentle toll of the hillside tower's bells, brought comfort and peacefulness to Christopher, Sarah, and Ellie. Forest Haven Parish and Our

Lady of the Pines Abbey are truly a sanctuary nestled amongst the pines, where the sacred and natural coexist in harmonious beauty, offering a serene refuge for all who enter.

Mother Agnes, the abbess, greets them as they enter the gate to the abbey. "Welcome," she says, "I have heard much about your visit here. I am Agnes Hartman, and I oversee the abbey and the nearby convent. I am honored to meet the three of you, Christopher, Sarah, and Ellie," she adds with a warm smile. Sarah responds, "Pleased to meet you, Mother Agnes. Your abbey is such a beautiful and tranquil place; it makes my heart sing with joy and appreciation for my many blessings." Mother Agnes responds with a joyous laugh; her laughter echoes through the courtyard, reminding all of the joy of being of service. "Well, I've never heard it described like that. Thank you. Yes, it brings joy to my heart as well." She looks at Sarah and thinks there is something very celestial about this young woman. I see the face of an angel and the innocence of a child. An otherworldly aura surrounds Sarah, reminding Mother Agnes of her days of enlightenment while becoming a Benedictine Sister of the church. The day she made her commitment to the solemn profession of vows for life, she pledged herself as a Consecration Virginitatis, mystically wed to Christ and dedicated to the service of the Church. She closed her eyes for a moment in silent prayer, and when she opened them, Sarah smiled at her with a knowing look as if she had pierced her very soul and read her thoughts. She realized at that point that this young woman was heaven-sent and that she was in the presence of the divine.

Mother Agnes gave them blessings and dismissed herself, walking across the courtyard and entering the abbey doors. Deacon Elias Crossford said, "Well, that's the tour. Thank you for allowing me to show you around. You can explore the grounds, buildings, gardens, and chapels independently. There are no restrictions here at Forest Haven. Let your faith be your guide." Christopher thanked him as Elias turned down the path back to the administration building. Elias turned and said, "See you all at dinner in the administration dining hall. We will dine at 5 pm." Christopher turned to Isabella and said, "Walk with us; we have much to discuss." She smiled and said, "Yes, thank you, Professor Daniels." Christopher smiled, "Please call me Christopher from now on, Isabella." The group leisurely strolled back to the parking lot to retrieve their luggage for the overnight stay. As they walked, the serene atmosphere of Forest Haven filled them with a sense of peace and purpose, preparing them for the challenges that lay ahead.

Christopher reached into his over-shoulder bag, still draped across his torso, and produced a leather-bound book, handing it to Isabella. "I believe this belongs to you," he said. Isabella took the book and realized it was her journal, which she had left behind at the institute, hoping that someone of high character would find it. Christopher had told her at their first meeting that he and Sarah had discovered it, and now, with gratitude, she knew the journal had come full circle. "Thank you, Christopher," Isabella said; tears welled in her eyes, and she felt unsteady. Seeing her emotional state, Sarah placed an arm around Isabella's shoulder to steady her and offer comfort. Sensing the magnitude of the moment, Ellie gave Isabella a warm hug. Sarah and Ellie brought support and comfort as Isabella regained her composure. Isabella said, "It has been a long journey since the fateful night I left the institute. I am so grateful and relieved that I am here with you. The sisters and clergy here have been very kind and caring, helping me escape my dark place. Now, I have direction and purpose in my life again." Sarah said, "You are part of our family now. Since we found your journal and are now meeting you, there is a connection between us that will never be broken."

Isabella thought how soothing Sarah's words were and how desperately she needed to hear them. "Thank you, Sarah," she replied. Sarah responded, "Christopher will not let anything happen to you. Your futures are intertwined." As she glanced at Christopher, her eyes penetrated his soul with knowledge and wisdom that transcended the moment. Christopher thought Sarah knew more than she was telling him. Arriving at the parking lot, they retrieved their luggage and overnight bags and walked up the pathway to the guest and visitors' quarters. Checking in, Sarah, Christopher, and Ellie were given simple, comfortable rooms with private baths overlooking the parish grounds. Isabella waved at the trio as she returned to her room just down the hallway from theirs. "See you at dinner," she called as she entered her room.

Isabella closed the door behind her, placed her handbag on the arm of the chair, placed her journal in her nightstand drawer, kicked off her shoes, and lay face up on her bed. Taking a deep breath and releasing it with a long sigh, she felt relief and gratitude. She said a silent prayer in appreciation, though fear of the evil forces that lay in wait for the alliance still lingered. She had faced that same evil in the past and escaped from it, but her resolve and faith told her that good would always triumph over evil, a lesson she learned from the sisters at the abbey. She thought about Sarah's words to her, "Christopher will not let anything happen to you." Isabella felt attracted to Christopher, wondering if it was because of his leadership role in the alliance, her vulnerability, or the fact that he had read her journal and its dark secrets. Christopher was handsome and attractive in a scholarly way and, at times, innocent in a playful manner.

She pondered the relationship between Sarah and Christopher, noticing how they looked at each other. She thought: There is something about her, and Sarah's connection with Christopher goes beyond just being a professor and assistant. The way they lovingly look at each other. However, Sarah also looks at her lovingly, and I noticed a strong connection between Sarah and Mother Agnes. Clearing her thoughts, she focused on her prayers, seeking guidance. Isabella had not been in a relationship for many years, dedicating herself to her work and, more recently, her rehabilitation and recovery. Yet, Christopher stirred emotions she hadn't felt in years. Isabella resolved to remain vigilant as a teacher at the seminary and a parish community member and committed to seeing this mission through to the end. She counted her blessings and remembered Sarah's words, "You are part of our family now. There is a connection between us that will never be broken." Isabella set her bedside alarm clock for 4 pm and closed her eyes, allowing her breathing to become calm and shallow, her body and mind drifting off into a pleasant sleep.

Senator "Ellie" Caldwell sat at her desk in her room, checking her voicemail and text messages. She read a text from her assistant, Susan, stating, "Senator Richard Hasting is trying to reach you, and you need to contact him as soon as possible." Ellie responded to Susan's text, "Inform him I am on sabbatical and will contact him upon my return. Thank you." Ellie then checked the remainder of her text messages, which consisted of work-related administrative items that could wait until her return. Checking her voice messages, she heard one from Senator Hastings: "Ellie, this is Rick Hastings; please call me when you get this; it is imperative. Thanks." She deleted it. Another voice message was from State Department official Sebastian Morland: "Hello, Senator Caldwell. Can you call me at your earliest convenience? Thank you." Ellie remembered Sebastian from a State Department briefing before returning to Salem. She saved the message until she could contact him when she returned to her Salem office. She texted Susan, "All is well, still on my retreat. The weather is lovely here.

Thank you for keeping me updated." Ellie closed her phone message app and plugged the phone in to charge. She undressed and stepped into the bathroom shower for a soothing cleanse before throwing on a robe, setting her smartphone alarm for 4 pm, and lying on her bed for a quick nap before dinner.

Sarah entered her room at the parish guest quarters, closing the door behind her. The room was simple yet functional, with a desk, a dresser, a bed, a small kitchenette area, and a bathroom. Perfect for an overnight stay. She placed her bag on the dresser and took a moment to appreciate the cozy, unpretentious space. The ceiling fan's gentle hum and the faint scent of cedar from the surrounding forest added to the room's peaceful ambiance. She undressed, entered the bathroom and enjoyed a hot shower. As she toweled off and put on a light, knee-length dress made of soft, breathable material, she felt a sense of calm wash over her. She relaxed on the bed, letting her thoughts drift over the day's events. The tranquility of Forest Haven, the warmth of the people they had met, and the connection she felt with Christopher and Isabella filled her with a deep sense of gratitude and purpose. She closed her eyes, allowing herself a few moments of quiet reflection before the evening's activities. Sarah felt Isabella would be the right person to help ease Christopher's mind when Sarah ascended. Although it will break his heart, Sarah will do her best to protect his heart, and with both herself in celestial form and Isabella in physical form by his side, he will get through the transition. She will lay the foundation for Christopher's and Isabella's future, ensuring their bond strengthens and they find comfort and strength in each other. Sarah's love for Christopher transcended her earthly presence, and she trusted Isabella to be his guiding light when the time came.

Christopher sat at the desk, gazing out the window of his room at the parish guest quarters. The peaceful courtyard below reflected the serene surroundings of the Mount Hood National Forest. The forest greenery and the soft rustling of leaves in the gentle breeze contrasted with the weighty thoughts in his mind. He contemplated the meetings earlier and the tasks ahead, feeling a mix of anticipation and resolve. Confident that the group hike tomorrow to the mountain's base would go well, he mentally prepared himself for the final conflict between the forces of good and evil and what they would encounter when they arrived. With Sarah by his side and the collaborated efforts of the clergy, they would carry the torch of hope to close the portal and restore the balance. The impending journey filled him with determination and a sense of solemn duty. He went to the bathroom, quickly showered, and dressed. As he gathered his thoughts, he decided to take this time to plan a strategy for tomorrow's hike, meticulously considering every detail to ensure their success. Once satisfied with his preparations, he felt a sense of calm and readiness wash over him.

Christopher checked the time: 4:30 PM. He left his room and knocked on Sarah's door. She greeted him warmly as Isabella and Ellie entered the corridor, exchanging friendly smiles. Together, they headed downstairs and walked to the administration building. The evening air was cool and fresh, the sky tinged with the colors of the setting sun. As they entered the dining hall, the comforting hum of conversation and the aroma of a hearty meal welcomed them. The table was laden with a sumptuous feast: beef and chicken plates, freshly caught fish, various vibrant vegetables, an assortment of warm loaves of bread, and a spread of ripe fruits. Fine parish wine flowed, enhancing the flavors and camaraderie.

Deacon Crossford, Father Green, Father Rossi, Brother Marco De Luca, and Mother Agnes were seated at the long dining table. Sister Helena from the Sacred Cedars Seminary also sat at the main table. A contemplative nun, she oversees the seminary's library. Her love for ancient texts and quiet reflection draws seekers of knowledge. Sister Cecilia, a talented musician, sat to the side, playing hymns on her violin. Her melodies echoed through the wooden rafters of the dining hall, lifting hearts toward the heavens and infusing the gathering with a sense of divine peace and unity. Joining the others for dinner, they shared camaraderie and strengthened their resolve for the challenges ahead. The unity and purpose of their gathering bolstered their spirits, each person drawing courage from the collective determination to face the unknown journey awaiting them.

Mother Agnes rises from her seat and moves gracefully to the dining hall door, opening it to reveal a striking woman dressed in modern Native American attire of natural earthen colors and sacred symbols. Colorful beads hang resting against her chest from a traditional tribal leather choker necklace. Her light brown, silver-grey streaked hair cascades down her back, and her piercing hazel eyes reflect her ancestors' spirit and resilience. "This is Aiyana Skye," Mother Agnes announces, her voice filled with respect and warmth. "She carries the wisdom of the Kaskali Tribe and the strength of Mount Hood. She has come to guide and protect our champions on their journey to the portal." Aiyana steps forward, her presence immediately commanding the room, embodying the powerful legacy of her people.

Aiyana speaks, "Hello, I am Aiyana Skye. My name means 'eternal blossom.' I am a skilled shaman and protector of my people's ancient traditions. I was raised in the foothills of Mount Hood, and I have a deep spiritual connection to the mountain and its secrets. Growing up in the Kaskali Tribe, I was trained from a young age in the ancient arts of my people, learning the sacred rituals, chants, and the use of powerful talismans. These teachings have instilled a profound understanding of the natural and spiritual worlds, allowing me to serve as a bridge between them. I have sensed the gravity of your mission and offer my services to guide you to the hidden portal at the base of Mount Hood. I recognize the impending threat of the forces of evil attempting to breach it. I have seen the portal with my own eyes, but I alone do not possess the power to hold back the malevolent forces. We can combine our powers to close the portal and protect our world from the darkness that seeks to invade it. With the strength of the Kaskali spirits and the courage of this alliance, we stand a chance to preserve the balance and ensure the safety of our future."

Sarah's gaze met Aiyana's, and at that moment, a silent understanding passed between them. Sarah's celestial intuition of discerning truth from deception told her that Aiyana was a spiritual guide and a formidable warrior skilled in traditional combat and mystical defenses. Her presence radiated a strength and wisdom that reassured Sarah. With a slight, confident nod, Sarah signaled her approval to Christopher, acknowledging Aiyana's vital role in their mission. The others at the table, observing Sarah's gesture, voiced their agreement with murmurs of approval and supportive nods. Recognizing the unanimous acceptance, Mother Agnes smiled warmly and extended her hand toward Aiyana, inviting her to join the main table. "Please, Aiyana, sit with us and share in our feast," she said. Aiyana gracefully accepted, taking her place among the group. As she settled in, the room buzzed with a renewed sense of purpose, united by the common goal of protecting the sacred portal and defeating the impending evil.

Sister Helena rose from her seat and addressed the group, "The Kaskali Tribe, named after their sacred mountain, flourished for centuries on the slopes of Mount Hood. Revered as guardians of the mountain, the people lived in harmony with nature, deeply respecting the land and its resources. They believed the mountain was a living entity, a powerful spirit that sustained them with its pristine rivers and fertile soil. Their society was deeply spiritual, with rituals and ceremonies centered around the mountain, which they considered the heart of their world. The tribe's elders, known as the Keepers of the Mountain, passed down sacred knowledge and traditions through generations, ensuring the preservation of their way of life.

At the heart of the Kaskali Tribe's spiritual beliefs was a secret portal hidden within the mountain's depths. According to their legends, this portal was a gateway to the spirit world, a place of immense power and mystery. The tribe dedicated themselves to protecting this portal, believing it maintained the balance between their world and the spirit realm. Warriors and shamans were entrusted with guarding the entrance, using ancient spells and powerful talismans to ward off intruders and ensure the portal remained closed to evil spirits from the realms beyond our physical world. Only a select few were permitted to approach the portal, each undergoing rigorous training to ensure their loyalty and strength. The Kaskali Tribe's devotion to protecting the mountain and its hidden portal defined their identity, shaping a legacy of resilience and reverence for the sacred." Aiyana smiled warmly, acknowledging the accuracy of Sister Helena's testimony and her deep knowledge of the Kaskali Tribe's history. Sister Helena returned to her seat, her expression one of quiet satisfaction. The others at the table thanked her, appreciating the valuable context she had provided for their mission.

Senator Ellie Caldwell was impressed by the group's collaborative efforts, noting how everyone brought unique skills and talents crucial to their success. She appreciated their calmness and spiritual approach in tackling the critical task of closing the portal. Grateful for the absence of departmental bureaucracy and government involvement, she felt a sense of relief and admiration for the group's unified, efficient efforts. She knew that after it was over, she would need to explain everything to her colleagues and file a comprehensive report. She knew her decision to leave certain government entities in the dark would not be well received. Despite this, she believed it was necessary for the success of their mission and was prepared to face the consequences of her unconventional approach.

Christopher had meticulously planned the hike to the base of Mount Hood for the following day and now shared the logistics with the group. They would depart in the morning after the morning mass, traveling in separate vehicles to the trailhead, where they would begin their hike. Deacon Elias Crossford, Father Green, Father Rossi, Sister Helena, and Mother Agnes would remain at the Parish to continue their support through prayer and coordination. The journey to the portal would be undertaken by Christopher, Sarah, Senator Ellie Caldwell, Isabella, Brother Marco, Brother Jasper—a parish seminarian—and Aiyana Skye. Christopher then presented the map given to him by Madam Elara to Aiyana, who scrutinized it. Together, they plotted a course based on her intimate knowledge of the terrain and the mountain's secrets. The group discussed and refined their plan, ensuring everyone knew their roles and responsibilities. With unanimous agreement and a renewed sense of purpose, they prepared themselves for tomorrow's journey.

Isabella could feel her journey coming full circle; closure was near, and she sensed it deeply. She knew it was crucial for her to journey with them to the portal and see this mission through. When the portal is again closed and the evil vanquished, the dark cloud that had hovered over her for so long will finally dissipate. With Christopher and Sarah by her side, she felt renewed strength and courage, ready to face the challenges that awaited them. She understood that whatever happened tomorrow would define her future, and she was determined to emerge from this ordeal stronger and free from the shadows of her past. Isabella glanced at Christopher, and he gave her a wink and a smile, a warm, simple gesture that made her feel stronger. She then looked at Sarah, whose radiant smile made Isabella blush in a good way; maybe Sarah sensed how she felt about Christopher, especially since she had assured her that he would protect her.

Deacon Elias Crossford said as dinner ended, "There will be a Sunrise Service tomorrow at 6 a.m. Join us in prayer as we ask for blessings for our sacred quest." Father Luciano Rossi will celebrate the mass in St. Sylvan's church." As the group stood and began to exit the dining hall, the Aspirant trainees, dressed in simple white blouses with their hair wrapped in sheer scarves, and the Postulant trainees in simple black jumpers and veils from the abbey, gracefully cleared the table. Their peaceful and graceful appearance added to the elegance of the gathering. As the attendees bid goodnight to one another at the door, Christopher, Sarah, Isabella, and Ellie took a stroll toward the guest quarters while Sister Agnes and Aiyana Skye headed toward Our Lady of Pines Abbey.

The late evening sky at Forest Haven Parish was a canvas of deep indigo, with the autumn air crisp and invigorating. The moon shone brightly through the cedars and pines that lined the walkway, casting silver beams on the ground below. The distant sounds of the forest— crickets chirping, leaves rustling—provided a soothing backdrop to their light conversation as they strolled up the pathway. Finally arriving at the guest quarters, they entered and climbed the stairs to the second-floor corridor. There, Christopher, Sarah, Isabella, and Ellie bid each other goodnight with gentle hugs, Sarah kissing Christopher lightly on the cheek. The smell of lilacs and lavender filled the air as they entered their rooms, bringing a sense of calm and serenity to the close of the evening.

❧ CHAPTER EIGHTEEN ❧

The afternoon sun shone through the windows of the Silver Ridge Institute's executive meeting room, casting long shadows across the polished table. The room held an air of anticipation and tension as four figures sat around the large conference table: Professor Edmond Thorne, a distinguished academic with a stern demeanor; Dr. Isadora Vale, whose piercing intellect was matched only by her cold, analytical eyes; Senator Richard "Rick" Hastings, a man of considerable influence and dubious morals; and Archon Heller from Germany, whose dark presence dominated the room. Standing guard were two of Senator Hastings' henchmen, Taylor and Parker, their vigilant eyes scanning the room for any threats.

Archon Heller was a figure of malevolent charisma, with dark hair, a Dali-style mustache, and a dark goatee, giving him a distinguished yet sinister appearance. His jet-black eyes seemed to pierce through the souls of those he looked upon, hinting at the dark ambitions that drove him. Heller was a man who thrived on chaos, weaving intricate plots to pit families and groups against each other. His true objective was a cursed relic, an artifact that granted dominion over life and death. To achieve this, he dabbled in forbidden rituals, invoking ancient spirits to aid him in his dark quest.

The group had gathered to discuss the Veil of Shadows portal and the Ruby Talisman, two elements crucial to their plans. The Ruby Talisman, which had been lost or stolen and which they did not possess, was believed to be in the hands of individuals determined to thwart their sinister intentions. These adversaries aimed to close the Veil of Shadows portal before Dr. Thorne and the group could reach it and secure the opening. The tension in the room was intense, as the fate of their dark ambitions hung in the balance, hinging on their ability to outmaneuver their opponents and seize control of the powerful artifact.

Professor Thorne's voice noted urgency and frustration as he addressed the group. "Our donors and benefactors are getting nervous. Local law enforcement has been snooping around the institute, and the locals' suspicions are increasing. We have been able to operate under the radar for a while now, but things are changing. Someone has informed the authorities about us and our activities. Even worse, a faction of the government besides Senator Hastings' group has become aware of our intentions, making it very dangerous for us and our benefactors from beyond the portal."

He paused, letting the gravity of the situation sink in before continuing, "For now, that faction of the government still does not know the extent or the location of the portal, but they are getting close to discovering our intentions. They are seeking the Ruby Talisman artifact as well. We cannot let them proceed in finding it. We must locate it first." The weight of his words hung in the air, a stark reminder of their precarious position. Dr. Isadora Vale's voice cut through the tense silence, her eyes narrowing with suspicion. "I am still suspicious of Professor Daniels and that assistant of his, Sarah! The professor is not telling us everything, and I don't trust his assistant. There is something about her that makes me feel vulnerable. I think she has powers that should not be ignored." Her words were laced with concern and a hint of fear, underscoring the precariousness of their situation. The mention of Sarah's potential powers added another layer of complexity to their already fraught mission, casting doubt and raising the stakes even higher.

Senator Hastings leaned forward, his voice tinged with unease. "I also have concerns. My contacts have told me that Senator Eleanor Caldwell was in the area earlier in the week. She is above reproach and a distinguished member of

206

the Senate. Her offices are in Salem, but it seems like an odd coincidence that she visited Silver Ridge, and when I tried to contact her, the Senator's assistant told me she was on a retreat. I have left several messages on her phone, and she has not responded. Maybe it's just me being paranoid. She has the ability and contacts to cause us concern." His words cast a shadow over the room, the implication of Senator Caldwell's involvement adding a new threat to their precarious situation.

Archon Heller spoke with a strong German accent, his voice resonating with a chilling resolve. "Our benefactors tell me that we are under attack by benevolent forces, just like we were at the end of World War II in Europe when the Portal that they opened up was ultimately closed by a holy alliance of the Keepers of the Ruby Talisman. In a bold and secretive move, the Keepers turned to the power of the Ruby Talisman to safeguard the delicate balance of spiritual energies. High-ranking clergy members journeyed to the heart of the European continent, where the portal pulsed with malevolent energy. In a climactic battle, the powers of good defeated our triple alliance and axis of power. Now, we face the same situation and must not let another holy alliance succeed. It is time to fight and unleash our dominions upon them."

Archon Heller continued, his eyes gleaming with dark determination, "You have all done well here, sending unsuspecting people with the lure of wealth, physical eternal life, and wishes fulfilled through the portal, trading their souls with souls from the other side, helping our forces to enter this world from other realms. Now, with our benefactors' help, we must not let the forces of good close this conduit. Dominance is our goal; it is our destiny!" His words ignited a fierce resolve within the room, a call to arms against the growing threat from those who sought to close the Veil of Shadows Portal and thwart their dark ambitions. Professor Thorne and the group decided that the best course of action was to head to the secret location of the portal near the base of Mount Hood, known only to them. They would take two vehicles to an undisclosed trailhead and hike the remainder of the distance—a path that Professor Thorne, Isadora, Archon Heller, and a handful of others had taken many times. This would be Senator Hastings' first time on the trek, and his henchmen, Taylor and Parker, would accompany them for protection. The plan was to leave after sunset, giving them plenty of time to reach the portal under the cover of darkness and avoid being seen.

The group prepared for their clandestine journey as the sun dipped below the horizon, casting long shadows over the institute. Professor Thorne and Isadora reviewed the route, ensuring they were prepared for any obstacles. While unfamiliar with the terrain, Senator Hastings exuded confidence, relying on his bodyguards' vigilance. The tension was evident, and so was their sense of determination. They knew reaching the portal before their adversaries was crucial to their plans. As the final rays of sunlight disappeared, they set off, their vehicles cutting through the darkness, leaving Silver Ridge and heading east on Highway 26.

Detective Brian Mitchell, a seasoned investigator with a keen eye for detail, parked his unmarked vehicle at a strategic vantage point, meticulously surveying the driveway and entrance of the Silver Ridge Institute. His attention was drawn to two sizeable black sport utility vehicles leaving the institute in tandem, heading toward the outskirts of town. With Professor Thorne at the wheel of one, Dr. Isadora Vale beside him, and an unknown figure in the vehicle's rear seat, Mitchell decided to tail them from a safe distance, ensuring he remained undetected. The convoy's route led them through a series of small communities, past the turn-off to Forest Haven and along

National Forest Road 2639, tracing the scenic Zigzag River route until the Hidden Lake trailhead was reached.

When the vehicles finally halted, Detective Mitchell discreetly positioned himself behind a bend in the road, killed his engine, and contacted Detective Karen Hayes by cell phone. In a hushed tone, he relayed his observations and suspicions about Professor Thorne and his group, hinting at a potential breakthrough in their investigation into the recent disappearances. Detective Hayes, acknowledging the peril of pursuing them further in the dark, advised caution. She would alert the Forest Service and State Police, arranging to reconvene at the Silver Ridge office and to return to the site with proper gear at first light. Heeding her advice, Mitchell started his vehicle, executed a U-turn, and retraced his path back to Highway 26, eventually arriving at Silver Ridge. The chill in the night air, combined with the hovering mist and eerie stillness, amplified the mystery and intrigue surrounding the missing person cases.

———

In her room at the Forest Haven guest quarters, Sarah stood at the sink, washing her hands and face. The cool water splashed against her skin, invigorating her senses. After cleansing, she reached for a bottle of lotion, smoothing it over her arms and legs with gentle, circular motions. The soothing fragrance enveloped her, leaving her feeling refreshed and calm. She changed into a comfortable nightgown, the soft fabric brushing against her skin, and climbed into bed. As she settled under the covers, she closed her eyes and whispered a prayer for guidance. The room was silent except for the rhythmic sound of her breathing. Sarah felt the day's tension melt away as she began to drift into a peaceful slumber. Suddenly, she felt a change in the air; the room's temperature rose, and a voice called her name. Startled, she opened her eyes and was greeted by a radiant figure. Archangel Kafziel, the divine angel of time and temperature, stood before her. His presence filled the room with a warm, celestial glow. Known as the ruler of the 7th heaven and the prince of the angel order called Powers, Kafziel was also the governor of Saturday. He had always been a great ally to Sarah in the celestial realm.

"Sarah, the time for ascension is near," Kafziel spoke, his voice resonating with divine authority. "Tomorrow, there will be a great disturbance within the forest, and you will need all your powers. Prepare yourself, for the time will be at hand. Call upon your guides and masters to assist you and your earthly charges. They will be there for you. Call upon the angels to battle alongside you to defeat the dark ones." Kafziel continued, "Archangel Orifiel will be by your side. He is the divine angel of the wilderness, guardian of nature, forests, and their inhabitants. You will know him by his bright aura of emerald. Pray for his guidance when he appears to you. He will protect you from the dangers of the wilderness." Sarah nodded, feeling a surge of determination. "Thank you, great one, and divine aid to Archangel Gabriel. I will take your wisdom and Archangel Gabriel's standard into battle." With a final, reassuring nod, Kafziel departed in a bright flash of light, true to the meaning of his name, "The Speed of God." Sarah closed her eyes and fell fast asleep, rejuvenating her body in preparation for tomorrow's journey into the forest to confront the forces of evil. As she slept, her dreams were filled with visions of angelic beings standing by her side, strengthening her resolve.

Christopher lay awake on his bed, unable to sleep. His thoughts raced, knowing that whatever happened tomorrow would change his future forever. They were on the edge of a precipice, and there was no turning back—nor did he want to. His journey had taken him this far, and he believed their quest would be successful with Sarah and the others by his side. He recalled the incantations he had read, and he mentally practiced the Latin phrases. He traced the route in his mind they would take, and with Aiyana Skye as their guide, he felt confident their journey to the portal would be easier. Still unsure what they would find waiting there, he told himself he would be brave and face his fears head-on. He would not hesitate in the face of evil, and he and the others would triumph. As he lay there, thoughts of Sarah filled his mind, and the scent of lilacs and lavender enveloped his senses. Gradually, his racing thoughts began to calm, and he finally drifted off to sleep, ready to face whatever the next day would bring.

Forest Haven Parish's clergy, staff, and guests began to stir and awaken just before the new day's dawn. There was a crispness in the air as dew drops mingled with mist upon the leaves and grass, creating a serene and refreshing atmosphere. The members of the holy alliance showered and dressed, each preparing for the day's events with a sense of purpose and reverence. As the first light of morning peeked over the horizon, they made their way to St. Sylvan's Church for the sunrise service. They greeted each other warmly at the door and shared quiet words and gentle smiles before entering the sanctuary. The soft light filtered through the stained-glass windows, casting colorful patterns on the floor as they took their seats, ready to begin the sacred rituals of the day.

Sarah sat next to Christopher in the pew, wrapping her arm around his left arm and moving closer to him. On his right side sat Ellie, with Isabella beside her. As Sarah moved closer, Christopher felt a warmth spread through him. She whispered, "I will always be by your side, Christopher; have no fear." Taking his hand in hers, she leaned against his left side, hearing him sigh. Christopher glanced at her, and their eyes met in a shared moment of peacefulness and love. Mother Agnes, Deacon Crossford, and Aiyana Skye sat in the pew directly in front of them, surrounded by other parish members and clergy. At the front of the church, at an oak and cedar wood altar, stood Father Rossi and Father Green, flanked by Brother Jasper and Brother Marco De Luca. A choir of sisters from the abbey sang hymns softly, with Sister Cecilia accompanying them on the violin. As the sun rose, the congregation settled in to celebrate morning mass, as birdsong blended harmoniously with the choir as the liturgy began.

Father Green began the service, saying, "We are gathered here on this Autumnal Sunday morning to give thanks for all the blessings we share. I am pleased to greet our new members and visitors to the parish. A special blessing to the members of our alliance who will embark on a journey of great importance today. Our prayers go with them." He introduced Father Rossi to the congregation, who would give the morning's sermon and prayers.

Father Rossi began the sermon by saying, "There has always been a conflict between good and evil in our world. Before the written word, there was a battle fought in the heavens, culminating in the casting out of heaven the evil ones to the earth and to other realms, blocking their entrance to the kingdom of God and limiting their influence over celestial beings. However, the evil ones corrupted the hearts of men and women on earth and worked their malevolence and control through manipulation and possession."

He continued, "Their presence and influence continue to this day. God cleansed the earth of the offspring of the fallen watchers, but the fallen angels remain between the celestial and earth planes. They have managed to open portals in which to travel between these realms, attacking, abducting, and possessing the hearts of humans. The benevolent forces of good, consisting of God's chosen Angels and Archangels, with the help of earthly holy alliances, have held back the malevolent forces, managing to close the portals and maintain a balance. They have been chosen to guide and look after humankind. An evil presence nearby has made us need to send forth our holy alliance against these forces." Father Rossi bowed his head and added, "Let us pray."

After a moment of silence, Father Rossi began to speak in Latin, "Virtute Omnipotentis, Angelorum auxilio, Et ascendentium suorum, Societatem nostram adjuva, Ad victoriam de malis viribus." Translated, "By the power of the almighty and the help of the angels and ascended ones, help our alliance to victory over the evil forces." He then added, "Benedicite fortes nostros et videte eos salvos in parochia nostra." Translated, "Bless our brave ones and see them safely home to our parish." Making the sign of the cross, he blessed the congregation. Father Green replied, "Amen," and the congregation echoed with a resounding "Amen." Sarah held Christopher's hand tighter, and Christopher reached out to take Ellie's hand in his; Ellie took Isabella's hand in hers. The four of them sat there with an energy pulsating between them, sending warmth and confidence through their bodies. From the altar, Father Rossi and Father Green could see a bright glow of celestial light surrounding Sarah, Christopher, Ellie, and Isabella. "Surely, he was witnessing a miracle," Father Rossi thought as he raised his arms to the heavens.

The sisters' choir began singing a glorious hymn, praising the angels in heaven, bringing the service to a close as the congregation rose to their feet. Departing St. Sylvan's Church, they were greeted by clergy who offered them pine branches and white rhododendron flowers. Brother Jasper appeared and began the yearly Blessing of the Animals. Once a year, parishioners bring their pets to receive blessings in the forest clearing at the church's steps. It is said that St. Sylvan's spirit watches over the church, the forest, and the animals surrounding Forest Haven. Some say that the pines sway in response when he is present, their needles rustling like ancient hymns.

After the Blessing of the Animals, Deacon Crossford, Father Green, Father Rossi, Sister Helena, Mother Agnes, and Aiyana Skye met with Christopher, Sarah, Ellie, Isabella, Brother Marco, and Brother Jasper at the administration building's dining and conference room for one last briefing before the team embarked on their day's journey to the portal location. Father Green presented the Ruby Talisman to the group, which he had secured in the parish admin safe. Brother Marco took it into his possession for the ritual they would perform at the portal site. Christopher nodded his approval, acknowledging the significance of the moment. Securing the other gear and provisions they would need and loading the two vehicles they would take, the alliance departed. Christopher drove one vehicle with Sarah, Ellie, and Isabella as passengers, while Brother Jasper, Brother Marco, and Aiyana took the other vehicle. With everything in place, they set out, the weight of their mission heavy on their shoulders but bolstered by their shared purpose and faith.

As they passed through the gates of Forest Haven Parish, Sarah felt a strange sensation of transformation in her body. She experienced a lightness as if the weight of her physical being was becoming less burdensome. Although she was still in her physical body, she knew it would not be long before she would ascend. The pines and cedars lining the road played in unison with the morning sun, creating a kaleidoscope of colors through the vehicle's side windows. Turning onto Mount Hood Highway, the procession traveled east, then took the National Forest gravel-paved Road 2639. Sarah's anticipation grew, and the beauty around them starkly contrasted with the gravity of their mission.

Ellie felt anxious but determined to see this quest through. Things seemed surreal in her mind, like a dream— unreal, fantastic, unworldly—but she knew they were facing something real and threatening, otherworldly. In her years of government service, she had witnessed many hidden things and secrets, but never something as tangible and paranormal as what they were about to encounter. Briefed and bound by a non-disclosure agreement about extraterrestrial and unidentified phenomena, she was always in the dark about whether these phenomena existed. Knowing about the portal made her believe that those secretive government files held truths she had never imagined. Here she was in a vehicle with three strangers she had just met only a few days ago, heading on a mission that even the government was unaware of. Her colleagues and staff believed she was on a personal retreat, yet here she was, playing a cat-and-mouse game with the authorities who trusted her to deliver the goods. Ellie knew in her heart she was doing the right thing for herself and the good of the government and mankind. She was determined to be successful and prevent the Ruby Talisman or the portal's power from falling into the wrong hands. Her resolve was firm; she would see this mission through to its end.

Isabella sat beside Ellie in the rear passenger seat, observing Ellie in deep thought. Occasionally, she caught Christopher's reflection in the rearview mirror as he glanced behind them, and sometimes she felt his eyes meet hers. Nervousness crept over her, knowing they would soon face the evil that had almost possessed her in the past. It was terrifying, but she knew this was the only way to find closure and dispatch the demons that had haunted her for years. She trusted Christopher, Sarah, and the others, confident they would protect her. Despite her fear, she believed in their strength and dedication to the mission. Isabella resolved to stay close to Christopher, feeling a sense of safety in his presence. As they journeyed toward the Veil of Shadows portal, her heart pounded with anxiety and determination, ready to confront the darkness and finally find peace.

After traveling for several miles along the National Forest Road and catching glimpses of the Zigzag River through the trees, the two vehicles arrived at the Hidden Lake trailhead turnout. The area, with gravel parking, trailhead information, some port-a-potties, and a couple of picnic benches, provided ample room for vehicles to park. A few vehicles were already there, likely belonging to Sunday hikers and tourists enjoying the Labor Day weekend. A truck with a horse trailer was also parked to one side, indicating that while the trail accommodated hikers, it could also support horses, though off-road vehicles were prohibited.

As the group parked and unloaded their gear, they noticed two identical black Sport Utility Vehicles parked at the turnout. Christopher felt a strong sense of apprehension as the vehicles seemed out of place for a day of hiking. He mentioned his concerns to the others, who had also noticed the suspicious vehicles and shared his unease. Looking around, he saw no forest rangers in the vicinity; perhaps they were at the ranger lookout tower further north of the trail, as he had seen on a travel map of the Mount Hood Wilderness area.

Aiyana stepped up and mentioned that the trail to Hidden Lake would initially involve a gradual climb but would become steeper past the lake. She explained that the forest would become denser, and they would need to leave the trail, hike into the trees, cross streams, and navigate some rock outcrops. She described the sound of gushing water from a hidden wellspring crevice and the haunting sound of wind through the trees, guiding them to a circular formation of stones. The group listened intently and then followed Aiyana as she led them into the Hidden Lake trailhead entrance, their anticipation and caution heightened by the unknown journey ahead.

❧ CHAPTER NINETEEN ❧

As they begin their trek along the trail, Aiyana tells them the story of Mount Hood, known initially as Kaskali Mountain, also the name taken by the Kaskali tribe, who have long considered it a sacred site. According to Kaskali legend, the mountain was created by the Great Spirit as a gift to the Kaskali people, providing them with abundant resources and a place for spiritual reflection. The mountain is known for its diverse wildlife, including elk, black bears, and various bird species. The area is also rich in flora, with towering Douglas firs, cedars, pines, vibrant wildflowers, and rare medicinal plants that the Kaskali tribe traditionally used for healing. Mount Hood is also considered an active volcano, producing frequent earthquakes, steam, and volcanic gases, mainly around Crater Rock near the summit. The last major eruption occurred in the late 17th century, and in the mid-19th century, early settlers reported fire, smoke, flying rocks, and steam escaping from crevices around the mountainside.

The trail they are on is called the Spirit Path in Kaskali folklore. This trail, winding through the dense forests and up the rugged slopes, has been traveled by generations of Kaskali people seeking solace and communion with nature. Mount Hood remains a place of great cultural and spiritual significance to the Kaskali tribe, who continue to hold ceremonies and gatherings on its slopes, preserving their ancient traditions and deep respect for the natural world. The air is thick with a sense of history and reverence as Aiyana's voice carries the weight of centuries-old stories and the enduring legacy of her ancestors.

The group hiked the pine needle-covered dirt trail, stepping over fallen trees and crossing creeks and overgrowth. Rhododendron bushes lined the path, their flowers gone, and the leaves turning to fall colors as autumn approached. There was a slight mist in the air as they ascended the trail. The sounds of birdsong, the soft whisper of the wind through the trees, and their breaths were the only sounds along the trail. Soon, they could see the outline of Hidden Lake through the Douglas fir trees and western hemlock. Once they arrived at the lake, bear grass and boggy reeds made it challenging to approach the water's edge easily. The water was clear and serene; dragonflies performed their rituals as they skimmed across the lake's surface. Waterfowl dotted the surface in some places, adding to the tranquil beauty of the secluded spot.

Beyond Hidden Lake, the main trail soon crossed a creek, which, even this late in the season, was running with cold, clear water, probably fed by one or more small springs somewhere above. A tree had fallen directly within the trail line, obscuring the path. Finding it difficult to climb over the fallen trunk, the group decided to bypass it, which proved a bad strategy as they lost the trail entirely. They retraced their steps and walked alongside and across the fallen tree branches. That worked, and Aiyana guided them back to the trail. After about two more miles, the trail wandered near the edge of the Zigzag River canyon, and at that point, they moved into the denser forest, leaving the trail behind them. Thick forest growth surrounded them as they moved forward single file; the eeriness and wonder of this hidden wilderness became apparent in their minds. The forest grew darker as the thick trees blocked out the midday sun, casting long, ominous shadows and enveloping them in an almost otherworldly silence.

As the group ventured deeper into the forest, an unsettling presence loomed over them. Hidden between the ancient trees of the dense forest, an evil shapeshifter slithered like a shadow. Its form shifted, blending seamlessly with the gnarled bark and twisted roots. Eyes like molten gold darted from tree to tree, scanning for any sign of pursuit. The air grew thick with tension as it moved silently, each step calculated to avoid snapping twigs or rustling leaves. The forest held its breath, aware of the malevolence that moved within its heart. The atmosphere grew increasingly oppressive as the group approached an outcrop of ancient volcanic boulders, oblivious to the sinister entity observing their every movement. The shapeshifter's presence was an almost tangible force, weaving through the underbrush with a predatory grace. Occasionally, a fleeting glimpse of its true form—a grotesque amalgamation of beast and shadow—would flicker between the trees. It watched intently, waiting for the right moment to strike, its dark intentions palpable in the stillness of the forest.

Suddenly, a large silver-grey wolf appeared, its eyes as blue as the sky. Aiyana called out to him, and he came to her side, responding to her presence with quiet familiarity. They communicated in a non-verbal language of hand gestures and eye movements, a silent understanding passing between them. At once, the wolf darted into the dense forest, disappearing behind the trees with a swift, fluid motion, leaving the group momentarily stunned by the suddenness of its appearance and departure. They heard a series of hideous screams and growls as the wolf caught the evil shapeshifter off guard, taking the shadowy beast down and rendering it helpless. After several moments, the shapeshifter became consumed by flames, leaving only ashes scattered amongst the fallen pine needles and leaves. A howling wolf's long, soulful sound echoed through the forest as Aiyana raised her arms into the air, offering a sacred tribute to the wolf and the Kaskali tribe's ancestors.

Passing beyond the outcrop of volcanic boulders, Sarah and Christopher could hear the faint sound of gushing water, becoming louder as they approached a vertical wall of stone crevices bleeding forth glacial water from the interior of Mount Hood. The water careened down into several shadowy streams leading into a clearing. The group paused just before the clearing, where the trees opened into a grassy meadow. Aiyana, Christopher, Sarah, and Isabella waited for Ellie, Brother Jasper, and Brother Marco to catch up to them. Aiyana said to the group, "This is the place. This is where we will find the circular stones and the portal." They could hear the gushing water and the wind through the trees and knew this was the place foretold in the legends and stories. They gathered their tools and relics and stepped into the clearing. There was an underlying sense of anticipation and mystery as they moved forward. The ground beneath their feet began to rumble. Sarah held Christopher by one hand as Isabella held his other. The trio moved forward cautiously, taking each step with care as the tension grew. Ellie, Aiyana, Jasper, and Marco walked stealthily behind them, scanning the area for signs of danger. Brother Marco held the Ruby Talisman outstretched in his hand, hoping the talisman would protect them.

As they approached closer to the meadow's center, a circle of standing stones came into view, and a small group of silhouettes encircled the stones. They stopped mid-step, realizing that they were not alone and recognizing Professor Thorne, Dr. Vale, Senator Hastings, and three other individuals, all engaged in a ritual of some sort. It became apparent to the group that Professor Thorne and the others were summoning the forces of evil as the air grew thick with the stench of death and malevolence. The once serene meadow now felt ominous and foreboding; the sense of dread intensified as they watched the ritual unfold, knowing they had to act swiftly to stop whatever dark power was being called forth. The ritual was an elaborate and unnerving spectacle set against the backdrop of the ancient standing stones. Professor Thorne, Dr. Vale, Senator Hastings, and another figure speaking in an obscure German dialect and cloaked in a red robe and hood stood at the center of the circle, their eyes closed, and hands raised towards the sky. The others chanted in an

220

unknown, guttural language that echoed eerily through the meadow. Three other individuals, dressed in dark, hooded robes, moved in a synchronized pattern around the central figures, their movements slow and deliberate, as if tracing invisible lines of power on the ground. In the middle of the circle, a large, flat stone altar was covered with strange symbols and runes etched in blood. Upon the altar lay various objects of dark significance: a blackened dagger, a scroll adorned with cryptic markings, and a bowl filled with a viscous, dark liquid that seemed to pulse with a life of its own. A cold wind whipped through the meadow, swirling the robes of the participants and carrying the scent of decay and sulfur.

The air around the standing stones shimmered with dark energy, and shadows seemed to writhe and twist within the circle. As the chanting grew louder and more intense, the Ruby Talisman in Brother Marco's hand began to glow, reacting to the malevolent forces at work. The ground beneath the altar cracked, and a faint, otherworldly light seeped through, hinting at the dark power being summoned from below. A portal opened at the center of the ritual, revealing the Veil of Shadows itself, and from its depths spewed forth entities from the other side—demons and unimaginable beings of grotesque forms and malevolent intent. The ground around them shook violently as these dark creatures emerged, their eyes glowing with an otherworldly light. The tension in the air was extreme, and the holy alliance members knew the incantations had unleashed something ancient and evil into the world. The air crackled with dark energy, and an oppressive sense of dread enveloped the group as they faced the horrifying reality of the portal and the nightmarish entities it unleashed.

As the portal continued spilling forth its monstrous entities, the holy alliance quickly realized they needed to act to prevent a complete breach of evil into their world.

With a resolute expression, Aiyana Skye turned to her companions and instructed them to form a protective circle around Brother Marco and the Ruby Talisman. The talisman, now glowing even more brightly, was their only hope of closing the portal. Christopher, Sarah, Isabella, Ellie, and Brother Jasper formed a tight ring, weapons and relics in hand, prepared to defend against the encroaching demons. Aiyana and Brother Marco began to chant a counter-ritual, their voices strong and unwavering despite the chaos around them. The air grew thicker with tension, each second feeling like an eternity as the demonic entities clawed and snarled, trying to break through the protective circle. After realizing their ritual was being opposed, Professor Thorne and his cohorts focused on the group, attempting to disrupt their efforts. Dr. Isadora Vale raised her hands, summoning dark energy to strike at Aiyana, but Christopher and Sarah intercepted, deflecting the attack with their combined strength. The battle was fierce and unrelenting, with every group member contributing to the defense and the counter-ritual.

A horde of malevolent demons and dark forces surrounded Sarah, Christopher, and the group as the first wave of demons descended upon them. Sarah and Christopher sprang into action, their movements fluid and synchronized as they engaged their foes with a combination of mortal skill and celestial power. As the tide of battle seemed to turn against them, Sarah's eyes widened with a sudden realization. They were overmatched, and the forces of darkness threatened to overwhelm them. Drawing upon her divine heritage, she raised her voice in a clarion call that echoed through the dimensions, invoking the aid of the celestial beings who watched over the realms of light and shadow. "Angelorum custodes et magistri ascensi, adiuvate nos in pugna contra malos et claudendum portam umbrae," Christopher intoned in Latin, his voice steady and resonant. The ancient words carried the weight of ages, reverberating through the battleground with a power that seemed to stir the air around them. His words spoken in English, "Guardian angels and ascended masters, assist us in the battle against evil and in closing the door to the shadows." As he spoke, the atmosphere grew charged with energy, crackling with an unseen force. Sarah and Christopher felt a tangible presence gathering, an assembly of ethereal beings ready to lend their strength.

In a sudden burst of radiant light, Archangel Orifiel, the divine guardian of forests and their inhabitants, materialized beside them. His presence was awe-inspiring, and his form was wreathed in an emerald glow that spoke of the natural world's enduring power. Deep and wise, his eyes took in the scene with a serene yet fierce determination. "Your call has been heard, warriors of light," Orifiel said, his voice like the rustling of leaves in an ancient forest. "We shall stand with you." Seeing the divine being, Professor Thorne and Isadora locked arms, channeling their combined power into a concentrated blast of energy aimed directly at Brother Marco and Brother Jasper. As the surge of power hurtled towards them, the Ruby Talisman in Brother Jasper's hand glowed with intense brilliance. Unfazed, Brother Jasper uttered the ancient Latin incantation, "Per potentiam rubini, claudatur velum umbrae," which translated to, "By the power of the ruby, let the Veil of Shadows be closed." The talisman absorbed the impact of the energy blast, transforming it into a flaming ball of light. With a blinding flash, the ball of light was hurled back towards its origin, effectively foiling Professor Thorne and Isadora's attempt to destroy the two holy brothers, reinforcing the brother's sanctity of their mission.

With Orifiel's arrival, the battlefield shifted. Guardian Angels and Ascended Masters began to materialize, their forms shimmering with celestial energy. Sarah felt her own strength surge as Orifiel placed a reassuring hand on her shoulder, his touch imbuing her with the life force of the forests he protected. The battleground shifted seamlessly between earthly and esoteric realms, the boundaries between dimensions blurring as Sarah, Christopher, and the holy alliance navigated the ever-changing landscape of their conflict against the forces of evil.

Guardian Angel Haiyael, the divine warrior, arrives with a majestic presence that instills hope and courage. His name, "God the Master of The Universe," reflects his immense power and authority. In Judaism, Haiyael is one of the Cherubs under the command of Archangel Gabriel. As the protector of God's divine weaponry, Haiyael wields a sword of discernment, and a shield formed from his radiant aura. These formidable weapons make him a fearsome adversary against the forces of evil. With his bright aura illuminating the battlefield, Haiyael brings the divine protection of God, holding back the tide of malevolent entities trying to enter the fray through the portal, ensuring the forces of light remain steadfast and resolute. Guardian Angel Yelahiah, known as the Warrior of Light, joins Guardian Angel Haiyael in the fierce battle. As one of the Malachims, Yelahiah serves under the command of Archangel Michael and is a member of God's Celestial Army. Protector of the divine law and all that is sacred, Yelahiah wields his sword with unwavering precision against the demonic entities approaching the holy alliance members. His sword, a beacon of divine justice, and his shield, an impenetrable barrier of light, stop and destroy the evil entities before they can harm the brave champions. Together, Haiyael and Yelahiah stand as an indomitable force, and their combined might be a bulwark against the darkness threatening to engulf the world.

As the battle rages on, the portal trembles and darkens, heralding the arrival of the fallen angel Arakiel. Once a revered Watcher with dominion over the earth, Arakiel was entrusted with the guardianship of every creature inhabiting the planet's lands, waters, and air. His once-divine purpose was to nurture and protect, but corruption and pride led him to forsake his sacred duty. In his fall, Arakiel was transformed into a demon, becoming one of the twenty Watchers who led 200 fallen angels into rebellion. Manifesting now, his presence exudes a sinister power, commanding the allegiance of countless other demons. His dominion over them is absolute, a dark mirror of the authority he once held over the natural world.

Beside Arakiel emerges Sariel, one of the angels of death and once an Archangel of the Earth. Sariel, too, succumbed to rebellion against God's will and became a disciple of Satanel, the first angel to defy the divine order. Sariel's transformation into a fallen angel marked him as a harbinger of death, his allegiance now with the malevolent forces that seek to overthrow the celestial realms. His dark power is formidable, and his presence alongside Arakiel signifies a dire escalation in the conflict. Together, they embody the fallen might of the celestial rebels, drawing upon their corrupted strength to challenge the forces of light. Their defiance is a testament to Satanel's enduring influence, the first Archangel and orchestrator of the eternal war between the angels of heaven and the forces of darkness. The appearance of these two powerful beings sends a ripple of dread through the battlefield as the champions of light brace for the onslaught of their formidable adversaries.

Together, Sarah, Christopher, and their divine allies launched a renewed assault against the forces of darkness. Orifiel wielded his staff, which sprouted vines and thorns that entangled and pierced the demonic entities. The guardian angels moved with blinding speed, their swords of light cutting through the darkness like beams of sunlight piercing through a dense canopy. Brother Jasper and Brother Marco stood resolute during the chaotic battle, their faces calm and focused amidst the storm of clashing celestial and demonic forces. Clasped firmly in their hands, the Ruby Talisman glowed with an intense, otherworldly light, serving as both a shield and a beacon of strength against the relentless onslaught of evil. The heat of the battle raged around them, scorching the earth and filling the air with the acrid scent of burning, yet the talisman's radiant aura repelled the searing flames and malevolent energies, protecting them from harm. With unwavering faith, they chanted prayers and invocations, their voices rising above the din, reinforcing the talisman's protective power and drawing upon the divine to bolster their defenses.

Amidst the swirling chaos, three figures were seen darting away from the circle of stones, making a desperate dash towards the outline of the nearby trees. Isabella and Ellie, their senses heightened by the urgency of the battle, quickly recognized one of the fleeing figures as Senator Hastings, accompanied by his two henchmen. Fear etched on their faces; they cowered from the conflict, their resolve crumbling in the face of the celestial and demonic forces clashing around them. Seeking refuge from the escalating battle, they disappeared into the dense cover of the trees. The ground quaked violently as steam and molten lava began to spew from crevices in the rock formations and at the mountain's base. Cracks splintered through the meadow, releasing scorching air that hissed and shimmered around the holy champions. Ellie and Isabella ducked down behind Christopher and Sarah, seeking shelter from the fiery upheaval. Aiyana stood firm her arms outstretched to the darkened sky as she called on the benevolent spirits of her ancestors to join forces with the holy alliance. As the earth roared and the heat intensified, the fallen angels, their eyes burning with malevolent intent, turned their attention toward the four of them, ready to unleash their dark wrath. The holy champions stood their ground, their determination unshaken despite the apocalyptic scene.

Appearing in front of them, facing towards the fallen ones, the Ascended Masters, beings of profound wisdom and power, chanted incantations that reverberated with cosmic resonance. Their words wove a tapestry of light and energy, bolstering their mortal allies' defenses and weakening their enemies' resolve. Kaskali ancestral spirits joined the alliance to form a barrier around Aiyana, Marco, Jasper, and the Ruby Talisman. Professor Thorne, still locked arm in arm with Isadora, came to a harrowing realization: all was lost for him, and redemption was beyond reach. Isadora, once a brilliant and formidable ally, had now taken on the grotesque appearance of a demon, her features twisted by madness and dark power. She cackled with deranged glee, her eyes wild and unfocused as she unleashed curses and bursts of chaotic energy toward Sarah, Christopher, and their allies. With each malevolent incantation and searing blast, her power grew, the air around her crackling with an ominous energy that seemed to feed off her insanity. Professor Thorne watched in despair as the woman he once knew became a conduit of pure evil, her transformation complete.

Unable to bear the destruction and torment any longer, Professor Thorne made a desperate decision. With a final, heartfelt plea to God for salvation, he wrapped his arms tightly around Isadora, his resolve unwavering despite the chaos surrounding them. Summoning every ounce of strength and courage, he leaped into the portal, dragging the maddened demon with him. The two vanished in a brilliant flash of light, their forms consumed by the portal's searing energy. The battlefield fell momentarily silent, the shock of their sudden disappearance resonating through the remaining combatants. Though the battle raged on, Thorne's ultimate sacrifice left a glimmer of hope that perhaps some small part of him might find redemption in the act, even as the forces of darkness continued their relentless assault. The demonic forces began to falter, their

227

once formidable ranks breaking under the relentless onslaught of divine power

As the battle reached its zenith, Sarah, Christopher, and the group, empowered by their celestial comrades, pushed towards the heart of the darkness where the Veil of Shadows loomed. The fallen ones, Arakiel and Sariel, unleashed a devastating cosmic energy burst aimed directly at Sarah and her group. In an instant, Sarah transformed, her divine wings spreading wide to shield Christopher and the others from the catastrophic blow. She absorbed the full force of the energy burst, her body giving way to her celestial form. Bathed in radiant, ethereal light, Sarah ascended above the group, her presence a beacon of hope amidst the chaos. Frantic and heartbroken, Christopher reached out to grasp the trailing edges of her celestial gown, his voice breaking as he screamed, "Sarah, Sarah, not now, it's too soon; please don't leave me!" His sobs echoed through the air, filled with anguish and despair.

Ellie and Isabella, moved by his grief, wrapped their arms around him, pulling him back as the air swirled upward with Sarah's ascension. Amidst the turmoil, Sarah turned, her face glowing with a loving smile and a knowing look. "Christopher, my love, do not be afraid; do not be sad," she said, her voice serene and comforting. "I will always be with you. This is our destiny; yours is to live; mine is to watch over you. Protect Isabella and keep her close. She will be your loyal companion. This is my wish and my blessing for you." With those parting words, Sarah turned toward the sky, her wings outstretched, her arms reaching heavenward. As she ascended into the heavens, her celestial form gradually faded from view, leaving behind Christopher with an enduring promise of her eternal love and guardianship. Christopher fell back into the arms of Isabella and Ellie, his heart broken and split into a thousand pieces. Isabella placed his head against her bosom and gently stroked his hair.

✎ CHAPTER TWENTY ✎

In the celestial realm above, the heavens themselves seem to weep along with Christopher as the battle reaches its climax, the cosmic forces of light and darkness locked in a struggle of cosmic proportions. Angels and demons clash amidst a tempest of celestial energies, their ethereal forms intertwining in a ballet of destruction that spans the heavens. In a climactic showdown of epic proportions, Archangel Orifiel, Angel Haiyael, Angel Yelahiah, and the other benevolent celestial beings gathered their remaining strength and unleashed a final, devastating wave of divine energy. The air crackled with power as their combined might surged toward the Veil of Shadows portal, which shimmered with chaotic energy. The malevolent forces within the portal struggled against the overwhelming onslaught, but the relentless force of the divine celestial beings proved too formidable. Slowly, the dark portal began to fold in upon itself, its sinister glow dimming under the relentless assault. The fallen ones, Arakiel and Sariel, including the red-robed figure, Archon Heller, were cast again into the fiery abyss from where they came. With a brilliant flash of light, the Veil of Shadows sealed shut, the mountain portal between dimensions closed forever.

As the final echoes of the divine blast faded, the battleground fell silent. The forces of darkness were banished, leaving the air clear and serene. The ground stopped shaking, and lava hardened, closing fissures and crevices, and steam no longer escaped to the surface. Christopher and the members of the holy alliance, their bodies, and spirits weary but triumphant, stood amidst their celestial allies. The light of the late afternoon sun on the horizon cast a warm, golden glow over the scene. Their victory was palpable, the air filled with a sense of hard-won peace and the promise of a brighter future. Christopher, his heart heavy with the recent loss of Sarah, looked to the heavens with a mixture of sorrow and gratitude, knowing her sacrifice had made this moment possible.

From the heavens above, a chorus of angelic voices began to sing, their harmonious melodies resonating through the air and filling the hearts of the weary warriors with a profound sense of peace. Guardian Angels Haiyael, Yelahiah, and Archangel Orifiel, their divine mission fulfilled, prepared to ascend to their places in the celestial realm. As they rose, their forms glowing with ethereal light, they looked down upon Christopher and the holy alliance, offering silent blessings and eternal gratitude for their bravery. Ascending to their divine posts, they resumed their roles as intermediaries between heaven and earth, their presence a constant reminder of the divine protection that would always watch over the world. As they disappeared into the celestial expanse, the Ascended Masters and the Kaskali ancestral spirits, who were instrumental in holding back the forces of evil, also faded into the ether from where they came; the serene meadow glowed with divine light as the sun shined through the trees.

Archangel Phanuel, known as the Angel of Peace, emerged from the center of this radiant divine light. His name, "The Face of God," reflected his holy purpose. Phanuel, the angel who fends off the fallen angels and forbids their presence before the Lord of Spirits, is one of the Angels of Great Counsel. In one of the most significant conflicts, the war in heaven, when the fallen Angel Satanel – also known as Satan or Lucifer, revolted against God and sought to destroy the agency of man, Phanuel, standing alongside Michael, Raphael, and Gabriel, played a crucial role in seizing, binding, and casting Satanel and the fallen angels into fire. As a divine patron of sanctification, a position shared with Michael, Metatron, Suriel, and Zagzagael, it was a great honor for him to appear before the group. Phanuel's presence was a beacon of peace and protection. His voice resounded throughout the meadow and forest, blessing the holy champions and pledging eternal support for their unselfish dedication to defeating the forces of evil and closing the Veil of Shadows portal. The brightness of his appearance caused the group to bow their heads in adoration and respect, their hearts filled with the profound weight of his blessing.

As Archangel Phanuel departed in the same way he arrived, as a bright light, the weight of their triumph and his blessing settled heavily upon the group's shoulders. They stood in silent reverence, absorbing the magnitude of their victory and the divine affirmation they had received. The future stretched out before them, free from the shadow of darkness, their bond as champions of the light forever forged in the crucible of conflict. Strengthened by their shared experience and the divine protection promised by Phanuel, they turned toward the forest and the pathway they had forged. Guided by Aiyana Skye, they returned to the Hidden Lake trail, their spirits buoyed by the promise of a brighter tomorrow. The serenity of the meadow and the divine light that had graced them lingered in their hearts, a constant reminder of their purpose and the celestial allies who watched over them.

As they hiked the trail, Ellie and Isabella whispered among themselves about Sarah's ascension. They wouldn't have believed it if they hadn't seen it with their own eyes. They both realized they had been in the presence of an angel on earth in human form, though they couldn't quite grasp the full significance of what they had witnessed. Isabella confessed that she had felt that there was something different about Sarah but could not put her finger on it. Sarah's relationship with Christopher made more sense to her now, explaining at least some of the mysteries surrounding them. Ellie marveled at the miraculous events they had experienced that day, admitting she had never encountered anything like it in all her years. The awe and wonder of the past few days weighed heavily on her mind, making every step feel surreal. Christopher walked ahead in silence, his grief visible. Isabella felt a strong empathy for him and hoped she could help him through his sorrow, sensing the depth of his pain.

Aiyana led the group, with Brother Marco and Brother Jasper taking up the rear. The two clergy members walked in silence, deep in contemplation and prayer, as they neared the edge of Hidden Lake. The late afternoon sun reflected off the still waters, creating a serene and calming backdrop. Dragonflies and insects darted across the surface, while the distant calls of loons and the rustling of small animals at the water's edge added to the tranquility. As they passed the lake, the trail became easier, signaling the final mile or two to the trailhead and the parking area. The descent was gentle, and the group moved in unspoken harmony, each lost in their thoughts. The day's miraculous events and the weight of their victory blended seamlessly with the natural beauty around them, providing a poignant end to their extraordinary journey.

As the group descended the final stretch of the trail toward the Hidden Lake trailhead, a sense of calm and introspection settled over them. The serenity of the surroundings provided a stark contrast to the intense battles they had just faced. Each step felt like a release from the turmoil, a gradual return to the mundane world, albeit forever changed by the extraordinary events they had experienced. Emerging from the Hidden Lake trail at the trailhead, the parking area was abuzz with activity. Christopher took a moment to gather himself, drawing in deep breaths of the cool, fresh air. His grief was still raw, but he felt a strange sense of peace, knowing that Sarah's sacrifice had ensured the world's safety. Isabella stayed close to him, her presence offering silent support.

Christopher immediately recognized Detectives Hale and Mitchell gathered at the rear of a Forest Service vehicle. Alongside them were the Mount Hood National

Forest Ranger Service members and several State Police officers. Christopher glanced at Ellie, and both noticed Senator Hastings and his two henchmen in cuffs at the rear of a State Trooper vehicle. Senator Hastings was rambling and protesting, swearing about the evil among them and something about a Ruby Talisman. When he spotted Ellie and Christopher, he screamed about a conspiracy to undermine his efforts to obtain the artifact for the government. His orders to the State Police to arrest them fell on deaf ears because the State Department had already issued a warrant for his arrest on multiple charges, including treason and misappropriation of government funds and assets.

Among the welcoming group was State Department official Sebastian Morland, who approached Christopher, Ellie, and Isabella. "Hello, Senator Caldwell; glad that you are safe. Now, tell me about this artifact. Were you able to recover it?" Ellie responded, "Yes, we did find the artifact. However, it was lost when it fell into a lava flow, was consumed by the lava, and disappeared within a fissure as it burned up; what was left of it was buried deep within the depths of the mountain as the lava cooled. There would have been nothing left of it to retrieve." Christopher nodded in agreement, and Sebastian replied, "That is a shame and too bad for our side. Sometimes, the dragon wins! It's probably for the best. We wouldn't want it to turn up in the wrong hands," as he winked and looked over his shoulder at Senator Hastings and his henchmen. Turning back to Ellie, he said, "Job well done, Senator." Ellie nodded and smiled as Sebastian turned and walked to the State Trooper's vehicle and his own to discuss the next steps with the State Police for the transportation of Senator Hastings.

Detectives Hale and Mitchell waved at Christopher and the group, offering a friendly salute as they returned to their vehicle, satisfied that their missing persons cases had been solved. The sense of accomplishment was tangible as the group dispersed, each member feeling the weight of their extraordinary journey lift slightly. Christopher, Ellie, and Isabella shared a moment of quiet triumph, their bond strengthened by the trials they had overcome. Ellie and Isabella exchanged a meaningful glance, silently agreeing to support Christopher and one another through the coming days. Aiyana Skye, having guided them safely back, offered a serene smile. "Our paths were meant to cross," she said softly. "Remember the strength you have found in each other and the light you carry within." Brother Marco and Brother Jasper approached Christopher, offering comfort and solidarity. "Her sacrifice will not be forgotten," Brother Marco said solemnly. "We must honor her memory by continuing to protect the world from the shadows."

In referring to the Ruby Talisman, Ellie asked Brother Marco, "Do you still have it?" Brother Marco tapped the front of his robe and said, "It is safe." Ellie replied with a nod of approval, "Very good, Brother Marco. It is in good hands with you and the holy church where it belongs." Brother Marco offered a reassuring smile, knowing the significance and power of the artifact now entrusted to him. Ellie felt a sense of relief, understanding the importance of keeping the Ruby Talisman out of the wrong hands. Its safety within the holy church was a safeguard against the forces of darkness they had fought valiantly to defeat. With a final glance at the scene around them, the group felt a sense of closure. The battle had been won, the Veil of Shadows had been sealed, and the Ruby Talisman was secure. They could now move forward with a renewed sense of purpose, knowing their efforts had protected the world from an ancient evil.

The sun began to dip below the horizon, casting long shadows across the forest as the group secured their gear and prepared to depart. With Isabella by his side, Christopher started the car's engine while Ellie and Aiyana climbed into the back seat, their spirits buoyed by the companionship they had found. After a final prayer for guidance and protection, the clergy members, Brothers Jasper and Marco prepared to leave in the vehicle they had arrived in. Driving away from the Hidden Lake turnout, Christopher couldn't help but glance back at the trailhead, a sense of closure mingling with his sorrow. "Sarah," he whispered, "I will carry on your legacy. I will not let your sacrifice be in vain." The drive back to Forest Haven Parish was filled with a quiet, reflective silence, fortified by their shared experiences and the bonds they had forged. The echoes of angelic voices and the divine light of Sarah's ascension lingered in their hearts, a reminder of their courage and sacrifice that had saved the world from the Veil of Shadows.

The journey back felt surreal, each mile a step away from the chaos and into a future shaped by the trials they had endured. The night sky stretched above them, stars twinkling like guardians watching over their path. As they neared the familiar surroundings of Forest Haven Parish, a sense of peace began to settle over them. They knew their lives had been irrevocably changed, but with the memory of Sarah's sacrifice and the unity they had discovered, they felt ready to face whatever life challenges lay ahead. Their bond, forged in the crucible of conflict, would guide them through the days to come as champions of the light in a world forever marked by their bravery.

Entering the gates of Forest Haven Parish, Christopher parked in the guest parking area, and the four weary alliance members walked up the path to the guest quarters. The air was filled with the scent of pine and the distant hum of night insects. The cobblestone path crunched softly under their tired feet, a comforting sound after their long journey. Christopher, Isabella, and Ellie entered the guest quarters building, their eyes drawn to the warm glow of candlelight spilling from the windows. Aiyana, however, continued along the path to the abbey, where Mother Agnes stood at the garden entrance archway, waving an appreciative welcome. The soft light of the rising moon cast a silver sheen on the scene, making the moment feel almost magical. As Aiyana approached, the moon's beams reflected through the pines, creating intricate patterns of light and shadow across the ground. Crickets sang in the gardens, their rhythmic chirping blending with the distant call of night birds, forming a natural symphony. It was as if the sisters themselves had instructed the creatures to sing songs of praise, welcoming the returning champions with nature's own music.

A table and chairs had been placed in the guest quarter's lobby, laden with fresh fruits, vegetables, loaves of bread, meats, and wine as a gift to the returning trio. Realizing they had not eaten in many hours, Christopher, Isabella, and Ellie sat down, partaking in the food and drink, grateful for the parish's thoughtful reward and bounty. The fresh flavors and hearty meal replenished their energy, and the wine warmed their weary bodies. A sense of camaraderie and relief settled over them as they filled themselves. Satisfied and content, they climbed the stairs to the second-floor guest rooms. Bidding each other a warm goodnight and a hug, they retreated to their rooms.

Christopher paused by the closed door that was once Sarah's room; the smell of lilacs and lavender filled the air just outside her door. Could she be close by? he thought. Maybe it was just the smell of her lingering in his mind. He reached out and touched the doorknob; turning it, he entered the room. Glancing around, he noticed Sarah's suitcase and belongings were nowhere to be found, and the bed, chair, and desk were undisturbed and clear of objects. He remembered that they had left their overnight bags and luggage in their rooms that morning when they departed for the hike to the portal area. Closing his eyes for a moment, he tried to hold back the tears, but they escaped when he opened his eyes, cascading down his cheeks, the saltiness of his sorrow reaching the corners of his lips. Turning, he departed the room, closing the door behind him.

Arriving at his room, he opened the door and entered. Kicking off his shoes, he collapsed on the bed, overcome with weariness and grief. The weight of the day's emotions and physical exertion pressed down on him, making it impossible to stay awake any longer. The soft bed felt like a haven, a brief escape from the sorrow in his heart. As his head touched the pillow, the tendrils of sleep overtook him immediately, pulling him into a deep, dreamless slumber. In the quiet of the night, the sounds of the parish grounds faded into the background, replaced by the gentle rhythm of his breathing. The moonlight filtered through the window's curtains, casting a soft glow over his resting form. For a few precious hours, he was free from the burdens that had weighed so heavily on him, lost in the oblivion of sleep.

Morning arrived at Forest Haven, sunlight filtering through the open window as Ellie awoke. She stretched, feeling the sun's warmth on her skin, then showered and dressed. With a sense of purpose, she packed her bags in preparation for her return to Silver Ridge with Christopher. Simultaneously, in his room, Christopher arose, showered, dressed, and gathered his bags. The prospect of returning to Silver Ridge brought a mixture of anticipation and reluctance. Isabella, who had made the guest quarters her residence over the past many months, also showered and dressed. She then walked to the administration building for the morning briefing. Christopher and Ellie met in the guest building's lobby after leaving their rooms with baggage in tow. They exchanged a brief, knowing glance, a silent acknowledgment of the journey ahead. Together, they returned to Christopher's vehicle in the parking area, loading their bags. The morning air was crisp, carrying the fresh scent of pine and the promise of a new day. With their tasks completed, they walked to the administration building, their footsteps echoing in the quiet morning.

Ellie and Christopher entered the parish administration building and were greeted by Deacon Elias Crossword, who led them into the meeting room. Seated at the large conference table, the other members of the holy alliance cheered as they entered. Handshakes of gratitude were exchanged around the table as Father Green recounted what Marco, Jasper, Isabella, and Aiyana had told him of Sunday's events and the miraculous closing of the Portal. A great service had been achieved for the good of all humankind. He gave his condolences to Christopher and those who knew Sarah, mourning her passing in human form while praising her ascension as a confirmation of her sainthood and true angelic nature. All bowed their heads in reverence, honoring her sacrifice.

Father Rossi then thanked the alliance members and champions for delivering the Ruby Talisman, scrolls, and manuscripts into the arms of the holy church, where they would be well protected for generations to come. The significance of their mission's success weighed heavily in the room, a mixture of solemnity and triumph. As the morning light streamed through the windows, casting a golden glow over the gathering, a sense of closure and hope filled their hearts. The meeting adjourned with heartfelt farewells exchanged at the front steps of the administration building. Christopher approached Isabella, noticing the tears forming in her eyes. "Isabella, pack a bag," he said gently. "You are coming with Ellie and me to Silver Ridge. I have plenty of room in my home and a very comfortable guest room with a private bath." He added, "There is still much work to do and things to sort out. Will you assist me with these things?" Isabella looked at Mother Agnes and Ellie, who both smiled and nodded their approval. With a joyful smile, Mother Agnes said, "Hurry, child, there is no time to spare; gather your belongings. You are going on a glorious adventure. The worm has indeed turned for you, my dear."

Isabella turned to Christopher, giving him a big hug and kissing him on the cheek. "Yes, I would like that very much. Thank you, Professor Daniels." Christopher replied with a warm smile, "Call me Chris." As Isabella hurried to gather her belongings, the sense of a new beginning filled the air. Shared experiences and mutual respect strengthened their bond, promising a future of collaboration and hope. With the holy alliance's blessings and the support of her friends, Isabella felt ready to embark on the next chapter of her journey, leaving behind the old and embracing the new with open arms.

Christopher, Ellie, and Isabella departed Forest Haven Parish, driving west on Mount Hood Highway 26 to Silver Ridge. During the drive, Christopher and Ellie planned to transition the Silver Ridge Institute into a more community-based college and campus. Christopher and Isabella were excited about leaving the past behind and forging a new future for the students, faculty, and the community of Silver Ridge. Ellie said, "I have much influence in the Senate and with the supporting board members of the Institute. I can get funds allocated for the remodeling of the institute and the startup of a new curriculum. With my recommendations, Christopher, you will be appointed the institute's new Director, and Isabella will become your assistant and Dean of Students." She asked, "How would you two like those arrangements?"

Christopher smiled and said, "It would be an honor, Ellie. but first, I will need to tie up some loose ends there," he winked and smiled at Isabella. Isabella tilted her head and, with a puzzled look on her face, asked, "Do I want to know?" Christopher replied, "You will know." Feeling blessed and included, Isabella said, "Thank you, Ellie, and thank you too, Chris." Christopher nodded, and Ellie said, "You're welcome, Isabella." The car continued down the highway with the promise of new beginnings and the determination to transform the institute into a beacon of learning and community.

Arriving at Christopher's residence, Ellie transferred her luggage to her own vehicle. After a brief but heartfelt farewell, she departed for her home offices in Salem. Ellie expressed her sincerity and purpose in helping transition the institute, assuring Christopher and Isabella that she would remain dedicated to their cause. Christopher opened the garage door, and Ellie backed out of the driveway, turning off Cascadia Maple Drive and entering the main street leading out of town. Her departure marked the beginning of their new journey.

Isabella and Christopher entered the house, and a sense of comfort washed over Isabella as she stepped inside. She was grateful for Christopher's generosity and support, silently vowing to be a loyal assistant and professional in her new capacity as the Dean of Students. Additionally, she promised herself that she would do her best to be a source of comfort to Christopher during his period of grieving, standing by his side through it all. Christopher showed her around the house, leading her to the upstairs guest room, conveniently located down the hall from his room so she would feel safe. Isabella felt safe and comfortable, reassured by her new home's warm and welcoming environment. After a late lunch on the downstairs deck overlooking the edge of the wooded area behind Christopher's house, Christopher and Isabella took a stroll on the main street of Silver Ridge. They passed by the same shops, cafes, and nooks that Christopher had frequented with Sarah and were no doubt familiar to Isabella from her days at the institute. Stopping briefly in front of Sarah's previous residence, Christopher pointed it out, mentioning that it was where Sarah had rented. He wondered if any of her belongings were still there, but in his heart, he suspected they had disappeared like her possessions at Forest Haven.

A little further along their stroll, they spotted a charming woven basket hanging in the window of a second-hand boutique. Isabella exclaimed, "What a lovely basket! May we stop in?" Christopher agreed, and they stepped into the store. Isabella inquired about the basket, and the clerk mentioned that it had just come in yesterday. "Would you like to purchase it?" the clerk asked. "Yes indeed," Isabella replied, purchasing the item. She ran her fingers over the smooth wicker weave, admiring the craftsmanship as she allowed it to hang gracefully under her arm. There was a subtle familiarity to the basket, though Christopher couldn't remember where he had seen it before. Perhaps it had been hanging in one of the booths at the farmer's market. Who knows, he thought. The basket's presence felt like a small but meaningful connection to the past, a symbol of continuity amidst change.

After departing the boutique, Christopher and Isabella arrived at the town's square and the steps of the Silver Ridge Institute. Sensing Isabella's fear and apprehension, Christopher suggested she sit on a bench in the town square's park area. Isabella agreed, grateful for his empathy. "I'll only be gone for a few minutes. Wait here for me," Christopher reassured her. She nodded, appreciating his understanding. Christopher entered the Institute, passed the reception area, and noticed Julie's absence since the institute was closed for Labor Day. He bolted up the staircase to the upstairs library. Ensuring no one was present, he found the hidden chamber's access lever and opened the bookcase entrance. He approached the pedestal in the center of the room, removing the Veil of Shadows manuscript and covering it with an old burlap bag he found in a corner. Quickly, he left the chamber, closing the bookcase entrance behind him. With the manuscript in his arms, he went down the stairs, out the front door, and into the inviting air of the town square park area.

Isabella was there waiting for him, a curious look on her face. He opened the burlap bag and told her it was the last loose end to be disposed of. Her eyes lit up with admiration for him, yet she also felt a wave of fear in the presence of the evil manuscript that had changed her world forever. Christopher said, "Have no fear, Isabella. I will not let anything happen to you. We will dispose of this properly when we return to our home. It is the last act of our faith and your hard-earned redemption." His words comforted her, reinforcing her trust in him and their shared mission. As they walked back together, Isabella felt a renewed sense of purpose and a deep bond with Christopher.

As the sun set on the town of Silver Ridge, Christopher and Isabella arrived home. Just as they settled in, Christopher received a call from Ellie, who informed him that she had arrived safely in Salem. She assured him that she would set the wheels in motion first thing in the morning, noting that the remodeling and construction at the Institute would take several weeks to get underway. Christopher expressed his gratitude before ending the call, feeling a sense of progress and anticipation.

Isabella went upstairs to refresh herself while Christopher opened the screens to the downstairs stone-faced fireplace. He carefully placed cedar and oak wood on the grate, adding kindling before setting the wood aflame. The fire crackled to life, filling the room with a warm, sacred fragrance as the cedar released its aromatic scent. He then opened a bottle of Cabernet Sauvignon. Its bold flavor profile filled his senses with notes of blackcurrant, cassis, and blackberries. It's a perfect wine to end the day. When Isabella returned to the downstairs living quarters, she found Christopher seated in one of the plush reclining chairs, the fire casting a cozy glow across the room. She joined him, sinking into the chair beside him, feeling a deep sense of peace and contentment. Christopher offered her a glass of the beloved red grape wine from the Bordeaux region. The soft light of the fire danced on the walls, and for a moment, the weight of their responsibilities lifted, replaced by the simple comfort of being together in the warmth of the wine and crackling fireplace.

Christopher opened the burlap bag and handed the Veil of Shadows manuscript to Isabella, who nervously accepted it, her hands trembling slightly. "Toss this into the fireplace," Christopher instructed gently, "so the sacred cedar and oak flames may consume it. In that way, you will have closure, and your future will be consecrated." With a deep breath, Isabella did as he instructed, watching the flames eagerly engulf the manuscript, reducing it to ashes. Christopher then tossed the empty burlap bag into the fire, the flames crackling as they consumed the remnants of the past, signaling the beginning of a new chapter in their lives. As the fire settled, Isabella raised her glass and said, "To the future." Christopher raised his glass and responded, "To our future, Isabella." Hearing those words, Isabella suddenly understood the meaning behind Sarah's words when Christopher and Sarah returned her journal to her: "Christopher will not let anything happen to you. Your futures are intertwined." Realizing that Sarah, as an angel, had foreseen this, Isabella felt a deep sense of love and protection. She smiled softly, thinking Sarah was likely watching over them, guiding them toward the future they were meant to share.

The evening gave way to night as the moon rose, casting a soft, silvery light through the living room windows. Feeling warm and at ease from their shared wine, the fire's ambiance, and the night's tranquility, Isabella closed her eyes and fell asleep in the reclining chair. Christopher covered her in a soft blanket, noticing how angelic her face appeared. He gathered the wine bottle and glasses and took them to the kitchen. Christopher, content and reflective, retired to his upstairs study.

Upstairs in his study, Christopher felt entirely in his element. among the bookcases, writing table, and oak desk, which exude a sense of order and quiet reflection. Through the half-open window, a gentle breeze whispered into the room, carrying with it the cool, crisp air of the night. As he stood in the center of the room, Christopher felt a strange stirring deep within his soul. The hairs on his arms stood on end as if electrically charged by some unseen force. Suddenly, he felt a soft, gentle touch on his cheek, like the flutter of a butterfly's wings—so subtle, it was almost invisible, yet unmistakable. It felt like the first time Sarah had kissed his cheek, a sensation so tender and familiar that it stopped him in his tracks.

Christopher initially thought it was just the breeze flowing through the open window until a familiar scent filled the room—the unmistakable fragrance of lilacs and lavender. The lovely smell enveloped his entire being, overwhelming him with emotions and memories. He reached out, feeling an energy swirling around him, almost as if he could grasp it. Overcome with a mixture of hope and longing, Christopher asked, "Sarah, is that you? Are you here with me?" There was silence for a moment, and then, as if carried on the air around him, a gentle voice responded, not just from one place but from everywhere, piercing into his very being and soul. "Yes, Christopher, I am here, my love, always." Her words wrapped around him, comforting and reassuring, as he vividly felt Sarah's presence. It was as if she were standing beside him. He knew she was…always.

In Perpetuum